Born in 1960, Ravi Sha... ...
Editor of *India Today* ...

He is also a political cartoonist and graphic artist. A collection of his short stories has been published in India, but *The Tiger by the River* is his first novel. His second novel, *The Village of Widows*, is now available from Doubleday. Ravi Shankar Etteth lives in New Delhi with his two dogs, Bosky and Thambi, and a cat named GurGur.

Acclaim for *The Tiger by the River*

'*The Tiger by the River* dazzles with its intricate plotting and stylish prose'
David Davidar, author of *The House of Blue Mangoes*

'A heady mix of mythology and myth-making . . . A rewarding, atmospheric read, laden with ghosts'
Time Out

'Full of stories and overlapping voices, teeming with history and myth . . . Etteth negotiates the cultures of west and east and the narratives of folklore and modernity with a rare and appealing skill'
Sunday Herald

'An outstanding first novel . . . beautifully handled in poetic, mystical and symbolic prose. From the first there is a sensation of being safely in the hands of a talented story spinner. This sad yet uplifting novel continues to haunt long after the book is back on the shelf'
Historical Novels Review

'A majestic novel of love and loss'
Books magazine

www.**booksattransworld**.co.uk

Also by Ravi Shankar Etteth

THE VILLAGE OF WIDOWS

THE TIGER
BY THE RIVER

Ravi Shankar Etteth

BLACK SWAN

THE TIGER BY THE RIVER
A BLACK SWAN BOOK : 0 552 77182 1

Originally published in Great Britain by Doubleday,
a division of Transworld Publishers

PRINTING HISTORY
Doubleday edition published 2002
Black Swan edition published 2002
Black Swan edition published 2003

1 3 5 7 9 10 8 6 4 2

Copyright © Ravi Shankar Etteth 2002

Set in 11/14pt Melior by
Falcon Oast Graphic Art Ltd.

Black Swan Books are published by Transworld Publishers,
61–63 Uxbridge Road, London W5 5SA,
a division of The Random House Group Ltd,
in Australia by Random House Australia (Pty) Ltd,
20 Alfred Street, Milsons Point, Sydney, NSW 2061, Australia,
in New Zealand by Random House New Zealand Ltd,
18 Poland Road, Glenfield, Auckland 10, New Zealand
and in South Africa by Random House (Pty) Ltd,
Endulini, 5a Jubilee Road, Parktown 2193, South Africa.

Printed and bound in Great Britain by
Cox & Wyman Ltd, Reading, Berkshire.

For my mother, Santha, who opened my eyes to magic,
and my teacher, Ipsita, who opened the door.

Swati:

INDIA

IN WHICH A WOUNDED PRINCE
RETURNS HOME TO A LOST PLAYMATE,
A TIGER, AND STORIES WRITTEN
ON PAGES OF BLOOD

The Spell of Forewarning

USED BY SWATI VARMA, THE LAST KING OF PANAYUR,
BEFORE HE STARTED HIS JOURNEY HOME

May the goddess Neeli manifest herself through the symbols and materials of this spell:

Grind one *nazhi* of rice from this year's harvest into a fine white powder. Mix turmeric and a black cat's milk into it. Dip the *athame* into the paste, then draw a pentagram on a black marble altar. Light four lamps at each corner of the altar: north, east, south, west. Keep one dried date-palm nut each on the eastern and the western corners; use a coral in the north and jade in the south.

Slice a lemon in two, rinse it with red turmeric water.

In the middle of the pentagram, hold the lemon, plunge the sacrificial knife into its heart, and turn the knife clockwise. Keep the little finger of the left palm pointing east while rotating the lemon between the thumb and the forefinger. Let the red juice of the sacrificial fruit fall upon the ground.

If there is thunder in the west, a great loss is predicted.

If a gecko chirps from the eastern side of the house, a homecoming is foretold.

The name of the goddess Neeli be blessed.

Source: Amavasyakandam,
Neeleebhagavadimantramala

Chapter One

'What is inside?' The policeman at airport security took the urn from Swati's hands. Swati's wife's red silk handkerchief was tied around its mouth. The policeman raised it to his face, and squinted at it.

'The Queen,' Swati replied, reaching for it.

'What did you say, sir?' he asked Swati suspiciously, moving the urn beyond Swati's reach. The policeman's hands were large and brown, with square fingers and bitten nails. Beneath the boredom in his voice, Swati could sense habitual impertinence.

'It contains my wife's ashes,' Swati, the last king of Panayur, replied, reaching out to take back the urn: the urn with the ashes of the queen of Panayur.

An aeroplane taking off outside the terminal startled the policeman. The vessel slipped from his fingers and Swati reached forward to catch it. He did not want Nina to fall again on this strange earth of Delhi, upon the concrete floor, which was coated with dust of unknown arrivals and departures. As he leant forward, clasping the urn in his fingers, he lost his balance and fell against the policeman. Swati was holding his beloved to his chest and he could feel her inside that small vessel of copper, a tender, unbearable weight that he was carrying home. The policeman flailed against him and they fell together, the vessel slipping from Swati's hands and rolling away.

'Nina!' Swati cried out her name. He saw the cartwheeling blur of strangers in the background – faces with unclear features and puzzled frowns. The fallen policeman disentangled himself from Swati's clasp, shook him away and tried to rise. The urn glinted at Swati in the light of the dawn coming in through the huge glass panes. It was intact but for a small dent on its side. A little bit of her had fallen on the floor – in a slim trail of ash like a farewell hieroglyphic.

Swati knelt beside it and carefully scooped it up in his fingers. She turned the side of his palm dirty grey. He rubbed her upon his chest. 'I'm so sorry,' Swati told her, holding the urn to his face and repeating her name over and over.

The policeman stood by, fidgeting. 'You should have checked it in,' he said, pointing at her gingerly. 'We can't be too careful. There are too many cranks these days.'

Swati interpreted his gaze, and could not help smiling at the policeman. He stood up, holding Nina close with both hands; she snuggled against his warmth. 'It is the last journey we will be taking together,' he murmured.

Swati opened his bag and put Nina back. Walking

towards the door, he felt the curious gaze of other passengers upon him. Two women muttered furtively to each other, pulling a child holding a teddy bear away from his path. The little girl stared at Swati – a tall man in black, whose long hair had a white streak at one side. Swati winked at her.

A short bald man with a huge woman smiled at him warily as he approached the door, standing aside, allowing him to pass. Swati caught his eye and smiled back. 'It's my wife,' he said, raising the urn slightly. 'She has this effect on people.'

Nina would have laughed.

Leaning back against his seat, feeling its texture against his head, Swati closed his eyes. He had placed the urn upon his lap, sensing her weight again after a week of death. He could feel her cheek against his shoulder, smell the fragrance of her fine, black hair, which fell to her waist, spilling over his. He could feel the rise and fall of her chest, the pressure of her soft breasts against his arm. Her silk rustled against him, and her perfume teased lightly. Swati surrendered to her, not daring to open his eyes – he was not sure of meeting hers. He was afraid to see her again, afraid to lose again that glimpse of her red mouth and the dimple in her cheek.

A diamond of sunlight flashed upon his eyelids. The plane was carving a circle towards the south, and Swati looked down at the Delhi he was leaving behind, green and neat, the Yamuna a gleaming sickle in the morning mist. 'Goodbye to all these years,' he whispered. 'Say goodbye, my darling.'

Under the belly of the aeroplane, the city was wet from the monsoon. The roads were shiny black ribbons upon which vehicles glinted. It had been raining for over a week; on the first morning of the rain Nina had woken him at dawn. She licked the rim of his ear and giggled. 'Let's dance in the nude,' she said tugging at Swati's nightshirt, 'in the rain.'

He saw that she was naked. In the morning light, her breasts gleamed, the heavy brown nipples like date-fruit. He felt the vertigo in the pit of his stomach that he always experienced whenever he saw Nina naked; he reached out and cupped one breast in his palm.

'Later,' she said, pulling away, drawing her hair deliberately across his face. 'Let's go out into the rain.'

Swati followed her, and Nina looked back and laughed. Her teeth gleamed at Swati, framed by the dark fall of hair. He saw the white of her slender arm upon which the gold of her bangle shone. She opened the door that led on to the lawn and ran out, squealing as the rain covered her. He grabbed her, taking her down with him on to the wet grass, Nina laughing and punching his chest. They rolled on the lawn, water falling on them, the incessant drumming of tiny feet, and he took Nina's mouth in his. It tasted of rainwater, dawn and her. She held Swati against her, inside her, staring widely at the indigo sky. 'Don't move,' she whispered. 'Can't you feel the earth move to meet the rain?'

The dawn was daubs of vermilion through the rain-clouds, the sky a great and pregnant presence spitting thin streaks of lightning. Swati lay on his back on the wet grass, drawing Nina to his shoulder, feeling the earth under him. Their unfinished house rose against the sky, the bedroom window a golden rectangle of light.

'Some architect you are,' he remarked. 'I wonder if I'll live to see this house finished.'

'Oh, you will,' she promised, 'and our children will bring laughter into its rooms.' She cupped his cheeks in her soft palms and laid his head against her belly. 'Do you hear him stir,' she asked Swati, with shining eyes, 'the prince of Panayur?'

The skin of her belly, its pressure against his cheek — Swati imagined the movements of his unborn child within her. He held her close, his heir against his face. The wind shivered on their skins.

'What kind of a world will he come into, this young prince?' Nina asked. 'I am afraid for him.'

'Into our world, the world of our mouths and our skin, into the safe umbrella of our sleep.'

'Swati, I am worried,' she mumbled.

He drew her upon him, naked on the grass, which was wet and clean with the rain. The morning birds sang far away. 'It is a beautiful world with you in it,' he said.

'Yesterday I dreamt that on our son's first birthday they started the nuclear war. Just like Nostradamus said.'

'Nostradamus was just a dreamer,' Swati tried to comfort her. 'There is going to be no nuclear war.'

'It began as such a bright dream.' She sounded wistful. 'There were streamers and balloons everywhere, and lots and lots of little children. I can recall the quality of that day even now – a bright blue sky lazy with white clouds, and the trees vibrant and green. All our friends were there: Mukul and Binita, Bubbles and Biren, Shammi, the Schmidts and the Jeejeeboys. We were drinking champagne and Mukul was cracking jokes. The children were outside in the garden, playing some silly game, and they all wore party hats. Inside the house Simon and Garfunkel were singing "Scarborough Fair".'

'I hate Simon and Garfunkel,' Swati said. 'Imagine hearing that in a dream!'

'Shut up, this isn't funny,' she replied. 'I was looking for you, but you were not there in the dream . . .'

'Great, some dreamer, you are. My son's first birthday and I am not even invited.'

'The children were in the garden and I brought the cake out. I can smell it now, Swati – it was chocolate and Binita had baked it for him and brought it over. "Happy birthday!" I said and all the kids turned and looked at me. Their party hats were black with soot, and skulls and crossbones were painted on them. All of them had the same burnt faces, like Edvard Munch's "The Scream" or something.'

'Hush, it was just a dream, Nina.'

'The sky was made of pewter, Swati, and the clouds

16

were all small red puffs of fire.' She hugged Swati fiercely, then drew away abruptly. 'Some mad general in Pakistan or some war-hungry mullah here, and we'll have Hiroshima here in Delhi. What will happen to the children, Swati?'

'There will be no war,' he whispered, his voice sounding like that of a stranger, hesitant, 'it was just a dream.'

Suddenly something occurred to him. 'What was his name, Nina? Our son's name?'

'I don't remember, darling. I can only remember the faces of the children. God, they were so horrible . . .'

Swati put his arm around her shoulder, and clasped the soft firm roundness. She buried her face in his chest. 'Promise me one thing,' her voice was muffled, yet fierce, 'you have to promise me one thing.'

'Anything, my pet, anything.'

'Promise me that if a war ever breaks out you will take me immediately to the house in Panayur,' Nina said, looking up at him, 'both me and our son. He will be safe there.'

To distant green Panayur, once the kingdom of his ancestors, nourished by the great river Papanasini, which flowed by the palace of his forefathers. Suddenly, everything seemed to be all right. 'I promise,' he whispered in her ear, inhaling the wet fragrance of her hair. 'I will take you to Panayur. Both of you.'

Nina and Swati had bought land a few miles away

from the city, ten acres of rocky red earth situated on a rise. From there they could see the Sohna hills and the green fields, which stretched out for miles; at night, on the other side, the lights of Delhi were a smoky, nebulous haze. Nina was an architect, but she did not want to finish building the house before moving in. She wanted the house to grow around them slowly as they lived in it, adding a room here, a wall there, putting up a marble fountain on the lawn, and a birdbath outside the portico. So they built a living room and a bedroom.

'Isn't it better this way? We can feel it opening around us as we go along,' she asked Swati in the morning, after breakfast. 'It takes shape in my imagination, like a great womb of warmth. I dream of nooks and crannies where we can make love, staircases I can sweep down, bejewelled, in a blue Kanjeevaram sari, and dazzle you.'

The rain had stopped, and cool sunlight came in through the door. Her neck was like the stem of a lily. Swati wanted to catch the sundrop on her lower lip, taste it.

It was the last time he saw her alive. Standing against the morning light Nina had the sunlit aura of an angel, the dark shape of her through the light cotton of her clothes, her skirt blowing in the morning wind, the gold chain around her neck a shimmering circle of fire. Her face was dark in the shadow, her hair blew in the wind, and she turned away with a laugh. He remembered her profile

18

pencilled by the morning, the curved line of forehead and the sharp nose, the clean, full lips and the rounded chin. Swati would replay the last twirl of her movement for ever in his mind, the rise of her breasts as the sun darkened them, the curve of her stomach and the soft swell of her belly. He felt a terrible ache as he watched her turn.

'Goodbye.' He waved.

She paused in the doorway, looked over her shoulder and smiled. The sun was in his eyes, and ever since he had tried to imagine what her last smile had looked like: the large kohl-rimmed eyes crinkling at the corners, the dimple, the orange mouth with the long, full underlip.

He was still thinking of her smile when he drove to work a few hours later, and saw her upturned car by the roadside. Glass like bloody sugar. A police jeep was parked nearby. 'Where is my wife?' Swati screamed. 'Where is Nina?'

The day darkened suddenly, and he heard the roar of the tiger far away in the sky. He knelt down by the car and the rainwater seemed red. 'The rain is falling on her blood,' Swati shouted. 'Nina's blood. Please help, help me . . .'

The rain ran over the road, branching out like a great red spider, mixing with the grass and the mud. He kept scooping the water into his hands to keep it from flowing away, but it continued to slip through his fingers in thin red streams. Swati felt a hand fall on his shoulder, and looked up at a policeman in a black raincoat. He held up his cupped palms, full of rainwater coloured with blood.

'It's my wife's blood. Where is she?' Swati asked.

The policeman did not answer. He held Swati's shoulder lightly, clumsily. The crowd enveloped them in silence. A small child stared at Swati from behind his mother's sari.

'She was coming around the bend when she skidded and hit a tree,' someone said. 'I saw it happen.'

Suddenly there was a babble of voices. Everyone was saying something to him.

'She was coming too fast . . .'

'I saw it happen . . .'

'I pulled her out . . .'

'Her eyes were closed, I saw it happen . . .'

'There was so much blood. Oh, the blood, the blood . . .'

Swati sat down on the road, where his wife's blood had mixed with the rain. It stained his trouser-legs. He was aware of the rain that fell on him, long thin messages of water that sluiced over his skin and through his clothes, and stung his face. The rain dimmed everything: the curve of the road and the trees, the people beside him, the policemen standing guard.

Swati got up. 'Where is she?' he asked.

The post-mortem report confirmed that she had not died alone. She had been two months pregnant.

My heir is dead, Swati thought, as he looked out

through the aircraft window. My son died in a choking whirlpool as the world tilted around him. Swati felt the earth careen, and closed his eyes tight. There was a roaring in his ears, a giant noise which filled him with a great humming throb. He opened his eyes: it was only the aeroplane tilting, its wing banking up in the air. Swati held Nina firmly on his lap. The sky was brilliant, the clouds faint indigo stains. He held his wife up to the window. 'We are going home, my darling,' he whispered, 'to Panayur.'

To Panayur, and the palace of his ancestors: his beloved shall swim in the Papanasini, the sacred river that runs by his palace, the river that is named the Quencher of all Sin. His heir shall swim with her as an unborn golden dolphin. Perhaps they will swim with the tiger of Panayur, who comes down from his cave in the Dhoni forests to drink from the river on *amavasya* nights: they will see the great head lowered to meet the water and the gleaming flanks in the glow of the stars. He will play with them as the noble beasts of the forest play with the spirits of the woods, his amber eyes seeking them out from the shadows mercurial with moonlight. The tiger by the river, the destiny of the royal house of Panayur, the beast its kings had hunted in vain, that his great-uncle, the regent of Panayur, had sought after Swati's father's death, when he had gone into the forest never to return.

A stewardess offered Swati coffee, which he refused. Outside was a timeless light, the blue sky arching to swoop down thousands of miles later over the palace on the banks of the river, the palace of his childhood, in whose grounds the kings and queens of Panayur had slept to the tidesong of the Papanasini. Northward from its banks were the green humps of the foothills and the thickening shadow of the forest as it climbed up Dhoni mountain. Once, the river had curved down from there, flowing below the railway bridge across the Tenkurissi boulders where one of his ancestors had hidden after he had been wounded in battle. As a child, Swati had stepped on to the bridge to stand upon one of the pillars, clutching the giant brown iron girders, waiting for the Madras Mail to pass – a dare on many a school half-holiday. The Mail passed at noon: a hooting length of shuddering, clattering carriages of brown and dirty yellow. Waiting for the train, he could look over the valley spread out below, and see the river flowing though the endless green paddyfields, dotted with black palmyra trees; the western wind flapped against them as it howled down the pass.

He had found a groove in one of the pillars into which he could snuggle, with his back against the soft cold moss on the stone. In the distance was the fort of Tipu Sultan, with whom Swati's great-great-grandfather had fought a battle and lost. Below the bridge, in summer, the river flowed away from its banks, unveiling stretches of silver sand. These were the battlefields of the armies of Malabar and the tournament sites of its knights. It was on these sands that the *chakorpada* fought their battles unto death: it was forbidden for them to return home in defeat. Sometimes the summer sunset would stain the sands with the blood of dead warriors and their cries could be heard in the wind. It was on these sands that the White Knight, Parangi Cheykor, had appeared one day, with his mane of hair, half blond and half black, one eye a blue ice chip, the other black quartz.

Sometimes Swati fancied he saw the Cheykor riding the tiger of Panayur upon the slope of a distant hill as he stood waiting for the train. But the mirages of summer afternoons shimmered and swept away his vision: under the great glass sphere of the sky golden filaments danced in shimmering spirals. Far, far away, he could see the spidery line of the railway track and the signal that blinked red and green near Palghat railway station. It was on the Madras Mail that his father had last come to see them before he went away to war. Swati remembered sitting on his mother's lap with Great-uncle as they drove up to the railway station in the Buick with the royal insignia of Panayur painted on its doors. The chauffeur wore a tuft knotted to the right side of his shoulder and a sarong with a border of gold brocade. Valiyamama, Swati's great-uncle, the regent of Panayur, sat erect in the back seat beside Swati's mother, the ceremonial dagger stuck into a red cummerbund around his bare belly. Beside the driver sat the gun-bearer, who held Grandfather's blue-barrelled Winchester with its gleaming walnut stock.

The car still flew the flag of Panayur on its bonnet.

'They tell me the district collector is upset about the flag,' Valiyamama had told Swati's mother. 'Only the government is allowed to fly flags, I believe.'

The gun-bearer chortled in his throat.

'What is the government?' Swati asked Valiyamama, and his mother smiled.

Valiyamama's grey eyebrows gathered in a small frown, but below them his brown eyes twinkled. 'I am the government,' he said, 'the ruler of Panayur. No little clerk is going to tell me what to do in my own land.'

The flag of Panayur was crimson and gold, with a leaping tiger embroidered on it.

'As if I am going to fly that Gandhi's flag,' the regent snorted. 'One of our *kudiyaans* has won an election with that Gandhi's party and is going around wearing white *khadi*. No king of Panayur is ever going to fly his serf's flag.'

Swati remembered his mother laying a comforting hand on Valiyamama's, her hand − so much like Nina's − with its long, slim fingers and the small, pink nails and the sapphire ring of Panayur's queen. The night Swati slipped that ring on Nina's finger, he had knelt down in front of her. 'It is the custom to kneel before the queen,' he whispered, 'just like my father did before my mother.'

Swati remembered Father getting down from the train, in his green army uniform with the colonel's epaulettes. He had knelt at Great-uncle's feet and kissed the old man's hand. Mother stood a few paces away, and Swati leant against her, looking at the tall man from the photographs who was his father. That was his earliest memory of his father, a tall man with a pencil moustache and a green beret, a man with laughing eyes.

As the train roared past the boy on the bridge, in a hot passage of coalsmoke and oil, he would try to scan the blurred faces of passengers at the windows for Father's familiar features. He tried to sniff his scent in the rush of the train, the fragrance of cologne and soap he had caught from the man in uniform who raised him up in his strong arms.

'My, my, Kalyani, how the little prince has grown,' Father exclaimed. Swati could always remember his voice, clear and loud on that distant morning.

Sitting on his lap, he had listened to his father explaining to Valiyamama that there might not be a war with China at all. 'Nehru and Chou En-lai are friends,' Father explained. 'Everything will be sorted out.'

'Chou En-lai is a Communist,' the regent said, 'and Communists are the worst enemies of their own country.'

'The Americans will support us,' Father said, 'and the Americans have the atom bomb. After all, the atom bomb was what brought the last war to an end.'

Mother was holding Swati's hand, and as Father spoke about the war she pressed the palm tight. Swati cried out and Father looked at him, then at Mother.

'Don't worry, Kalyani,' he consoled her. 'There will be no war.'

Valiyamama snorted. 'I do not trust that Patel. He tricked the Junagarh kingdom into being part of his plans,' he shouted, 'and that Malayali Englishman, Krishna Menon, is a fool. After all, it is the *kudiyaan*'s party that is running the country. I don't see why Panayur has to get involved in this. And you are the heir.'

Father told the old regent that Panayur was no longer a kingdom on its own. Great-uncle flew into a rage. 'Are you telling me that this *kudiyaan*'s party is ruling *me*? Never!' he thundered. 'In their silly white uniforms, and that Gujarati shopkeeper's multi-coloured flag? And then the other day a group of youngsters came with a *Namboodiri* to see me. Said they were Communists. I would not have let them into the courtyard if I had not been told that it was Udayan Namboodiri from Chandanathara Illam who was seeking an audience with me. Even the Brahmins are mad these days. In the old days, Choorikathi Kombiyachan would have chopped off their heads.'

'What did they want?' Father asked, suppressing a smile.

'Damned Communists behaving like Tipu Sultan and Haider Ali. Even Tipu Sultan did not impose his *rowka* rules on Panayur. Everywhere else in Malabar women had to cover their breasts, but not in Panayur! What a king as great as Tipu didn't do, now the Communists want to, I believe!'

'What has Communism got to do with breasts?' Father said.

'They wanted me to order that women should not go around bare-breasted any more, especially the low castes. They said it was against the pride of the working class. The pride of the working class indeed!' Valiyamama spat betel juice through the open window of the car.

'And what did Your Highness say?'

'I asked, "Are their breasts so ugly that you have to keep them under wraps?" ' the regent said, 'and that Udayan Namboodiri flew into a rage. He warned me that Mother Russia would seek revenge on Panayur. I asked him, "Do the breasts of my subjects belong to Mother Russia or to me, the king?" '

Father threw back his head and laughed. Great-uncle turned on him in a rare rage. 'I told him to tell his Russia to declare war on Panayur. If I see him again, I will not keep in mind that he is the son of Maitran Namboodiri and the grandson of Uttaman Namboodiri who was the court scholar of Panayur. I will chop off his head.'

'And did it stop the women working bare-breasted?' Nina had asked Swati, when he told her the story.

'Only architects who belong to the present king of Panayur have to work bare-breasted,' he answered, with a smile, pulling her towards him and placing his palm on her breast. She raised her lips to him, her hands slipping around his neck. They were cool and

27

soft. She rubbed her palm against Swati's cheek, moving it in little circles. They were sitting on the stone steps of the royal bathing enclave, which led into the Papanasini, watching the sun's margin bruising the horizon.

'There is sunset on your lips,' he said.

He leaned forward to kiss her, and she drew away with a teasing laugh. The evening was a great dome that curved away into the distance, disappearing behind the great hills, which were China-green and smoked with wandering cloud. The river was just a thin strip of red and silver, obscured by the grass, which now grew wild on its marshy bed. The wind hissed in the paddy like a million snakes. To their left, in the small shallow harbour, was the wreck of a ship. On its broken topmast, tatters of sailcloth still fluttered in the breeze.

'The ship of the mad king, Choorikathi Kombiyachan.' Swati pointed to it. 'The only land-locked navy in the world.'

Nina's face was intense with curiosity. 'A ship!' she exclaimed, and his heart lurched at the bellsound of her throat. 'Is it ours?'

He laughed at her enthusiasm and she stood up and held out her hand. 'I want to board it,' she said. 'Let's repair it and sail on it. It will be just like time travel.'

'On this river?' he asked, waving at the dry riverbed with its shreds of water.

'If the ship can sail again,' Nina called, 'the river will return.' She was already climbing the stone steps.

Swati followed, catching up with her and linking her arm in his.

Together they reached the ship, a fallen dinosaur of wood and moss. 'How do we get on it?' Nina asked.

'We cannot,' Swati said, pointing at the mast. A great cobra was entwined around it, resting on the perpendicular shaft, its hood raised at them questioningly.

Nina shuddered. 'A cursed ship,' she said.

Swati drew her close. 'Those are not our curses,' he said. 'Our voyage is different.'

Chapter Two

Climbing the grey stone steps of the Panayur palace was like ascending to another plane. Swati shook off his loafers, and walked barefoot upon the marble floor of the veranda, feeling its coolness spread along his toes through the patina of dust. He paused by the tall wooden pillars supporting the rafters to caress their roughness, trying to distinguish the familiar, long-departed touches of his mother, his father, and his great-uncle. Nina's, too. The palace settled around his arrival like a great craft of presence. Time had left behind its debris, altering the shapes of the shadows and leaving behind ancient, almost imperceptible echoes.

Swati carried his luggage into the sitting room in which his great-uncle, the regent of Panayur, had once received visitors. He placed the small urn he had carried with him from Delhi upon the Queen Anne table in the drawing room, under Great-uncle's portrait. The smell of the monsoon was in the wind, a familiar portmanteau of scent: of fresh leaf and coarse paddystalk, grain, mud and mango flowers. A lizard chirped from the rafters. The years were gathering within him like a flock of tired birds.

'Who is there?' a voice asked him.

Swati turned to see a woman, perhaps near middle age, her hair streaked with mild grey and a sandal-paste mark across her forehead. 'It is I, Swatiraja,' he answered. 'Who . . . ?'

She stepped into the light, and he saw her face, with its dark, heavy-lidded eyes.

'Antara?' he asked tentatively, in wonder, not fully believing that it was she, the playmate of his child-hood, the daughter of his mother's attendant, Fatima.

'Your Highness,' she exclaimed, her voice like feathers drifting to the floor. 'After such a long time.'

Swati reached out and took her hand, the skin rough with the years, although the palm was soft. 'My friend,' he said, and Antara was crying softly.

Suddenly they heard something fall in the attic, and a window, which had come loose in the wind, hitting the wall, a staccato sound.

'Too many bats in the attic these days,' Antara complained and turned to go inside.

Swati followed her. They climbed up the great staircase, its mahogany banisters shining in the gloom. The palace seemed like a three-dimensional map in a dream, known yet arcane. At the foot of the attic stairs a box lay open on its side and cowrie shells were scattered all around it on the floor.

'The sorcerer's box!' Antara gasped, her hand flying

to her mouth. Swati noticed the familiar crease on her forehead. 'It is an omen,' she said.

She held out the black wooden box to Swati. A bat flew out of the attic door, swishing past them into the dusk, leaving a pungent odour of leather and pollen in the air.

Swati took the box, feeling its old weight upon his hands, his blood sensing the quicksilver movements of the soothsaying spirits that dwelt within it. 'Come,' he said to Antara, with a smile, placing the box aside and holding out his hand to her.

In the loft, to which Swati and Antara climbed, holding hands like the children they had been thirty years ago, was Markandeya Varma's trunk. It squatted like a heavy black coffin covered with dust, festooned with cobwebs. It was full of documents: mortgage records, stamp-papers and letters. Swati picked up a mouldy diary that lay among them, and dusted off its sides. A photograph fell out of its unstrung pages. It was of a man he did not recognize, with clear smiling eyes and raven hair, in a dark suit. Beside him was a strikingly beautiful European woman, whose light hair spilled over her shoulders. On her lap was a baby in a round-collared tunic, buttoned up to the neck. The baby's eyes reminded Swati of Father's. On the back of the picture, in fading blue ink, in a neat sloping handwriting it said: 'Rama Varma, Else and Jai. Berlin, September 1935.' Swati held it up to Antara, searching her eyes with his smile.

'Raniyamma, your mother, used to look at that

photograph often,' Antara told him. 'She used to hold it up to her mask, and I have often felt the sigh that rose within her body.'

'Who are they, Antara?' Swati asked, with sudden apprehension.

'They are family. Your mother used to go to the front door often with the photograph in her hand and stand looking out, as if waiting for someone to return,' Antara replied, 'and I would go and stand beside her. "This is a family to whom no one returns, Antara," she would tell me in a voice that was barely audible. "It has been so ever since Queen Ponni was forced to flee from her husband."'

'Choorikathi Kombiyachan, the cruel king of Panayur?' Swati said, with a little laugh. 'I remember Mother's tales about Ponni and her white lover, Gomez. And their son, Parangi Cheykor, who later became king of Panayur. All that was such a long time ago, Antara. What has it to do with that photograph?'

'It is the curse of Panayur that its kings went out, never to return, and those who were left were taken by the tiger.'

'There is no tiger of Panayur,' he said, taking the picture from her and looking at it again. The man had clear eyes that seemed to hold Swati's gaze from across the years.

'Don't say that about the tiger,' Antara warned softly. 'It is sacrilege.'

Swati put his arm around his old playmate. 'It is just a charming myth of the eighteenth century,

Antara,' he said, 'in which Amma also believed.'

'The queen was waiting for your father to come back from the war, so that he could take you to the forest and hunt the tiger,' Antara said. 'It is the royal custom that the king must teach his son to hunt the tiger.'

'But Father didn't come home from the war,' Swati said, 'and Mother changed into someone who didn't seem real to me, most of the time.'

Swati's father, Markandeya Varma, the previous king of Panayur, was a lieutenant colonel in the Aksai Chin incident, India's ill-fated battle with China. Inside the great bedroom of the palace where the kings had slept, there hung a framed photograph of him in uniform, debonair, with a pencil moustache, one arm around his wife, the queen Kalyani. The day a telegram arrived from army headquarters on a calm Wednesday afternoon in late 1962, Kalyani had sat down at the German sewing machine that Swati's great-uncle, the regent, had brought home from his travels, and stitched a hood for herself from white linen. She would take it off only on the day of her husband's *shraddham*, when the ritual of comforting the dead was over. With Swati, she would bear the consecrated offering on fresh plantain leaves to the riverbank: milk pudding seasoned with cloves and palm sugar, red hibiscus petals upon it, like a salad of blood. She would place it on the golden sand, then step away from it, raise her face to the sky and clap her hands, calling the crows to her.

'*Kaake, kaake, vaa.*' Little rough birdwings of sound flew from her throat, tremulous and rusty from lack of practice.

The crows were the spirits of the ancestors, hungry and lawless, who flew over the bleak landscape of the dead, hearing the summons of those they once loved. As she called them, the birds would arrive one by one as if from nowhere. They would hop around her with the cautious insolence of crows, their arrogant beaks gaping and closing, heads cocked to one side. The queen would take a few steps further away from the food on the ground, and the crows would swarm upon it, cawing furiously. She would watch them with a remote calm, her slender, fair hands clasped loosely before her, long black hair untied in the wind.

But there was one fat white crow, Swati recalled, who would not eat. It always arrived last, and would sit at a distance away from its hungry companions, staring steadily at Queen Kalyani until she became motionless and quiet under its gaze. As if by some trick of light her features sharpened into a silhouette sculpted by grief. A great distance had cast itself around her, lulling Swati into a trance. It was the frontier of another death. Across it no wind blew, and the river flowed silent and deep. His mother stood at its centre, a frail woman with thick hair that fell to her ankles, her slender form wrapped in white linen.

The other crows, satiated, would take wing and fly up in a black caw-cloud into the sky. The white crow would hop up to her, peck her outstretched palm,

35

drawing blood, and then, with a rough cry, take wing. Swati would wake from his stupor to see that Mother had fainted. He would sit beside her, holding her hand to guard its wound, listening to the purl of the river, until she woke into the evening and her blindness.

Behind him, the palace was a great ship moored on the bank of Papanasini, its black outlines wet with the blood of sunset. In the western corner of the palace grounds slept the ancestral dead of the house of Panayur. The queen's *thozhi*, Fatima, had lit the little prayer-lamps in the headstone nooks of their graves, the flames licking the western wind. The day after Swati's mother went into mourning, she collected her husband's belongings and placed them upon a bier in the burial ground: Markandeya Varma's uniforms and medals, his green beret, his letters, his coin collection and tennis shorts, his spare cartridges and all his shoes. She woke Swati early, bathed him on the stone steps that led down to the river. Dawn was opening a crimson eyelid at the edge of the sky. The stars were still shining and he was a small wet boy, shivering in the wind. She led him barefoot to the royal cemetery and told him to light the pyre. Above the crackle of the flames a crow cried in the distance, harsh and lonely.

She thrust a black oblong box into Swati's hands; he could still recall its touch. It was made of old teak and bonded with gold. One of its compartments held cowrie shells and the other an astrological almanac, inscribed on palmyra leaves. Great-great-grand-father's hobbies had been necromancy and astrology, which had become the pastimes of the house of Panayur. Mother had told Swati about the mad king of Panayur, Choorikathi Kombiyachan, whose perverse lust for power had led him to court the dark powers of sorcery. He kept numerous sorcerers among his retinue: the *odiyans*, who could turn themselves into savage, carnivorous bulls, *kuttichathans*, who were malicious, murderous poltergeists, and *paraya* priests who worshipped Neeli, the dark goddess of the hills. He would conduct *mahishayagnas*, buffalo sacrifices, in the hope of gaining immortality.

'The buffalo is the familiar of Yama, the god of Death,' Mother had told him, 'and the rituals were conducted on the first night of the lunar eclipse.'

Sometimes, waking up in the middle of the night, when the wind brought the river's flow to him, the child heard in it the occult moans of buffaloes: desolate animal sounds taut with spectral agony. When he mentioned this to his mother, she ruffled his hair and smiled sadly at him. 'The blood of the sorcerer kings of Panayur runs in you too, my son.'

The morning after his father's belongings, now a molten lump of metal and ash, were collected from the bier and buried in a small silver urn, the court astrologer, Puliyeri Panikker, came to teach Swati the royal pursuit.

* * *

37

'Raniyamma told me that you had a great aptitude for astrology,' Antara's voice broke in. 'You must tell me my future some time.'

Swati laughed and said he was out of practice. He didn't have much use for a future.

'I have something to give you,' Antara said, turning to the man she had met again after so long. She saw his tall spare frame, the wide shoulders and restless hands, the long black hair with the white streak. She studied the face of her old companion as if it belonged to a stranger, looking for familiar signs in the cool, dark eyes and strong jaw. Her heart beat fast with gladness as he smiled, showing even white teeth.

Old playmate, the last keeper of the secrets of Panayur, Swati thought, my mother's constant companion of the twilight that swims within the crumbling palace of my ancestors, this labyrinth of memories and shadows to which I have returned.

They walked together to the queen-mother's room, the great master bedroom of the kings of Panayur. Great-uncle had slept here, and before him his father and his, and the great White Knight Parangi Cheykor, who was betrayed by the British, in his doomed war with Tipu Sultan. It had also been the bedchamber of Choorikathi Kombiyachan, who loved to watch killer elephants crush the heads of his captives and held tournaments in which gladiators fought crocodiles and tigers to the death. The crackle and hiss of leaves blowing outside held eerie echoes of long-dead conversations. Swati laughed uneasily to himself, trying to dispel the ghosts.

Antara opened a drawer of the antique mahogany desk and took out an envelope. It was fat and yellow, and bore a London postmark with a magenta stamp of a young Queen Elizabeth with her shy, tight-lipped smile. Printed on the left-hand corner were the words: Baulmer and Baulmer, Solicitors, London.

'What is it?' Swati asked.

Antara smiled a hooded smile and pointed at the photograph in Swati's hand. 'More secrets, Your Highness,' she said. 'At the end of every journey one returns to the secrets that always wait for one.'

Inside the envelope he found folded sheets of yellowing paper strapped together casually with a red rubber band. Tucked within them was a note addressed to Swati from his mother. 'My darling son Swati . . .' it began.

Swati took the papers to the mahogany chair by the bay window and sat down. He had to sit down: his shoulders felt heavy, as if a thousand years had unloaded their burdens upon him. Antara came to stand behind him. Her soft hand touched his shoulder briefly. She reached across Swati and switched on the ornate reading lamp that Great-uncle had brought back from London; its twin cherubs held up the silk lampshade that now cast a moon of light upon the papers he held.

'I'm not sure I want to know any more, Antara,' he

said, thinking of the urn that stood upon the table in the drawing room.

Antara laid her small hand upon his shoulder and Swati looked down at the letter, at his mother's writing. With slow fingers he caressed the script, as if he was hearing her words once again. Too many memories, too much loss . . .

My darling son Swati, the last king of Panayur,

This will be the last story I will ever tell you. In the days when you were a child you used to put your little head in my lap and hear the tales of Rumpelstiltskin, and Vikram and the Vampire. Only this time it is a real story about the family of Panayur – and one that you will not have heard before.

Once upon a time, in the late 1920s, a young king of Panayur called Rama Varma left for England. He was your grandfather. He left behind his young wife, Queen Sarada, and your father, who was only a small boy. Five years later he returned to Panayur on vacation. With him was a German woman named Else. Queen Sarada saw Else with your grandfather and understood. The men of Panayur have always had a weakness for white women. She turned away and went upstairs to the zenana, where she summoned her lady-in-waiting, Antara's grandmother. She asked for the yellow kolambi nuts, which grew wild in the garden, to be gathered and brought up to her. Sarada locked the door from inside, and ordered the poisonous kernels to be

40

ground into a paste mixed with jaggery and honey.

In the morning, with Else beside him, Rama Varma drove out in the Bentley, flying the royal flag of Panayur on its bonnet, to Thekkady, to hunt. He did not know Queen Sarada lay dead in her boudoir, her sightless eyes looking out at the morning sky through the latticed window. By the time he came back from his hunt, with the collector's Bedford truck trailing behind, loaded with the spoils of his day – spotted deer and boar, skins of leopards and a tiger – Queen Sarada's funeral was over. Your father had lit her pyre. He was eight years old.

Rama Varma left for Berlin with Else. Antara's mother, Fatima, who was only a girl then, remembers her – she was fair and had hair like the beginning of sunset, golden with tints of red to come. She was not haughty like most parangi women and she did not know of Sarada's suicide. But your grandfather was terribly upset. Before leaving for Berlin, he appointed his younger brother, your Valiyamama, as the regent of Panayur.

'You killed her, Rama,' Valiyamama accused him, as they were leaving. 'Do you think Sarada's ghost will rest?'

'The kings of Panayur have always had many wives,' your grandfather answered. 'Why did Sarada have to do this?'

'She loved you,' the regent said. 'She was waiting for you to return. She wanted you to take your son to the forest, to teach him to hunt the tiger of Panayur.

And instead you came home with that accursed white woman.'

'Stay your words,' your grandfather said. 'I will return soon, and then I will take my son to the forest to look for the tiger. But for that he has to reach fourteen years of age, you know that.'

Your father told me all this. He was hiding behind the great pillar in the patio watching the men talk. The tiger hunt was the customary rite of initiation into manhood of the princes of Panayur, when the king took his eldest son into the forest in search of the great cat. It is said that the princes of Panayur went into the forest as boys and returned as men.

Your father rarely spoke about your grandfather, and the few times he did I saw the bitterness in his eyes. They were full of a poisonous longing. His pupils would change colour to a translucent green, and it appeared to me that his eyes belonged to someone else. They were eyes that remembered things he could not have witnessed. But later he could not take you, either, into the forest to hunt the tiger.

Read these letters, which I received one day from London. Your grandfather wrote them to your father. I received them a few days after your father died, so he was not able to read what his own father had to say to him. But there is a journey in here for you, a journey of initiation, a hunt that every man has to endure at least once in his life, in which things lost may return. Strange are the ways of ghosts . . .

A crow cawed outside the window. Swati leant out and looked at the river: in the twilight, the water glimmered through the tall, white-tufted grass, which grew wild among the rocks where the Papanasini of his childhood had once flowed without interruption.

Antara, who stood beside him, gave a little cry. 'Look, my lord.' She pointed to a patch of red earth that the rain had sloughed up. There in the middle, slowly collecting the water of the Malabar monsoon, was a gigantic pugmark.

Chapter Three

Antara left Swati by the window with the sheaf of his grandfather's papers in his lap. He felt trapped: he was not ready for this journey, which had been thrust unexpectedly upon him. When he had returned with Nina to the palace, he had imagined that his travels were over, but now a dead man was about to speak to him from across the years, to reveal secrets he was not sure he wanted to hear. They were the secrets of his grandfather: messages, pleas and admonitions. They were meant for someone else. All Swati wanted was to release the ashes of his wife and his heir into the waters of the Papanasini. When he had discovered Antara, he had felt that in the picking up of broken threads of incidents and conversations of long ago, in the repetition of the rituals and memories of child-hood, he might lay his ghosts to rest, but it seemed his mother had left another door open for him. Swati felt a twinge of resentment towards her.

You pass through one door and you find other locked doors waiting, he thought. It never ends.

He called to Antara to bring him the bottle of Lagavulin and some cold water. She left them for him upon the Louis XIV table that Great-uncle had brought home from Paris. She had brought water in the old crystal jug that Valiyamama had drunk from, and his Bohemian crystal tumbler, upon which Panayur's royal insignia was embossed.

The whisky was golden and warm, and settled comfortingly in his stomach. Swati was reluctant to begin reading. He played with the envelope, balancing it on his palm. He raised it to his face and breathed in the musty smell of time. Outside, the young night was full of crickets. Birdcalls flew across the trees. He could hear Antara far away in the kitchen, the sounds of pots and pans; the smells of cooking came to him. He drank a deep draught of whisky.

'Müggelseedamm 11, Berlin, 17 April 1937 . . .' Swati began to read. The words were like runes.

I will be dead by the time you get this letter. I do not know what calamities lie ahead in these coming years. I am worried that the royal house of Panayur itself might not survive. The world is going to be at war, and Britain may lose to a powerful Germany because her leadership is weak. And if that is the case, the kingdom to which you are heir will fall into the wrong hands. I do not know if by the time you get this letter there will be still a king of Panayur, or even a kingdom. But, by then, I suspect it would be too late for me. The Nazis would have sent me to one of their labour camps, if they do not shoot me instead. I can hear jackboots outside the window. It is night now. I am truly sorry about your mother, Sarada. I do not seek forgiveness from you, nor do I offer an explanation. We all live with our ghosts, and we return to them when we die. My wife, Else, has started dreaming about a woman in white. This woman has long black hair and shining eyes. The rest of her features are lost in a mist that swirls constantly around her lips. Her eyes are sad. I know it is Sarada, and God knows that Else is innocent. I do not expect you to forgive us – Else and I – but as I sit at my desk hearing the soldiers outside on the cobbled streets, I am afraid. Not for myself, but for the house of Panayur, and for my wife. And afraid that you will never see me, or swim with me in the waters of the Papanasini. I had promised your mother when I left for Germany that I would take you one day to seek the royal tiger of Panayur, when you were grown-up. The tiger is our myth, our mascot, and in searching for it the kings of Panayur learn what it is to be a man. My father took me when I was fourteen, and it was the most frightening journey of my life. The woods were alive with sounds and movements that a fourteen-year-old boy could not understand, sounds of a forest full of life. We followed the trail of the tiger, to the great cave of the beast. I returned without my father, a king at fourteen, and I cannot tell you what I saw. If you survive what you see, then you will learn to live without fear for ever. It is what a warrior is taught. You will have to see for yourself.

If we cannot escape to England, I am sure one day we will be put on the trains to the labour camps. But after that journey into the lair of the tiger, all other journeys seem harmless. But it is not so for Else. My wife is awake, lying on the bed. She is afraid. She is pretending to be asleep so that I may be comforted, but no Jew can sleep in Germany. Yesterday the police came for our neighbours, the Goldsteins, in a long black van. Through the window your stepmother and I saw that Frieda Goldstein was crying. She is pretty. She has a delicate Jewish face with high cheekbones and large soft brown eyes. Her hands are white – she plays the piano very well. Else and I have heard her play on many a night when we would be lying back in the bed after making love, sipping from a glass of cold white wine. We won't hear Frieda any more, I am sure of that . . .

Swati felt the presence of his grandfather Rama Varma, joining the clamour of the ghosts that had gathered in the room, pleading with him to read on. But he tried to distinguish Nina's voice among the chatter of the dead – hers was the only voice he wanted to hear. The moonlight made strange shadows outside, the river rustled low in the grass and in the distance a bus groaned along, laden with people returning home.

I feel homesick; you and Sarada are often in my thoughts [Swati read on]. I realize the gods have

47

chosen for me to die in Germany. But I have a secret to share with you, my prince. You are the heir to the kingdom. I have to inform you that Else and I have a son, your half-brother, and his name is Jai. I have smuggled him across to America with help from a friend, Fred Kramer. I have no hope of escaping from Germany now. If Else and I die, I have left instructions for my ashes to be brought to Panayur. Even if I am thrown into an unmarked grave, I am sure I will be found: the bones of the mages send out their signals. The remains of a sorcerer king of Panayur cannot be abandoned in some distant, heathen land. I need you to perform the rites for me and give my remains to the Papanasini. I want you to erect a stone for me beside those of our ancestors, and I want your wife to light a lamp beside it every evening. I want to rise up on the nights of the full moon and watch the river flow by our palace. I want to see the tiger of Panayur come down from the forests to drink . . .

Swati called Antara's name, and she came quickly into the room. Her face was worried. Swati held out his arms to her and she went to him, cradling his head against her breast. She smelt of *thulasi* and clean cotton.

'Hush . . . What happened?'

'More secrets,' Swati mumbled. 'My grandfather's bones . . .'

'I know,' Antara said. 'Your mother told me. They will come to Panayur one day . . .'

48

The ghosts milled around them, deepening the twilight, and Antara stood like a priestess guarding her king from them, but faces of mist insinuated themselves beneath Swati's closed eyelids, their voices speaking strange names. Swati shut them out, clinging to the warmth of his old friend, his childhood guardian . . .

'How will you find your grandfather? Are you going to look for him?' Antara asked.

Swati looked up at her, searching her eyes. He understood by her smile that his mother must have spoken to her. It seemed as if long before he had even begun to suspect, the queen-mother had been charting a course for him, an ethereal map he was destined to follow in search of an unquiet ghost.

'But I have just come back,' he said. 'And where do I begin my search?'

'Perhaps you could start by writing to these lawyers,' Antara pointed to the address at the bottom corner of the envelope. 'Write to Baulmer and Baulmer in London. But before you go anywhere, you have to discover what it is that you came back to. And where you are going from.' She picked up Valiyamama's diary, which Swati had put on the table. 'There is much to know,' she said, gesturing at the papers in his hand, 'about the past and the present.'

'And the future?' he asked. 'I came back to heal.'

'The future will wait. As it always does.'

He leant his weary head against her. 'Where do I start?' he asked.

'The past,' she answered. 'To seek the future, you always start in the past.'

'Take me there.'

'Remember the temple, Your Highness, where your forefathers worshipped, that your mother visited every morning to read the royal records? You will find all your answers there.'

Chapter Four

Swati had not visited the Papanasini Temple since the very first *shraddham* day of his father. Mother had taken him, freshly bathed in the river, a ritual streak of sandalpaste smeared on his forehead, and bade him bow down to the god. The god was an ancient standing stone, its aboriginal texture lustrous in the glow of oil lamps. The royal records of the house of Panayur were kept in a wing of the temple, as were the mystical horoscopes of planets, rivers, countries and other esoterica the court astrologers and sorcerers of Panayur felt were necessary for study.

The temple belonged to the house of Panayur and stood just within the palace grounds. It had been given to the kings of Panayur by the Chola emperors when the land was part of their southern empire. Much later, when Parangi Cheykor became king of Panayur, he built a mosque on the eastern side of the palace. It was a mark of respect to his friendship with Tipu Sultan, but it was also meant to annoy the British who occasionally held services at the church built by

Choorikathi Kombiyachan. From his personal harem, Tipu gave Muslim ladies-in-waiting to the household of Panayur – Mysorean women, well versed in the arts of amusement. They were accomplished conversationalists and singers, and could play both the *veena* and the harp. They knew the secrets of distilling perfumes and herbal cosmetics, and waited upon the queens of Panayur. And the queen's lady-in-waiting was made the royal keeper of the palace records. Parangi Cheykor insisted that only her perfumed hands might touch the ancient documents that had been preserved so carefully since the first days of the kingdom. This was how Antara – like her mother, Fatima, before her – had become the curator of the royal documents.

As Swati walked towards the temple, he saw that the place had changed little since his childhood. Palmyra trees marked the borders of paddyfields, holding up thorny bamboo fences around thatched dwellings. Small houses with concrete walls and cement roofs had also sprung up, built by one-time serfs who had become landowners after the Land Ceiling Act had been passed in the 1950s by the Communist government. Once it had all been paddy and areca-nut, part of the Panayur royal estate. This Act had inflamed the regent of Panayur, who did not sleep on the night that the local police inspector informed him apologetically that he could no longer demand payment from the serfs: there were no more serfs, the regent was told. He walked up and down the front veranda, screaming for his guns to be cleaned and the car to be brought out so that he could drive to the state capital and shoot the Communist chief minister.

'That renegade Brahmin, that Sankaran Namboodiri,' the regent raged. 'Why couldn't he leave Panayur alone, when he had all of Mother Russia to piss in?'

Swati's great-uncle had a long-standing feud with both the Congress Party and the Communists. The former he regarded as a bunch of hypocritical snakes who wore Gandhi's cloth and sang foolish songs, the latter he saw as a bunch of dangerous outcasts who wanted to take over their land.

Swati walked into the temple compound, past a small tea-shop with a yellow thatched roof and earthen veranda. On the roof a small red flag fluttered in the wind; two men sat on their haunches, smoking beedis and reading *Patriot*, the Communist daily paper. They looked at him with the habitual suspicion of the provincial Communist. He smiled and walked round the temple to the archives room where the parchments were kept. With the key Antara had given him he opened the heavy wooden door and stepped inside.

A bulb with a white porcelain shade hung down from a thin black wire. A spider swung from it sleepily. Swati switched on the light, and sat cross-legged on the grass mat spread upon the floor. It was cool. The old records had been stacked neatly within palmyra scrolls and folds of thick vellum paper on a low shelf placed against the wall. Antara had kept them clean, he noticed.

Swati touched the palmyra rolls, then ran his fingers along the hieroglyphic ridges of calligraphy that detailed the horoscope of the river Papanasini, its history and myth. The bulb swung slowly in the breeze, and rings of light swayed hypnotically, intersecting the ochre-dark shades of the room as he read.

When the destroyer Siva flew into a rage and slew his consort Parvati for having disturbed his meditation, parts of her body were flung all over Bharatam. Breaking into the terrible dance called the *tandava*, his third eye opened into a great ball of fire, melting the primordial ice of the Himalaya. His rage became the hood of a great, fiery cobra which opened above the land, setting its skies on fire.

As the goddess Parvati's head was severed from her body, the first teardrop of pain fell from her eye upon a great rock in Sivamala, the mountain of Siva in the Western Ghats. The stone split apart with great force, and a gigantic womb of water sprang up. Blue and green algae appeared like primeval ink as the newborn river thundered and frothed its way downwards. White sand spread itself to greet the water's advancing course as fresh green grass sprouted on the virgin clay of its shores, and fish were born in flashes of silver light. The rock lizards and chameleons that slept in the summer sun were baptized by the flow, and metamorphosed into giant crocodiles. In the chaos of its search for the calm blue waters of the Arabian Sea, the river sculpted its dance upon rocks that the earth disgorged in its furrowing. Later, at each bend of the river, between Pollachiand Shoranur, fifteen *sivalingas* were found, and fifteen Siva temples were built around them. Lepers who bathed in the temple creeks were miraculously cured, and harlots, cleansed by the stream, became virgins once again. The goddess appeared to each of the fifteen priests in a dream and commanded that the river be named Papanasini, the Quencher of all Sin.

Papanasini's course ran through rich loamy land, whiskered by the green of paddy and coconut palms, spreading out to join the river Bharatapuzha, which, passing the small town of Shoranur, flowed down to meet the Arabian Sea near Calicut. Two hundred years after the Portuguese adventurer Vasco da Gama landed in Calicut for the last time in 1524, a group of sailors took a boat upriver in search of fame and fortune. Their leader was Fernando Gomez, a tall twenty-six-year-old Portuguese whose great-great-grandfather had sailed with da Gama all those years ago. Gomez had grown up on the stories his ancestor had told which had been passed down through the generations: tales of gold, of walls of silver inset with rubies in the Samorin's court, and of dusky, supple women who hid their nakedness behind garlands of pearls. He had piercing blue eyes and a scar on his right cheek attributed to the knife of a savage at Mozambique – in reality, it was the result of the bite of an irate parrot, the pet of the fair Melinda, which Gomez, one drunken night, had tried to fondle, thinking it her breast. The sailors had sneaked away at night without telling their captain, who had laid down strict rules about drinking, looting and women. As they rowed upstream, the Malabar moon gleamed on the adventurers and the wind from the Nilgiris tickled their necks under their collars.

'Brrr, it is a night for foreplay,' grunted Gomez. 'Row harder, da Cruz, and pray to Mary that we find a harem full of virgins and rooms full of gold.'

All along the river, the palm trees swayed in the wind, a huddled conspiracy of black-green shadows. In the water their reflections were distorted by the wake of the boat, and the stars in the heavens crinkled in the ripples. Unknown to the sailors, the planets Shukra and Sani, Budha and Kartika were watching them, with the distant detachment of eternity. They had winked their mischief upon these men, had watched their duels and serenades with amusement and charted their passage across the ocean, from Portugal and the coast of Spain to the green coast of Calicut.

Now they watched the boat moving upstream through moonmade liquid silver. The houses on the riverside were dark and the temples dozed under the *bodhi* trees. The Malabar coast was sleeping early that night, and no one saw them except a Namboodiri on his way to his nightly *sambandham* at the house of his young Nair paramour who had just turned eighteen that night, and an old woman who had come out to defecate on the riverbank.

'*Aaravo*,' shrugged the Namboodiri. 'Must be the Panayur king's navy.'

It was a joke. The only landlocked kingdom in Malabar to have a navy was Panayur. One Sunday afternoon its king, the navy's founder, Choorikathi Kombiyachan, had received an English priest, Father Thomas Charteris. The king bade him sit down and talk to him about England.

'Is it bigger than Panayur?' asked the king.

'Slightly,' said the priest apologetically, because he did not want to offend the king: he eyed the short-sword lying at the king's side. A cloud pulled away from the sun and the blade winked at him maliciously.

'Bigger than Moolathara?' persisted the king, because he had a long-standing feud with that kingdom.

'Much bigger,' the priest answered slyly.

This seemed to satisfy the king.

'Is everyone in England white-skinned like you?'

'Yes,' the priest said proudly, 'but we are all God's children.'

'Is your king also white-skinned and yellow-haired?'

'Our King George is powerful and wise,' Charteris replied, suddenly driven by a desire to boast. 'Even our queens were great. Like mighty Elizabeth!'

'Then her cunt must be pink,' the king said, with amazing clarity, 'with yellow pubic hair.'

The priest said nothing, but his lips tightened.

'How does she go to war? With her *onnara*?' the king asked contemptuously.

The *onnara* is the linen undergarment worn by Malayali women. Father Charteris was angry, but he was also a coward. However, Choorikathi Kombiyachan's remark about war gave him an opportunity to silence the king. 'England has a mighty navy,' he announced, his pigeon chest swelling with pride. 'Her most famous admiral was the great Sir Francis Drake who defeated the Spanish Armada. Our navy still is mightier than Spain's.'

'What is Spain?' asked the king's minister, a thin, nervous Nair with a bald pate and a tuft.

'It is a country with which England has often been at war,' answered the missionary.

'Is Spain bigger than Panayur?' asked the king curiously.

Records do not exist on how that afternoon durbar ended, but by the time the indigo shadows of the mango tree lengthened and flowed up the palace steps, and the sun became an introverted orange ball sinking into the Ghats, the missionary had received the king's permission to advertise his God in the kingdom of Panayur. He was given, by royal decree, land on the riverbank to build a temple, but the king stipulated that he could not conduct his service until after morning prayer in the king's own temple, and that before the priest started his worship he must bathe in the Papanasini. 'It is the holy river of

Panayur, she cleanses our sins,' the king said. 'And every priest should cleanse his sins before he takes care of the sins of others.'

Charteris was a Yorkshireman, who hardly bathed. He had grown up in a small two-roomed cottage on the moors where the wind howled like a demented dog and cleaned itself on people's bones. The well was inside the cellar, under the house, and the family, which consisted of his gruff father who always stank of ale, his unwashed mother and seven brothers, kept warm in winter around a fire built in the middle of the room. When he had come first to India, the priest's nose had hurt in the spicy air of the Malabar coast, assailed by the scents of oil and flowers, the rough fragrance of the paddy and of Kerala's rain-sloughed red earth. He acquired a habitually surprised look, his nostrils flared like those of a horse which has heard a sudden noise. The king's conditions annoyed him, but he dared not show it: Choorikathi Kombiyachan had a reputation for chopping off heads at whim, and the Englishman had no desire to be buried headless in Malabar, far away from home. So he bathed every morning in the balmy waters of the Papanasini. Today, the tradition still survives, and even after the church was destroyed in a fire, and a new Panayur Church of Our Lady was built a few miles upstream in 1955, the parish priest always performed his morning ablutions in the river before he celebrated mass.

People became accustomed to seeing Charteris's

pale body and wet blond hair in the water, the freckles on his back and his narrow bony shoulders. But the missionary did not mind. He discovered to his astonishment what everyone on Panayur had known for centuries: that throughout the year, whatever the time of day, the water was always of the same temperature. The clear green water flowed warm and benign, cooled by the shadows of trees that grew alongside.

The masseuses of the king were taught to swim early, long before they grew breasts or experienced their first menstrual cramps. They learnt to swim along the undertide of the Papanasini, to cavort underwater so that their bodies became supple and knew the river and its drift. They were taught to swim with their arms held along the current, so that the course of the river flowed along the lines on their palms. And when they grew older, their breasts were stroked by the river's flow, and their hard-tipped, palm-dark nipples were instructed in the logic of the wavelets. The masseuses of Panayur were famous. Old court records show that a pair were once sent as a gift to the court of Emperor Akbar, where both perished, unfortunately, due to indigestion, Mughal food being too rich for them.

Then, one day, Choorikathi Kombiyachan summoned Father Charteris to the *kovilakam*. Beside him stood a girl, barely sixteen, with hair thicker than a monsoon cloud, which spread down to her tiny waist. Her fingers were like lilies restless in a tide, plucking at the hem of her *kasavu*-bordered *mundu*.

Her breasts were large, her nipples the colour of dark honey. Her eyes looked like midnight.

'This is Neeri,' the king said, 'my best masseuse. I give her to you, in return for something you must teach me.'

Charteris eyed Neeri slyly, his loins thickening uncomfortably. 'A priest of England cannot take a woman as his wife,' he protested.

The king studied the priest's face. Charteris looked at Neeri's nipples and licked lips that had suddenly dried. Neeri knotted strands of her black hair in her fingers and looked back at Charteris shyly.

'Come here,' the king said, stroking his silver moustache. The great tufts of his eyebrows were gathered together over his domed forehead and his thick hair flowed down to his shoulders and gleamed in the sun. The priest went to him hesitantly, nervously eyeing the sword. The king leant over, grabbed the Englishman by one bony shoulder and whispered in his ear.

Charteris did not answer, but his face paled. The king's minister saw the blood beating under the skin of his shaven cheeks and, later that night, told his wife that the white man's blood was also red. 'White skin must be a disease of pigmentation,' he said.

Charteris left the king's audience, his head bowed; Neeri followed a few paces behind him.

Choorikathi Kombiyachan watched them with a small gleam in his large bloodshot eyes, and a smile trembled at the corners of his mouth. That evening the king summoned the royal carpenter, and sent a team of three hundred woodcutters to the Dhoni mountains to fell timber to bring back to Panayur.

It is not known what the king said to the priest to make him walk away with Neeri, but a month later, Choorikathi Kombiyachan began to build his navy. The logs arrived, floating down the Papanasini from Dhoni, and were hauled up to the banks by thirty elephants. Charteris supervised the building of the ships, the cutting of the canvas sails and the polishing of the masts. The king's workmen laboured on the ships through one hundred and seventy-five days and nights; the priest often woke to the sounds of their hammers and the trumpeting of the elephants as they hauled the heavy logs from the riverbank. He would see that Neeri was awake, watching him with sleepless feline eyes. Her smile was wet, spreading moonwater. Her hair was fragrant and swam across the bed and she would trail it over Charteris's face and chest, creating in him the sensation of drowning in some dark scent. Her earlobes shone like pale shells in that nightdrift, and her hands fluttered over his body. She flowed over him, breasts and nipples nestling against soft parts of his body, her mouth enveloping him until he felt he was swimming in the river itself. He felt the fish tease his skin with their silvery scales, ripples lapping against hidden places, the pleasure unbearable, and as the torrent welled up inside him he screamed his God's name in hopeless ecstasy.

On the shore of the Papanasini, in the curve of the bay, Kombiyachan's newborn ships rolled in the tides, anchored and restless. The river heaved beneath them, and the wavelets whispered.

It was some of these ships that Fernando Gomez and his small band of adventurers came across. With Gomez there were four others: da Cruz, Eduardo, João and Omar the Moor, who was seven feet tall, black, and had foul breath. He wore a huge scimitar in a scabbard clotted with innumerable maroon patches and greasy stains. Nobody dared speculate whether these marks were blood, or how many belonged to his victims and how many to Omar himself. It was rumoured that Omar had once been a pirate, and had signed on with the captain after having lost his soul to the seaman in a tavern game of arm-wrestling at Mossel Bay. In truth, Omar was a butcher's apprentice who had run away to sea, sickened by the continuous bleating of the sheep he had to slaughter. He couldn't bear to see the beasts' eyes rolling in terror as they were dragged to the knife; his own eyeballs had developed a similar roll which made him look especially fearsome, a towering, inky giant with a surly, drunken glare. But long after he had left the butcher's shop in Santa Helena behind, there remained around him a haze of blood, a miasmic vapour that gave him a faint carmine aura. Wherever he went, Omar carried this mist, translucent in the tavern lights or in the starlight upon the deck where he stood, watching the ocean swell under the ship.

Gomez had seen in him an invaluable fighter: fear of death and his aversion to blood made the Moor want to finish a battle quickly, and the strength of his great arms as he flailed his scimitar, mowing down those who came in his way, struck terror into the hearts of his enemies. The sailors kept away from him, crossing themselves as he passed. Omar was used to this: the blood on his hands and its sickly sweet smell had made him an outcast long ago. Even whores in the ports they stopped at were reluctant to accommodate him; those who did charged him extra.

Eduardo and João were from Lisbon, barely past their teens; their swords had yet to taste blood. They were in awe of Gomez chiefly because he was first mate, and had the manners of an aristocrat. He could whistle romantic ballads through his fine white teeth, and he kept the ends of his moustaches waxed and pointed upwards like a chevalier. He was the only person who treated the big Moor with any amiability. When he first set his eyes upon the solitary giant, Gomez had decided that Omar would be of great use; in those days, strength was a man's greatest asset. Gomez was ambitious; he was no longer content with his share of the purse whenever they returned to Lisbon. Born in a small village three days by horseback from the city, he was the illegitimate son of a Portuguese count and a seamstress, and the shame of his bastardy had driven deep into him the need for gold. Gold gave men acceptability and fine clothes; it gave them entry to the king's court.

'Ships!' Gomez whispered. 'Ships!'

Three vessels were moored to the pier that the king

had built upon the Papanasini, their sails down and tied.

'They look English,' grunted da Cruz.

Fernando gave the sign for the men to rest their oars. He fingered the pommel of his sword.

'Do we attack them, Cap'n?' João asked, his face pale in the excitement of his first fight.

'Silence!' Gomez hissed, thinking furiously. 'English ships?'

The craft looked sleek and fast. The breaking dawn outlined their masts with a sharp silver, varnishing their wet sides.

'Row up slow,' Gomez decided, 'and we'll board them. You boys take the first, da Cruz and I will board the second, and Omar . . .'

The giant grinned, and the stench from his mouth made da Cruz wince. 'I'll take the last,' he growled.

Omar dived into the river, a great seal entering the water silently, sword gripped between his teeth. He swam with powerful strokes, not looking back, the top of his shaven head gleaming in the morning light.

Gomez raised his hand once more. 'Let Omar tell us what he finds,' he said. 'Until then we wait.'

They watched him clamber up the anchor chain and Gomez felt a strange dread clutch his throat. Prayer bells rang out from the temple of Siva and a cloud reared up in the sky, a great hood curling up over them. It began to rain heavily. Long silver needles stabbed the water around them and a great swarm of crows rose up, cawing furiously.

Omar vaulted on to the deck, landing on his feet in a crouch, his right hand on the hilt of his sword. The ship had been swept clean and it shone in the morning light. Something twinkling on the floor caught his eye, and he went across to pick it up: a little amulet of gold lay discarded beside a porthole. Grinning, the Moor slipped it into the pocket of his pantaloons and entered the main cabin.

The rain stopped as quickly as it had begun and Gomez lit a cheroot. He had been so intent on watching the ship Omar had boarded that he had not noticed the soldiers lined up along the riverbank. A horse whinnied behind him. He turned, cursed and reached for his sword. 'Row back!' he shouted. 'They are too many for us to fight.'

The soldiers on the bank were Panayur's army. They held long spears and carried gleaming short-swords. The officers were on horseback, and wore long shining belts of steel around their waists. Gomez was to learn later that these belts of steel – called *urumis* – could shred a man to ribbons. But as he turned away his boat towards Calicut, his thoughts were of escape.

'The Moor – what about the Moor?' someone cried. Gomez thought it was João. But his thoughts were not of Omar as he saw another ship bearing down upon his little boat.

'We are trapped!' da Cruz shouted. João and Eduardo flung themselves into the water and swam towards the forest on the opposite bank of the river.

The Papanasini was a full half-mile wide, and Gomez did not see Eduardo sink half-way across – his fair head bobbed up a couple of times, and then he was gone with a feeble wave of one hand – for he and da Cruz were staring at the ship bearing down on them. It was a galley, and they could see the frowns of the oarsmen as they gritted their teeth and pulled against the current. Gomez's eyes caught the curious gaze of a white man who stood at the stern, dressed in a black cassock. His thin fair hair was blowing back in the wind, and under his eyes were black pouches of sleeplessness and dissipation. Beside him stood a half-naked woman with dark eyes; the sun gleamed golden on her naked breasts.

'Holy Mother!' swore Gomez, as the ship rammed into his boat. The world churned, and darkness swam up to meet him, drawing him down like a witch-woman's hair into a spiralling whirlpool of sleep.

Later, much later, and only moments before his death, Fernando Gomez remembered that morning, and grinned ruefully. Then he had thought the last sight he would see would be that black prow hurtling down upon him. How wrong he had been. Now he stood naked, buried upright in the king's courtyard. The fierce summer sun hurt his eyelids.

This is fate, he thought, as he watched the giant black foot of the king's elephant raise itself over his head. The earth around and below his waist was wet and sticky, and he knew he had emptied his bowels. Tusks gleaming with their rings of gold, the elephant trumpeted insanely, and as Fernando Gomez watched the huge dark foot descend on him, he saw with great clarity the wrinkles around the ankle and the dirty ivory-coloured nails . . .

At the time of the attack on the river, Omar had been about to turn away from the forecabin of the ship he'd boarded when he heard a woman's moans followed by a man's deep growls. He turned back silently and crept to the corner of the aftway. The sounds were coming from a cabin to his left. The door was ajar, and he glimpsed the ivory skin of a woman. He opened the door wide and entered, scimitar raised. A short, naked man with long silver hair was lying on top of the woman.

Choorikathi Kombiyachan looked up at the black giant and cursed. He had just come back from the war with Moolathara, and his navy had taken the Achan's army by surprise. Since there had been no reports of troop movements, the unsuspecting Moolathara were in their beds when the soldiers of the Panayur expedition had landed on the riverbank. The annexation of Moolathara was over by morning, the Achan impaled on his bed with a spear, his head removed and mounted at the door of the harem. The Panayur army had returned only the night before, and Choorikathi Kombiyachan was celebrating his victory on board his favourite ship, making love to Queen Ponni, his prize from the raid of Moolathara.

Now as Ponni looked up at Omar, her eyes caught

the Moor's and the heat in them turned him immobile. Kombiyachan's hand had been between her legs, his lips had turned her nipples to dark, stiff coral, and Omar stood transfixed, his erection like an oar. The king glared at him with speechless fury. The Moor did not see the black shadow that slid silently from its perch behind him, and he barely heard the rush of air as Kalan, the king's pet panther, launched itself at him. Then he felt six furrows of fire cleave his back, and turned to see the flat-skulled black face of the beast next to his, its rotten-meat breath choking him unconscious.

When his senses returned, he was lying on straw in a lightless room, his feet chained to the wall. His back was raw and crusted with dry blood. Beside him, da Cruz slept in a deep faint, his mouth open, hands suspended over his shoulders from gyves nailed to the walls. Omar's eyes met those of Gomez, who smiled at him weakly. Gomez was spreadeagled on the floor, his limbs tied down to pegs. But he could raise his head to look at Omar and had been watching him come awake.

'Rotten luck,' he said. 'Our only hope is that the captain comes looking for us.'

'Not likely,' Omar grunted. 'I doubt he will have time for deserters. He might come looking for us, but only to hang us.'

'You cheer me, my Moor,' said Gomez. 'I think we have visitors.'

It was Kombiyachan. The king was accompanied

by Father Charteris and a woman whose gaze Omar recognized. She was now dressed in a white linen *mundu*, edged with gilt brocade. Her chest was covered with gold, and her hair fell to her knees in a thick black plait. She looked past the chained Moor and her eyes fell on Gomez, who was staring intently at her. For Fernando Gomez had never seen anything so utterly beautiful. Queen Ponni felt his gaze on her. Her eyes opened wider and a small blue vein on her right eyelid quivered.

Kombiyachan did not notice the look that passed between his new queen and the captive, for he was gazing at the Moor. But Charteris did not miss it.

'A remarkable specimen,' Kombiyachan remarked to the priest. 'He would have killed me were it not for the cat.'

Kombiyachan often referred to his panther as a cat, sometimes calling it a kitten, his *poochakutty*. The priest always found this a little gruesome and funny.

'He is strong and big,' Charteris said. 'We can use him for the tournaments.'

The king prodded the Moor's biceps with his foot and grunted. 'He looks stronger than the savages we trap in Lakshwadeep.'

'Let's try him out with the ape that the Dhoni chieftain has sent us,' suggested the priest, with relish.

'Good idea,' the king said. 'Or should he be wrestling with the crocodiles?'

'Or even baby elephants.' The priest pursed his lips.

There was a stirring in the shadows behind the king: da Cruz was waking. The king jumped, and swung his sword. The Portuguese's head flew up in the air and fell on Gomez's chest. Its dying eyes seemed to look into his with a deep sense of hurt, and a long sigh escaped its lips, followed by a froth of blood. Gomez screamed.

The priest swung round, glaring at him, with demented, opium-hazed eyes. 'Kill him, too, Your Highness!' he screeched.

Gomez caught the sly gleam in the king's eyes.

'Oh, no, he is a sailor, and the captain of that boat.' Choorikathi Kombiyachan laughed. 'Tomorrow morning he starts training my navy, the white man's way.'

Gomez caught the gleam of hatred in Charteris's eyes and shuddered. He had to escape – and soon. He looked at the long-haired queen who stood beside the king. She had turned back to look at him as she followed her new master out and there was a softness in her eyes, which answered Gomez's crooked, bruised smile . . .

All this had come to Gomez as the foot of the king's elephant descended towards him. Time unfurled like a sail slowly filling with wind. He wondered if his head would remain alive even after it had been crushed like one of the coconuts the priests at the temple broke before the stone penis of Siva. Or if his brain and sinuses, blood and bone would mingle in the red earth of the king's courtyard. The creature's foot was a spreading umbrella, shading him from the sun, and there was a coolness on his face which reminded him of something, something near-forgotten but beloved. He felt the first touch of death as the elephant's foot met his head, and remembered what it was.

His last thought was of the coolness of Queen Ponni's navel as he laid his cheek against her belly and felt his child growing inside.

Chapter Five

Swati realized that Antara had come into the room while he had been reading, and had stood by the door watching him. The words had cast their sorcery on him, hesitantly at first, then in a rush of voice, blood, love and laughter, and he had not noticed her arrival. He turned towards her, smiling, and she sat down next to him, smoothing her clothing over her hips. 'I have read these so many times that I know them by heart,' she said. 'Read them to me now.'

Swati looked at her face, softened by the lamplight and opaque shades.

'I want to hear you read,' she said shyly, 'to hear your voice.'

'Gomez remembered watching the elephant's foot descend on his head for a moment after he died,' Swati began. 'In that cusp between pain and oblivion, packed in his own excrement and wet mud, the memory of his lover's belly swollen with his child, a ripe, sweet melon full of their shared life, gave him hope . . .'

*   *   *

Queen Ponni's fingers teased Gomez's hair and the diamond on her ring caught in it and pulled it. Gomez sat up on the bed. Outside, a boatman was punting home in the night – the sound of the water against the boat came to them in the wind.

'It is becoming dangerous in the court,' Ponni said. 'If Kombiyachan learns of our love, he will slaughter us. Can't we go to Portugal?'

'We do not have the ships and the crew,' Gomez answered. 'We would have to escape to Chittoor first, to your father's house.'

'Will Omar come?'

'I doubt it. Since he slew the bear in the ring, he has become a great favourite of the king.'

Ponni shuddered. The vision of the Moor, his arms wrapped around the huge animal, his face buried in its hairy neck as he gnawed at its jugular, still haunted her. Above the roar of the crowd, and the bear's scream of rage and pain, had come Omar's victorious shriek as he ripped away the animal's throat, his broad sweat-shined back livid with bloody horizontal scars. She had not been able to distinguish man from beast. She watched as the dead animal fell at Omar's feet. The towering Negro stood in the middle of the ring, panting, his face covered with blood. The ivory of his eyeballs gleamed against his dark skin while his huge fists were clenched with exertion. Ponni noticed Kombiyachan, who was sitting next to her, lean forward, his jaw dropping, his shoulders slumping. The crowd roared in bloodlust, but Ponni heard a small sound escape the king – a slow purr that rose and fell. He was snoring.

She started to laugh. Her eyes were filled with tears of mirth. She saw Omar collapse in a blur on the dead bear as Kombiyachan's snores continued to rise and fall. Her belly hurt. It was her laughter that woke the king, rather than the din of the crowd and the neighing of the horses. His hand gripped the hilt of his shortsword. 'Chop his head off,' he growled. Ponni was now almost hysterical with laughter. The king turned and slapped the side of her face; her lip tore and began to bleed. Kalan, the panther, glanced up at her, scenting blood, its amber eyes fixed on her torn mouth. The crowd fell silent. Ponni felt as if the sun had dropped down into the pit of her stomach.

Kombiyachan leant forward and licked the blood from the corner of her lip. 'I'm sorry, you startled me,' he said.

Ponni's eyes were misty, her vision specked with red dots, but she saw Gomez start forward, the frown on his face making him look thin and dark. His hand went to his sword, and she shook her head at him, warning him to keep away. She noticed Charteris glance at Gomez; in the priest's eyes she detected the shadow of speculation.

That night, she woke from a wounded sleep to find Gomez standing by the window, brooding. The casement balcony overlooked the river, and he had swum along the bank and hauled himself up by the roots of the banyan tree that grew adjacent to the wall. She held out her arms, smiling, and he went into her embrace, kneeling down to lay his head on her breast. 'We must escape,' he said.

From the window, they could see the river's great curve and the church Charteris had built. The sky was pale grey, the moon hidden. A frame of light – a window – shone against the black wing of the building in which the priest lived.

'The Englishman suspects us,' Gomez said, 'and that mistress of his with the oily gaze . . .'

'It seems the very walls are spies,' Ponni whispered.

'Sometimes I feel the walls watch me, day and night,' Gomez said, 'as though they are full of the king's eyes.'

'They say Kombiyachan is also a sorcerer,' Ponni said. 'When he rebuilt the palace, he buried people alive in the walls. He commands their souls, and the walls see for him. On each turret of his fort dead men stand as his sentries where they have been walled in, disguised in brick, doomed to watch over the kingdom.'

Gomez laughed uneasily. 'There is no such thing as magic,' he said, stroking her hair. 'Not for white men.'

Suddenly a bat flew into the room, a quick leathery flutter that circled in the air above the lovers. Ponni suppressed a shriek. Gomez struck out at it.

'Leave,' Ponni said urgently.

There were footsteps outside, and a knock on the door. 'Your Highness, the king desires an audience,' a guard's voice announced.

Gomez got up and went quickly to the window. It was too risky to dive into the river – he would be heard by the sentries – so he lowered himself along the banyan roots and stood against the tree, his feet planted sideways upon the brick ledge. Along the palace wall, further down, there was a smell jetty where a few boats had been moored; they grated against the bricks as the tide tossed them about. The shadows of the banyan hid him, while the rush of the river and the creaks of the boats would mask any sound he made. Gomez spotted a *thoni*, which had drifted on to a sandbank between the tree and the palace. For a moment he contemplated dropping down into the water, clambering on board the little boat and escaping to the far shore, but the fear he had seen in Ponni's eyes rooted him.

He watched the king enter Ponni's chamber, the panther gliding swiftly into the room behind him. Ponni curtsied. The great cat went up to the window and stood with its paws on the windowsill, staring at where Gomez was hidden. Its yellow eyes sought him out, its gaze locking on to his contemptuously. It growled softly in its throat. Ponni stifled a gasp and Kombiyachan went up to the window and peered into the shadows. 'No one is there,' he told the cat. Then he turned to Ponni and paused. 'Is anyone there?'

Ponni smiled at him; her mouth hurt as it stretched.

Kombiyachan went up to her and sat down on the bed. 'I am sorry I struck you,' he said, 'but you should not have startled me.'

'I would like to visit Chittoor for a few days,' Ponni said.

'You should not talk,' the king said gently, his hand caressing her naked breast. 'It will hurt. Ah, but your breast is like a fig carved in ivory.'

'I would like to see my father,' she said. 'He has not been well.'

'Hush,' the king said, and stooped to take her nipple in his mouth. He sucked on it, making whistling noises.

'Your Highness, I am not fit to be touched today,' she whispered.

Kombiyachan sat up and peered into her face. His breath smelt of sour *arrack*. 'Or you do not want to fuck me,' he demanded, 'because I hit you.'

Ponni looked into his face, and smiled seductively. She lowered her heavy-lidded eyes, and looked up at him through her lashes with the glance she knew would inflame him. 'How could Your Highness say that?' she asked softly.

Kombiyachan looked at her darkly, his frown burning her skin. Then he laughed. 'All right. When?'

'The day after tomorrow, my lord,' Ponni said, 'I will wait for you.'

The king got up, patting his rounded belly. Ponni could see his erection bulging against his sarong. At his waist, the hilt of the dagger stuck into his cummerbund glinted with diamonds. He looked very tall, and the shadows in the room gave him the appearance of a statue. He leant forward and gently touched the queen's lower lip. 'Lucky Ponni,' he said, with a tender wistfulness that surprised her. 'I hate being woken suddenly from sleep. I might have chopped off your head.'

Ponni smiled again, but her eyes gave her away. Kombiyachan absorbed her glance in his, and a small smile ticked at the corner of his mouth. He collected her hair in one hand, raising it high so that he could smell the jasmine. 'And that would have been a pity, my queen,' he said, stroking the nape of her neck.

The panther growled again. It sensed Gomez shifting his position on the wall. The Portuguese had pressed himself against the trunk of the tree, trying to make himself invisible from the panther's gaze. He had found a nook where the tree grew into the barrier: its branches hung down thick with leaves, its roots spreading over the brickwork.

'There is nobody there, Poochakutty,' the king called. 'It must be the ghost of the old Achan visiting his wife.'

Ponni gave a small sob, which seemed to please the king. 'Missing him, my dearest?' he asked, bringing his face close down to hers. He still held her hair in one hand. Ponni did not answer; she did not dare struggle. 'Tell me, am I not a better fuck than he?' he asked.

Ponni did not answer. The big cat turned and padded up to sit beside the king. It squatted on its haunches, purring softly, its saffron gaze fixed on her face.

'Answer me, my queen,' Kombiyachan commanded.

The panther's eyes hypnotized her.

'I must tell you something I haven't told you before,' the king said. 'When I killed your husband, I looked at his dick. It was so small he could not have fucked a parrot with it.' He released her hair, and peeled away his sarong from his waist. His erection stroked her cheek, curved, hot, with a strong aroma of its own. He rubbed it against the cut on her mouth, and Ponni winced. 'You can't fuck because you are bleeding from your cunt,' he said, 'but you can suck me.'

Ponni's eyes widened, and the horror in them excited Choorikathi Kombiyachan. He took her face in his palm, digging his fingers deep into her cheeks. He thrust himself into her open mouth, and Ponni choked as he filled her throat. The cut on her mouth bled afresh, and Kombiyachan bunched her hair in his fist, pulling her face to and fro along him. Blood ran down the side of Ponni's face, mixing with the dribble on her jaw. Then her mouth filled with Kombiyachan's semen, which mingled with the blood and spittle and flowed down her neck to her breasts.

The king stood frozen, one large palm holding her face against his navel. He stroked her hair with the other. 'You are beautiful.' His voice was soft. 'Fucking you is like fucking a hibiscus.'

He released her and Ponni fell back on her bed. Her throat burned and her head throbbed. She felt disembodied, her spirit distanced from her pain floating somewhere in the air as a weightless leaf. A strange

80

droning filled the room, beginning softly, then rising until it filled her ears.

The panther was purring a hideous lullaby.

From his precarious perch among the shadows of the tree, Gomez watched Kombiyachan leave the queen's room; the king's swaggering retreat filled him with helpless hatred. The great cat turned to look back into the night once more, its eyes seeking Gomez out in the shadows. He did not realize that his own lips were drawn back in a feral snarl. He heard the guttural summons of the king to his pet, and waited. He wondered if it was a trap. He could see Ponni lying upon the white linen bedcloth; her chest rose and fell, interrupted by spasmodic shudders. Time seemed to stretch far into the night, curling around his limbs like a sluggish serpent. Eventually, hearing no further sound, Gomez climbed cautiously back on the ledge and hoisted himself into the room. 'Wake up, my darling.' He shook her. 'We have to escape.'

Ponni groaned. Her eyes opened, and her head fell back on the pillows. Gomez knew it would be useless to try to wake her: she was in shock. He lifted her on to his shoulder and climbed over the windowsill. Slowly and carefully, he lowered himself and Ponni on to the sandbank, and into the boat . . .

The heat woke Ponni; she felt the sun on her face and saw the sky and the clouds moving above her. The sound of water had pierced her dreams. Gomez's shadow fell across her eyes and she saw that his face, browned by the sun, was tender and anxious.

'Where are we?' she asked.

'We are approaching Chittoor,' he answered. 'Help is near.'

Ponni slid back into sleep, the pain a distant margin. When she woke again, she was in her girlhood room in her father's palace. Shadows of her childhood and adolescent nights formed familiar patterns, telling stories on the walls. The window opened on to a perfumed night; the wind was full of half-forgotten scents and sounds. Crickets chirped in the fields beyond the palace grounds, and the palm leaves rubbed against each other in the breeze. The river came to her, too, the mantra of passage, lapping and heaving against her consciousness.

Ponni had forgotten the pain. Shadows moved over her, a blanket of soft darkness that soothed her bruised face as the moon travelled its arc. They were making the walls come alive once more – a great tapestry revealing long-forgotten shapes and contours. Her mother was leaning over her, and she could smell the *kayampoo* on her skin. Ponni whimpered, and remembered the night of her first menstruation when she had woken frightened by the wetness of the sheets and her thighs – woken from a strange arousing dream in which a monstrous elephant loomed over her, the great fans of its ears flapping in the dreamwind, its ivory tusks scraping her belly as its rough and fibrous trunk pushed between her thighs.

'Hush, my daughter, my little princess,' her mother crooned over her. And she remembered she had refused to recognize she was awake, her eyes clenched shut at the memory of that nightmare and the blood.

Now, as Ponni lay in her father's house, she recalled how her mother, the queen of Chittoor, had hanged herself from the tamarind tree outside her daughter's window. There was a message in her death that Ponni strove to understand.

'It is blood, that red language of pain,' she had said in her sleep, a sleep from which she knew she had woken a long time ago.

'It is nothing, my daughter,' her mother whispered, stroking her brow, gently blowing on the tiny beads of sweat forming on her forehead. 'It is the beginning of being a woman. And being a woman is the beginning of pain, inaugurated with blood.'

Now, as she watched the ghost in the air, an empty space trapped within the fine dust and pollen, shaped by the breeze, she whimpered again. The pain of a woman begins with her blood; it flows deep from her womb like a forewarning of what lies ahead.

Ponni had never understood why her mother had hanged herself and left her father to mourn. He did not have many wives, unlike so many other kings, and he did not take another after Mother had died. Sometimes Ponni came across him looking thoughtfully out of the window, at the empty space that Mother's presence still occupied. She wondered whether Father could see the ghost, too, but she doubted it. One of the things about being a woman was not to show pain to your men – your fathers and husbands and sons – but to keep it hidden in your heart until your fingers turned red from clenching. She knew it was this pain that she now dug with her painted nails into the soft cushion of her palm, a pain more original and fresh than that of Choorikathi Kombiyachan's penis in her mouth, a pain composed of memories.

But now all that mattered was her pain's sharpness blending into faceless grief: it had her mother's farewell in it, her father's bereavement, her lover's execution. She knew that more pain lay ahead. It was as if the flight had opened her to her final destiny of pain.

Pain has its own bewitchment, Ponni thought, and she longed for Gomez to be at her side to read her its runes. But Gomez lay in an exhausted sleep in the dungeons of the king of Chittoor, a prize to be given by him to Choorikathi Kombiyachan. The king, Ponni's father, knew Kombiyachan would come looking for his runaway queen and her lover, and he had no desire to do battle with his strange and volatile son-in-law.

The kingdom of Chittoor had been exhausted by a previous war with the neighbouring chieftain of Pollachi, a battle won at the cost of many *chakorpada* Nairs. It had taken place on the banks of the Chittoor river, with the invading *pandis* arrayed on the other side. They had constructed a bridge of coconut-palm trunks lashed end to end and the king's stomach had churned at the thought of fighting those dark-skinned Tamil warriors with red waistcloths and flashing swords. The *chakorpada* was the last line of defence, a small cluster of silent brown men waiting patiently behind the king's footmen. The king's heart went out to them, the suicide-warriors of his land about whom bards sang and women wove orgasms while mating with their husbands. In peacetime they fought tournaments on *angathattus*, the raised platforms of mud, the elegant and deadly dance of *kalaripayattu* which was the origin of all eastern martial art, practising their skill to die.

But that night, when the army of Chittoor faced the Tamil army, the king's heart was heavy. Chittoor was a small kingdom – a province, really – but its *illams* were rich and the *Namboodiris* had hoarded much gold and jewellery. But, more important, Chittoor held the key to the land beyond the Kuthiran mountain ranges: Calicut, Travancore and Cochin. Anyone who overran Chittoor could cross through the mountain pass and plunder the east of Kerala. The facile treaty that the king had first signed with the British and later with Haider Ali had left the kingdom untouched by invasion. The only condition that Haider Ali, the swarthy giant from Mysore, had set was that the women of Chittoor wear cloth over their breasts. It was a demand the king had accepted gladly in return for freedom. And Haider's army had marched through Chittoor, a never-ending sequence of fierce shapes in the dust, bent upon taking the riches of the Zamorin of Calicut. The king heard stories of how the entire army stopped for prayer, spreading mats and turbans on the road, their glistening spears and swords laid down beside them as a harvest of death, their whinnying horses pawing the ground. As one great form, Haider's warriors knelt towards the black stone of Mecca, the sultan in front, prostrate upon a rich red-gold Persian carpet, a wave stooping slowly to the earth, foreheads touching the soil of Chittoor.

'*Allahu Akbar . . .*' A vast and strange cry from a thousand throats ascended into the clean skies of that little kingdom, the red dust settling over the land, horses falling silent at the name of a new desert god.

Haider died later in Mysore, while Tipu Sultan chased the British all the way to Calicut. But Tipu was called back, his campaign interrupted by his father's death. And after the sultan fell at the battle of Seringapatinam, Malabar returned to its old ways: the *cherumis* scythed the green paddystalks and sang while the summer sun glowed on their bare breasts, which shone like brown apples.

Spies brought home the news of the death of the Zamorin of Calicut, who had screamed curses while he ran along the burning rooms and balconies of his palace, abusing the invaders from Mysore and calling down damnation on their souls. The king of Chittoor mourned. Later, as Tipu passed through Chittoor again, chasing – like his father before him – the whiteskins of the East India Company all the way to Calicut, the king retreated into his palace. Sequestered in his chambers, he waited for the flames to reach him, the poisoned juice of *kolambi*, sweetened with palm-extract, poured into small silver goblets, to be drunk by his daughter, Ponni, and himself.

But Tipu passed without a glance at the Chittoor king's palace, riding his white charger hard in pursuit of the British, who were fleeing towards the ships docked at Calicut. It was the second time the East India Company had fled from the family of the sultans of Mysore. The first was when Haider Ali had driven them to Fort St George in Madras, then turned back without laying a finger on the garrison. And this time, too, while the English cowered in fear of slaughter, Tipu turned back. Haider Ali lay dying in Mysore. But the king of Chittoor was not to know that had either father or son succeeded the history of India might have been a little different. The rich red earth of the little province he ruled – the corridor of empires – bore the spoor of many such war journeys. Only later, much later, when he met Tipu Sultan face to face on one of his passages through Chittoor, did the king ask the outsider: 'Why did you turn back? Would your father have wished you to return unfinished?'

'It was more than the death of my father,' the sultan replied. 'It was a sense of unfinished destiny against which I had no mortal power. Once I turned back, I knew we had lost.'

The king of Chittoor sat with Tipu in the sultan's

tent, pitched on the hillocks overlooking the village of Palghat. The fort was being built by labourers from the neighbouring provinces with help from the *pandis* of Pollachi and Coimbatore. It was an immense structure of black stone, whose presence seemed alien to the king's eyes. It was too formidable an edifice, more intimidating and despotic than anything he had ever seen. Tipu smiled and stroked the end of his moustache. He was a man of medium height and slim build, wearing a turban of gold and pearls and an embroidered shirt. But the hilt of his sword was plain and unjewelled; it had the lethal comfort of a warrior's much-used ally.

'Why do you need to build something like that?' the king of Chittoor pointed at the fort. 'You have either conquered or made treaties with most kingdoms here. No one has the strength to attack you.'

'It is not against you,' Tipu replied sorrowfully. 'We have fought so long with ourselves that we have admitted our nemesis already. The white man is coming to stay.'

Tipu Sultan's strongest ally was Choorikathi Kombiyachan, with whom he had an uneasy pact. The sultan was aware of Kombiyachan's reputation for cruelty, but he also knew that the despot had a vast network of spies that extended all the way from Tamilakam to the borders of Travancore. In return for his independence, Kombiyachan gave the sultan valuable information – which in time was to prove Tipu's undoing. For the priest Charteris had begun to anticipate the arrival of the Company again, and during the last days of Tipu's reign over Malabar, had instructed his spies to mislead the sultan about the movement of the British troops.

It was Charteris that the king of Chittoor remembered as he lay on his carved wooden cot staring into the night. He was aware that his daughter was in love with the foreigner imprisoned in the dungeon below. He was also aware that the white man had saved Ponni from Kombiyachan. If it had been only Kombiyachan, he might have pleaded for his daughter's life and exiled her lover, but he knew that the priest did not tolerate other white men at court. Charteris had to be the unique ambassador of his pigment in Malabar, and he had developed a contempt and hatred for Gomez. It was the priest who had begun to poison Kombiyachan's mind against the Portuguese, insinuating that he had stolen Ponni's affections.

After Gomez was freed from prison, he proved himself an excellent sailor in Kombiyachan's navy, and became his untitled admiral. He brought to Panayur's mariners his vast experience of the seas, introducing them to the arts of ocean warfare, stealthy landings and surprise guerrilla attacks. Charteris saw that Gomez was turning the king's navy into a formidable fighting force, and that Kombiyachan insisted the Portuguese seaman accompany him on all his raiding expeditions. The priest sensed the dependence of Kombiyachan on Gomez, and was aware, too, of the attraction between the sailor and Ponni. This, he knew, would prove to be Gomez's undoing.

And Ponni's father, the king of Chittoor, had no strength to fight the wiles of Charteris and the army of Kombiyachan together. The king remembered the morning of that battle long ago as he waited for the *pandis* to cross the palm bridges, dismay and a sense of doom filling him. He had sent word to Kombiyachan's court, seeking help, but the messenger had returned without a clear answer. As the dawn had shuddered into silver over the Western Ghats, the king was startled by the sudden cry that rose from his army. Around the bend in the river appeared Kombiyachan's fleet, heralded by the thudding rhythm of oars, topsails fat with the western wind. The Tamil army, which was about to begin its charge, paused in bemusement at the sight of ships that bristled with armed men. Kombiyachan's navy dropped anchor at a little distance from the battle sands and the king of Chittoor could see Kombiyachan standing on the deck of the leading ship. The king raised his sword in salutation and Panayur's tyrant waved back.

'Charge!' he shouted, leaping on to the bridge of palm trunks with his army behind him. The king was sure that Kombiyachan's soldiers were already disembarking to join him in battle. The *pandis*, surprised to see ships full of soldiers bearing down on them, had heard of the fierce king who chopped off heads and had a navy that patrolled the river. The Tamils were thrown into confusion and, before they could recover, the Chittoor army was upon them. But both sides realized quickly that Kombiyachan's army was a mere spectator to the fighting. As the king of Chittoor parried a thrust from a *pandi* soldier, his eyes met Kombiyachan's across the distance. In a fleeting moment of recognition that distracted him, he saw the autocrat's eyes glitter like stones that fed on blood. Too late, he could not avert the oncoming spear – although his sword deflected its force – its shaft slamming into the side of his skull. As he fell, with the roar of screaming men and clashing weapons receding from him, he caught the curious gaze of Kombiyachan, who was standing on the prow of his ship, slapping his thighs and watching the battle as if it were a tournament.

When he woke he was in his room at the palace, and night was already fading. Ponni sat by his bedside; he saw that she hadn't slept. 'Have we lost?' he asked wearily.

Ponni sobbed in her throat and from the shadows the king heard Kombiyachan's voice, deep and throbbing: 'No, Father-in-law, you won. And it was a great victory.'

The king sank back into his sleep, nourished by the knowledge that the *pandis* had been beaten back. It was only later that he was to know that most of his army had perished along with the invaders and it was his stand of *chakorpada* Nairs that turned the last hours of the battle into victory. All along, Choorikathi Kombiyachan and his army had waited and watched, spectators to a bloody regatta taking place on the sandy banks of the Papanasini.

'I had no quarrel with them,' Kombiyachan explained later.

'But you are my ally, my son-in-law,' the old king said, in wonder and sadness. 'If you had joined us I wouldn't have lost so many men.'

Kombiyachan stroked the head of his panther. It looked up at him and winked its amber eyes as if sunlight glinted in them. 'It is not my way,' Kombiyachan said. 'And why do you need an army when I am with you?'

And so, as his daughter lay in her tormented sleep, her lover incarcerated in the dungeons, the king realized he had no army now to fight his neighbour if he came looking for them. If he did not yield his daughter to Kombiyachan, the Chittoor king was sure that his palace would be razed and he would be hanged at the main crossroads of Panayur. He wished his wife were with him: she would have soothed his throbbing temples with her soft palms and calmed him. He got up and walked to his daughter's room, half expecting his dead queen to be beside Ponni's sick-bed. As he opened the door to Ponni's room he thought he imagined a flicker of white in the moon-light that flapped away through the window . . .

Swati was interrupted by a loud hammering on the door, and he got up to open it. Engrossed in the story of the doomed queen and her lover, Antara and he had not realized how time had flown. Night had fallen, and a crowd of men stood outside the temple, some carrying sticks.

'Who are you?' one demanded.

'It is the king,' he heard Antara say from behind him.

'It is I, Swati Varma,' he said. 'What is it that you want from me?'

There was an abrupt silence. Then, suddenly, a few of the men prostrated themselves on the ground, touching their foreheads to the earth.

Swati was embarrassed. 'Please do not do this,' he said. 'It is very awkward. There are no kings now.'

He was interrupted by a sudden babble of protest that broke out from the crowd.

'We thought it was a thief who had broken into the temple . . .'

'The Communists these days are stealing idols and blaming the Muslims so that they can start a riot.'

'Please forgive us. We did not know that the king had returned.'

Swati came out of the room and faced the crowd. 'Muslims have always come to this temple,' he said. 'It is the custom of the royal house of Panayur that its records be maintained by Muslims.'

'Times have changed, Swatithampuran,' someone from the crowd proclaimed ominously. 'Since we demolished their mosque in Ayodhya, we have not been able to trust anyone.'

Swati sensed Antara's agitation.

'Swatiraja, do you know who the legislator from here is, these days? A Marxist!' someone spoke out.

'A Marxist whom the Muslim League is supporting!'

'It is Razack, the tailor's son. And we are told he will be the candidate for Parliament in the next elections.'

'Imagine, a Marxist tailor in Delhi! A Muslim too! Shame upon Panayur!'

Swati held up his palm, asking for silence. 'Why shouldn't Muslims or tailors go to Delhi and represent Panayur in Parliament? I have been away from home for such a long time that I do not understand local politics,' he said. 'I do not have any idea how things have changed.'

'You are our king. You must stand in the elections against the Communists,' someone shouted.

'We are members of the Hindu Sabha of Panayur,' a young man raised his stick in the air. 'We want you to be our leader!'

Swati winced. 'I have come here to rest, and be at peace. Let us talk later.'

The crowd dispersed slowly, muttering and shaking their heads. Some of the younger men lingered to look back at Swati, who turned to Antara in bewilderment. 'I am sorry, my friend. I did not realize Panayur had changed like this.'

Antara did not answer, and Swati saw her wipe her eyes with the tip of her *thorthumundu*. He noticed an old man who had remained behind, standing behind

Antara and peering at them in the darkness. 'Who is that?' he asked.

Antara stood aside. The man was bent and thin; he wore a shabby white shirt and sarong. He hobbled up, dragging behind him a leg swollen with filaria. 'I am Chandu,' he said. Swati detected a defiant pride in his voice. 'My great-great-grandfather was once the umbrella carrier to the king of Chittoor.'

'Let the king be,' Antara said gently. 'Come back to the palace. I will give you something to eat.'

'Those days are gone,' the old man muttered under his breath, to no one in particular, 'when the king held an umbrella over the carrier, too.'

Swati watched the man turn and follow Antara, limping. 'Chandu,' he called softly, 'wait.'

It was Antara's eyes that turned towards him first, bright in the night and gleaming with questions. Swati smiled at her, and asked Chandu, 'Why don't you look after that leg?'

The man laughed without mirth. 'It was a gift,' he said, 'from the royal house of Panayur.'

'I do not understand.'

'After my great-great-grandfather Unnikuttan went to the forest with his king, he returned with a swollen leg,' Chandu said. 'And after that all the men in our family have elephant-legs.'

'Tell me about it,' Swati motioned Chandu to sit down.

Ponni moaned softly, and the king, her father, saw

her wounded mouth in the early dawn. The old man was far away from sorrow, and ever since the death of his wife and the decimation of his army he had behaved as if he were living in a dream. His ministers saw that his mind was drifting, and he took little interest in daily matters of the kingdom. Often he walked to the battlefield upon the riverbank, his long white hair flying in the wind, his small brown face shrinking into a network of lines. Unnikuttan, his loyal umbrella carrier, was behind him, holding up the red canopy to protect him from the sun. As they walked on the sand that had once gorged on blood, he heard the king mutter to himself that it was time for the sun to set. The words of his ruler puzzled the umbrella carrier, since it would already be sunset by the time they reached the riverbank. The river shimmered, its depths dark red in the setting sun – it reminded the umbrella man of blood in the rain.

When he was a child he had seen a dying cow lying on its side on a grass bank, its brown stomach heaving. It raised its long face to him as he approached. Unnikuttan saw the cow look at him with round, frightened eyes that were as yellow as egg yolk, the rims flecked with foamy blood. Blood flowed from its mouth and its anus. It had begun to rain: long thin lines of sharp water that attacked him. The water mixed with the blood on the grass and turned a rusty red. Unnikuttan, who was witnessing the first death in his life, squatted on his haunches beside the dying animal. Its horns were pointed towards the sky and he noticed that one was slightly bent. All around them the world was silent – an eerie gloaming stillness, as if everything had ceased for the time being in honour of the twelve-year-old boy in the presence of his first evidence of mortality. The cow fixed his eyes with its endless stare, trapping them, and in the grape-coloured bovine pupils was an inexplicable mesmerism. Unnikuttan found he was leaning closer to the creature, his face almost touching the animal's as it bled in the rain that now thickened and drummed on their bodies relentlessly. Suddenly the cow shuddered, reached out and nipped at his fingers, bit off one, fell back and died.

Unnikuttan felt the pain of his severed finger only much later. It was the first time he had seen much of his own blood, which spouted from the stump on his knuckle into the bloody mud. He was fainting, surrendering to a soft whirling eddy that had begun to spread inward from the sides of the landscape like a cloak. He let himself go into its embrace, his head full of cotton clouds tinged with red, falling unconscious upon the dead cow.

Unnikuttan whimpered at the memory of that pain. He realized that the royal umbrella had fallen on to the riverbank. He noticed that the king was on his haunches upon the sand, examining something that shone in his hands. Each day, as they walked on the bank, the king discovered some remnant of the battle with the *pandis*: a broken sword, a piece of armour, an amulet that had failed to save its wearer. Beyond the river to the west were the mountains that grew shadows eastward into the night as the sun sank among their dark promontories. To the east, across the plains and the black palmyra, Tipu's fort sat like a huge dark animal, licked red by the Malabar sunset. The king stood up with his souvenir, gazing into the coming night at the bend in the river along which he knew that, sooner or later, Kombiyachan would come sailing for the head of Gomez and the body of his daughter.

'Look!' He held it up to Unnikuttan. 'The broken hilt of my sword. If only I had died . . .'

The umbrella carrier bowed and did not reply; it was not his place to answer the king. But he guessed what went on in the sovereign's mind.

Everyone in Chittoor knew that the Princess Ponni had returned one night, carried ashore from a boat in the arms of a white man. There were rumours that she had escaped from Kombiyachan's palace with the foreigner and expected terrible retribution from the king of Panayur.

But retribution did not come immediately: it took Kombiyachan almost five months to arrive in Chittoor with his navy. A complex string of agreements and wars with the nearby provinces of Malampuzha, Knassery and the tribes of Dhoni had kept him occupied. Omar had become commander-in-chief of Kombiyachan's army, and was winning the battles the despot fought along the banks of his river. Papanasini had become the royal river of Panayur – which Kombiyachan had announced as far as Dhoni by sending out criers and drummers.

After Charteris received a spy from the East India Company one night – he appeared in the church in a missionary's habit – Kombiyachan was told that Tipu's days were numbered, though it was not to happen for many years. The British were gathering their forces in the north, but Tipu had completed the tunnel from Palghat fort to Seringapatinam. Kombiyachan, who had acquired from his spies the plans to the fort and the Sultan's escape route, agreed to sell them to the British in exchange for being allowed to function as a free princely state once the Company had taken Malabar. He had learnt to speak fairly fluent English from Charteris and had insisted that the women of his household and his numerous children also learn the language. It was thus that the first English school was founded in Panayur, perhaps the first in all southern India; the children were taught by two teachers whom Charteris claimed had arrived from England. Both were Company spies, whose information was to prove invaluable to the British in their conquest of the southern tip of India.

The day before Kombiyachan enquired of Charteris, 'What is the Portuguese word for *decapitate*?', the king of Chittoor had woken from a dream in which his dead wife appeared and urged him to flee to the mountains with Ponni. His daughter's belly was swollen in her eighth month of pregnancy, and she had withdrawn into herself. She refused to speak or smile, and had fashioned a rough shroud with which she covered her face. The maids who were attending the king told him that the princess was perhaps going mad, that her mind had travelled inwards and that she made noises that echoed the gurgling in her womb.

The king took Gomez into her room, hoping he would be able to rouse Ponni from her stupor. Gomez took her face in his hands, looked into her eyes and recoiled at the blackness he saw in them. The princess was absent from her own face. He knelt by her bed and placed his ear to her swollen belly. He felt his son inside, but Ponni did not respond to his touch. He spoke to her in urgent whispers about their love, about his loneliness in the dungeon and his love for their unborn child. But Ponni did not move, and, as the guards dragged her lover from her, screaming and crying out her name, she lay still, lost inside the world of her womb.

The next morning Kombiyachan's navy docked at the riverbank. When he and his panther, guided by Omar, entered Chittoor palace all they found was Gomez in the dungeon, chained to the wall. The king of Chittoor had put his pregnant daughter on his horse and was already half-way into the forest of Panayur when Omar walked down the steps to the near-deserted dungeons and heard Gomez crying.

'So here you are, Kapitan,' Omar the Moor said softly, and began to chuckle. The sight of his old captain in rags, his eyes sunken, face unshaven and dirty and hair infested with lice, amused him.

A flight of hope crossed the Portuguese's eyes as he saw his old comrade. 'Help me escape, Omar,' he pleaded.

Omar picked a louse from Gomez's beard and cracked it between his thumbnails.

'Kill me, then, please. I don't want to be taken alive by that monster.'

'That would be helping you,' Omar said, 'and that I cannot do.'

When he discovered that Ponni had fled Kombiyachan's rage was terrible. He ran through the rooms of the palace searching for his fugitive wife and her father, his sword drawn and the panther trotting beside him. The rooms were deserted; he slashed at the copper lampstands and velvet canopies, plunging his sword into beds and cushions while screaming for his unfaithful queen to be brought before him. He had brought the bullock cart of royal punishment with him on the ship, drawn by twin oxen whose sides shone fat and white in the sun. They had tassels of gold strung on their painted horns. A plough of teak was attached to their necks with banded red rope, the end sharpened to a keen point. It was meant to go between Ponni's legs, entering her vagina and severing the joints of her thighs as the oxen backed into her, slowly pushing into her womb and her stomach, collapsing her lungs and spearing her heart to emerge, glutinous with blood, bile and phlegm, through her broken throat. The disappointment drove Kombiyachan insane with rage and he ordered the soldiers to ransack the palace and burn it down.

When he saw Omar dragging a chained Gomez towards him, he almost swung his sword at the Portuguese's neck. 'No, white dog.' The king checked himself. 'You will die too quickly. I will find my queen and you will die together, slowly and painfully. I will prepare a festival for it.'

Gomez looked at Kombiyachan sitting on the throne of Chittoor, which had been dragged into the front courtyard of the palace. By now the building had been torched and the flames now framed Kombiyachan. Gomez spat at him and screamed, 'Now there are three of us. Try killing us all.'

Kombiyachan's forehead grew black with fury. 'I will find her and your bastard!' he shouted. 'And I will scoop the rat out of her belly with my sword!'

Gomez grinned at him, through his filthy lice-infested hair and the caked blood at his mouth. He knew he had won.

Ponni was far away in the forest, sitting on her father's horse as the old king painfully negotiated the overgrown path. Her swollen womb pulled her spine forward with each jolt of the horse. Unnikuttan walked behind, the royal umbrella held over her head to protect her from the leeches that dropped from the slimy, moss-rotted branches of ancient trees. Snakes swayed down in lazy question marks, their flat heads poised against the advance of the party. Their tongues flickered in the moist forest air, and Unnikuttan tightened his grip on the stem of the umbrella. The king held his drawn sword in one hand, and the reins of the horse in the other. Occasionally he would stop and look back at some sound the forest made: the fall of a stone on the hillside or the crackle of a twig.

Later, Unnikuttan was to sit around the steaming pot of pig-intestines and spicy codfish in the *arrack* shops of Chittoor and Panayur and recount his tale of the royal flight. 'The night was green, the leaves of the forest filtered the moonlight, which shimmered with opaque shadows. Walking into the forest was like diving in the Papanasini . . .' the umbrella carrier's stories would begin.

Rogue elephants screamed in the distance. At every twist of the narrow path, Unnikuttan expected the great beasts to come charging at them. The mountain road crawled along narrow boulders, skimming the tops of precipices below which Unnikuttan heard the river roaring its way down to Panayur. The way was slimy with mushrooms and toadstools. Reptiles slithered across their path and leopards watched from the cool heights of trees. Many times the king stopped and brandished his sword in front of him as a snake appeared in mid-air from the foliage above, hissing at the intruders. But the old man was weary with travel and his shoulders drooped. Ponni alone seemed unaffected by anything: she sat on the brown horse like a swollen statuette, her long hair loose like the goddess Mahakali's and her large black eyes shining with a fever that burned deep within her.

'Then what happened, umbrella carrier?' his listeners asked. 'Tell us about the tiger of the Panayur forest.'

Unnikuttan stretched his swollen leg and swatted away the flies. He had been bitten by mosquitoes in the forest, and the day after he came back to Chittoor, he woke screaming from a nightmare. He had dreamt that he was in the court of Chittoor, holding the canopy over the king as he sat on his throne. Suddenly, everything around him began to change, and the faces and limbs of people began to rot. Decay surrounded him. Skin and flesh putrefied and fell away, as black vines grew up the crumbling walls of the palace. The king's face began to melt, and the white bone of his skull gleamed through his skin. There was a terrible stench in the air. Far away people were screaming. Unnikuttan was screaming, too, in his dream and in his waking, for he could not move his leg. He struggled to sit up on the grass mat and saw that his leg was swollen. It smelt rank and wormy. As days went by, it turned black and was bloated like an elephant's penis. He drank a lot of *arrack* to ease the pain . . .

The umbrella carrier picked up his earthen pot, and took a huge mouthful of the bittersweet fire. Fire like the striped flame that shot out from the dark night between the trees. The night was torn by the screams of the rogue elephant who stood ready to attack, inflamed with musth, his trunk raised in a war cry. The king's horse neighed in panic and reared. The princess fell to the ground, clutching her belly. Unnikuttan's umbrella dropped from his hand, and caught in the horse's reins. The animal broke loose and plunged down the hillside, taking the umbrella with it. Suddenly separate realities of sound and sight coexisted in that night and, as the umbrella carrier turned to run, he felt as if he was moving very, very slowly. His arms and waist were heavy, his legs weighted down with lead. He heard the horse lose its feet on the hillside and then its pain-crazed neighing tore through the night.

From the corner of his eye Unnikuttan saw the princess on the ground on her back, hair spreading out behind her like a black fan. He saw the immense elephant towering in front of them, its trunk raised in a raging arc, the terrible, demented trumpeting rending the night. As Unnikuttan began to run, he turned back briefly to see the old king, who had charged the elephant with his sword, being raised skyward, impaled on one of the beast's tusks. The old man's sarong had fallen away and he was a gnarled, naked figure in the air writhing in his death spasms, but still hacking wildly at the brow of the elephant. The last thing he saw – or imagined – was the great tiger leaping out from the shadows, roaring at the elephant as it buckled slowly to its knees under the sword of the dying old king of Chittoor. Unnikuttan did not see the tiger stand guard over the princess, who had begun to shudder and scream at the sudden unbearable pain shredding her from within. He did not wait to see the birth of the bastard prince of Chittoor, a child with hair half blond and half black, who came into the cold forest night howling and kicking as he split his mother's thighs. Many years later the child remembered the cool darkness of the cave in which he lay against the warm sides of his foster mother and sucked on her teats. Her flanks were striped and furry, with white tufts along the sides that retained the familiar smell of her harsh milk. He remembered his foster father walking into the cave and nuzzling him as he lay against his dam, the great head with its endless green eyes looking at him with tender majesty. He remembered roaring into the night, his man-throat swelling as he answered the tiger of Panayur from an unseen distance in the forest.

Unnikuttan the royal umbrella carrier heard it, too, on occasions, as he walked back home dragging his swollen leg. He would pause by the roadside to listen, realizing his fate was inexorably entangled with the destiny of the two kingdoms of Chittoor and Panayur like a fly trapped in two webs, that he had somehow become a party to the making of a legend. And it was his tale of what he had seen that night, told in the *arrack* shops of Chittoor and Panayur, which reached the ears of Choorikathi Kombiyachan as he sat watching the women of his harem fondle one another's breasts.

'A tiger coming down from the forest with a child on its back to drink water from the Papanasini?' Charteris scoffed. 'Native rubbish, my king!'

'The child is half white and half black,' Kombiyachan said. 'I know whose child it is.'

Charteris laughed. 'For God's sake, do you think any child of Gomez would have survived in the forest?'

Kombiyachan got up and struck Charteris with the flat of his palm. The priest fell on his back, his mouth twisted in fear and anger. Charteris had grown fat and sloppy.

'Get up, you fat whiteskin,' the king ordered. 'I go to hunt the tiger.'

In the folklore of Panayur, that was how the legend of the tiger and the royal hunt was born – of the tiger who comes to drink from the Papanasini on full-moon nights, of the child warrior who rides on its back with a sword in his hand and his two-coloured hair sweeping behind him. Choorikathi Kombiyachan went into the forest with a hundred men and after three months came back alone. The royal horse stumbled into the palace yard, lame in its hind leg, its reins trailing. The courtiers ran out to help the king down from the saddle. One fell back as Kombiyachan's sword sliced through his windpipe. Then Kombiyachan leapt down, holding his sword pointed out in front, feeling the space around him with its tip.

Choorikathi Kombiyachan had no eyes. The sockets were empty, and buzzing with flies.

Chapter Six

Morning slid across Swati's face through the window
as it had when he was a small child. After Father had
been left to his eternal solitude upon the distant
Chinese ice and Mother had taken to her white linen
veil, he had had to sleep alone in the great room facing
the river. The first nights were full of whispers and the
chirping of crickets. The wind hurled itself at
the black palm fans along the mud-dark ridges of the
paddyfields, then on the trees in the courtyard.
Sometimes the roll of thunder was followed by roots of
lightning that cleaved the sky. 'Hear the gods going to
war,' his mother said, and Swati imagined the great
chariot wheels of the Kauravas and the Pandavas
rumbling along the sky as war-elephants screamed
their savage cries. After Father died, thunder always
reminded Swati of a distant cannonade.

One evening a year after Great-uncle had taken his
gun and gone off into the forest to look for the tiger,
Swati and his mother finished dinner and went to
their bedroom. Shadows merged with the portraits on

109

the walls and the familiar old furniture waited for them with sleepy warmth. Mother turned the lamp down low, and her elongated shadow fell against the golden lustre of the wall, a strangely poised goddess without features. The boy took her soft palm and placed it on his chest. 'Aren't you coming to bed?' he asked.

Mother shook her head gently. 'It is time for you to sleep alone from now on, my darling,' she whispered.

Swati sat up in bed and held on to her hand tightly. 'No, no, Mother, I cannot,' he had cried.

'It is forbidden for a prince to be afraid,' she replied. Now he remembered his mother's words, spoken as she sat beside him in the night's speckled light. He could see the moonlight upon the ridge of her nose and her cheeks, the rise of her slender neck above her breasts.

'Mother,' the boy whispered, 'can't you sleep beside me as usual? At least tonight.'

She did not reply but continued to stroke his head, almost absently. Swati knew she was on the threshold of another beginning. That evening, he had seen her turn away from her vigil for Great-uncle at the top window of the zenana. A new tautness was in her walk. Mother's first watch had been for Father; it had lasted nearly ten years. After Father had gone off to Aksai Chin with his valet, Nooruddin, who was a *subedar* in the same regiment, Mother would stand at the eastern window on the second floor, which looked out over vast spaces of paddy and water. Standing a few feet away from her was her lady-in-waiting,

Fatima, Nooruddin's wife. The twilight of Palghat was an eldritch cape, a translucence that hung over the land burnishing the palmyra trees, which stood like djinns against the red-stained sky. Beyond the Papanasini, the rise of the temple and the ruined church, the paddyfields stretched out, green and gold. The cranes flew home silently and slowly through the mist of dusk.

Along the railway track, which ran through the fields, all the way from Calicut to Madras and beyond, the evening train would emerge from the Valayar tunnel, puffing its smoke. Its hoot brought an alertness to Mother's stance. She waited for the train to stop at Panayur railway station, which could be seen from the palace – a small platform with a banyan tree growing over it. It had been built in the colonial days for the king of Panayur to board the trains that went to Madras, but nowadays they rarely halted there. (When Great-uncle went to Cochin or Madras, the train would stop for him as an old courtesy.) Even long after the newspapers reported that the war with China was over, Mother continued her twilight vigil, waiting for the train to stop and for Father to step from one of the carriages in his beret and green military uniform. And after Valiyamama went off into the forest, Mother watched again, scanning the road for him to return from the last hunt.

'Valiyamama will not be coming back,' the queen-mother said, sitting beside her son upon the bed. 'Now you are the king.'

'I do not want to be king,' Swati sobbed. 'I want you to sleep beside me.'

'It is time for you to learn to be alone,' Mother said.

'But Great-uncle can't leave us like that. He will return,' he said, with a cry in his throat that he was afraid to release. 'Can't I sleep beside you at least until he comes back?'

Mother was still and, under the linen that masked her features, Swati perceived an intense withdrawal. The wind seemed to come from far away, full of indistinguishable murmurs. It seemed as if it carried the flapping of burial clothes and the scent of freshly cut paddy. Swati could see the shadow of the mango tree like a great, intricate fan, the moon a luminous witness. The boy shut his eyes tight and curled up into a ball; he felt his mother's touch leave him. That was the start of his loneliness. The night began to spread around him like a gigantic, dark flower. Smothered in its fragrant, velvet pollen, he was doomed to lie, listen and feel all by himself, as the palm of his mother left his cheek and her weight lifted from his cot. It was as if her handprint had dried on Swati's cheek and parted from his face as a piece of skin, a tattoo that only he could see, a parting that marked the end of his childhood. Each footstep she took away from him somehow enlarged the night, and when the door closed softly behind her, the boy felt its darkness come in through the window and enfold him in its soft pleats. Swati opened his eyes to this new night, learning to be afraid.

An owl hooted. As he lay there, he wanted to breathe softly so that the night could not hear him. The sounds of darkness became more distinct. There were shifts of temperature as the breeze swirled and eddied, and the flow of the Papanasini grew and pulled with it. The moon shifted and the mango tree entered the room, its shadow stretching to touch his cheek where his mother's palm had been. It had a cotton weight to it, and Swati sat up on the bed and offered himself to its embrace. It seemed to hold him with the regretful wispiness of a ghost, and he felt himself pulled to the window.

'Sit on my branches,' it echoed, in Father's half-forgotten voice, 'to see the navy come sailing by.'

'And where shall I go?'

'Looking for the tiger.' Father's voice was a small persuasive drumming in his ears.

Father of the night, preserved in the ice of the Himalayan slopes, speaking to him, into him, into his memories of childhood. Later, when Swati grew up, he learnt that in the narrow aisle between wakefulness and sleeping there was the sorcery of another attention. And that sleep was as full of longing as his dreams were. After Nina died, Swati had no nightmares, only dreams of her: delicate sketches in coloured pencils, her hair and her smile, the reality of her body in the vision preventing him waking with its unbearable weight of grieving radiance. And that is how his art of dreaming had begun, on the night of his abandonment. Thus he was taught to dream by his

113

mother when she left him marooned, without warning, in that silent night to the enchanted embrace of an ancient childhood tree. And, in its shadow, his father's form was calligraphed as he rose from his frozen sprawling and came to Swati in the past of this sleep.

'Get up and look towards the river,' came Father's voice, urgent and soft. 'Look for the boats of Kombiyachan's navy.'

In that sleepwalker's stupor Swati had got up and walked over to the window. His bare shoulders shivered in the western wind and his white dhoti clung to his legs – he could still remember that night, as we remember the beginning of any change. Sleep was leaving him, and his mind was full of a fresh wakefulness. Outside, the river was a gleaming belt of water. Sitting under the mango tree, leaning against its side, was a little girl Swati instinctively recognized.

A nightbird cried, harsh and lonely, and a shooting star raced down the sky. It detached Swati from all the residues of sleep, and the night acquired the quality of a play. It was Antara who sat under the mango tree, the little girl with the pigtails and the large eyes who was the daughter of his mother's lady-in-waiting. He remembered that Antara's father had accompanied his own to the war and had not returned. He was full of curiosity about this child, who wore hibiscus flowers in her hair and on some afternoons played skip-the-squares by herself in the shade of the trees. Occasionally, when he sneaked into the kitchen to raid the cook's banana fritters or *unniyappams*, Antara would be there with her mother, sitting by herself in the corner by the big clay oven. Her eyes were as dark as soot. At her mother's sharp look she would get up, curtsy to the prince, and leave.

Swati wanted to ask her what she was doing by herself in the middle of the night, sitting under the tree. The palace was asleep as he opened the window, swung his leg across the sill and dropped down to the veranda. Antara did not hear him approach, and afterwards Swati could always recall her profile as he saw it on that night of moonlight and cool wind, her hair with its lunar fringe of silver and cheeks with their soft girl-fuzz. She was crying softly, her shoulders hunched, arms wrapped around her legs. The water's slow lapping was a sister to her sobs, as if her crying was part of a secret riversong. He squatted down beside her and reached out to touch her hair. Antara leapt up in fright, her eyes wide and gleaming in the moonlight, a hand flying to her chest.

'Why are you crying?' Swati asked.

'The prince,' she stammered, bowing down. 'You touched me!'

'Why do you say that? Are you dirty?'

'It is forbidden,' she stammered, her eyes firmly fixed at her feet. 'You are the prince of Panayur. How can you touch a mere retainer?'

Swati caught hold of her hand and tugged at it. 'Where does it say that a prince may not touch another?' he demanded.

'The gods will be angry,' she said, in a small, trembling voice.

With the assurance of his thirteen years, Swati held her hand even more firmly, pulling her down to sit beside him. 'Your name is Antara,' he said.

She looked at the prince, raising her eyes to his. They held a mixture of fear and inquisitiveness. 'Your Highness knows my name . . .' she said in wonder.

'I have heard your mother call you Antara,' he answered. 'But, Antara, why were you crying?'

Swati could smell the jasmine she wore in her hair. Something in him stirred, a strange new feeling, as if his chest had acquired an uneasy fullness. He felt strong and renewed.

'I miss my father,' she said.

Father of the ice, Swati thought. Fathers of the ice. Antara's and his, journeying across the white land to the Chinese border, sleeping inside the permafrost that had become their tomb, the indestructible ice. He gathered the girl to him; her little form was slender and soft. 'I miss my father, too,' Swati whispered.

'They say that His Highness the regent will find them,' Antara said, 'that is what my mother says.'

'How will he find them in the forest?' he asked.

Antara looked up at him sharply, responding to the scepticism in his voice. 'Mother says our fathers returned from the war to hunt the tiger,' she answered. 'Mother says the house of Panayur belongs to the tiger.'

116

'But Father died in the war,' Swati said, the re-iteration of the knowledge somehow making death seem unreal.

Antara glared at him and broke away. 'Don't say that, Your Highness. My father is not dead.' Her voice was full of fire. 'He has gone to hunt the tiger with your father. They will come back.'

The river heaved against its bank, responding to an unexpected tide. The moon seemed to grow longer for an instant, an ellipse, a nocturnal mirage.

'Antara, what will you do if they don't?'

'I will find them,' she said. 'I will bring both of them back, your father and mine.'

Swati put his arm round her, drawing her to him, subject to prince, child to child, mourner to mourner. The fireflies danced over the river in mystic loops, and far away a crow cried in its nest. In that covenant, the night cooled around them and their skins acquired an awareness of their own.

So are the first chapters of loneliness learnt, the first understanding of the balm that comes from un-familiar touch, sometimes the caress of a feminine stranger. Throughout Swati's life, the memory of Antara's skin against his remained an encoded lesson. Later he realized that a little teacher by the river had unconsciously begun his education in adulthood.

Now Swati heard the broom in the courtyard, smiled and stretched. He walked across to the window and opened it. Great-uncle had, as a young man, acquired a taste for louvred windows and British bathtubs, and had returned with both from a trip to England. The huge white bathtub with its bronze claw feet and porcelain taps had been installed in the bathroom of the master bedroom, and Swati planned to draw a hot bath and soak. The auguries said that he should perform Nina's last rites the next day. He looked at her sitting on the little table in the corner and smiled. Thin, buttery slices of sunlight fell in strips across her. The urn gleamed. He picked her up, this time feeling that all the pain had happened to someone else and not to him. Coming home was the end of his memories, he told himself. The palace was a great shell, a magical atmosphere that banished all the aches of previous times.

'Tomorrow morning, my dearest,' Swati promised Nina, touching the cool rim of the urn to his lips. 'You shall continue with the Papanasini.'

He placed the urn back on the table, and turned to see Antara standing by the door. She wore a small regretful smile, her eyes inscrutable.

'You must miss her a lot,' Antara said. She had bathed early, and her thick black hair, now silvered at the temples, was bound back in a long plait.

'In a way that is very strange,' Swati said, 'I do not feel she is dead. I just feel that she has changed.'

Antara looked at the tall man with the white streak across his head, took in the greying hair on his broad chest and the love handles of middle age that had begun to show at his waist. She searched his eyes for an old understanding, the recognition that lay in that first night they had sat by the river as children and sought their fathers in the myth of the forest that had been guarded for centuries by the tiger of Panayur. The tiger that had suckled the great White Knight, Parangi Cheykor, that had leapt into the last battlefield of Panayur and saved its king from a Mangalorean soldier's blade. Yet it was also the creature that haunted the royal house and teased the princes with its spoor.

'Do you know why they hunt the tiger?' Swati recalled Mother asking him.

'For revenge, and for honour,' he said proudly. 'All the kings have hunted the tiger when the time comes.'

'No, it is fate. For the princes of Panayur it is also the secret of manhood,' Mother answered. 'Fate has many reasons, hidden within each other in a chain-link of stories. And, Swati, there is also a story behind every story . . .'

And so Mother would begin, and he would trace the smile on her mouth under the white linen veil with the tip of his finger, and sometimes she would nibble the tip gently. 'Tiger Mother, don't bite,' Swati would say laughing.

Tiger Mother of the stories, now playing in the wind outside the palace, a formless motherhood present in all the rooms and the air over the palace.

'Parangi Cheykor, as Queen Ponni's son, was the heir to the house of Panayur. Kombiyachan did not have any other sons,' she began her story. 'After Choorikathi Kombiyachan returned blinded from his hunt, all he wanted was to capture the bastard son of the Portuguese adventurer, Gomez, and Ponni. He sent small expeditions to the forests, hired white mercenaries who took with them their guns and native beaters. The drums sounded through the night, pulses of sound coming from far across the river, torches burning like distant forest fires.'

'Did they find the tiger, Mother?'

'Few of the hunters came back, my little prince. Those who did returned raving mad, babbling about caves hidden by waterfalls, and a boy suckled by tigers and frolicking with the beasts of the jungle. Among them were native mercenaries, whose weapons the boy had examined with great interest, lifting the heavy blades and unwieldy *urumis* with instinctive ease. They bargained for their freedom by teaching the man-tiger the lethal art of *kalaripayattu*, under the constant eye of a gigantic tiger. There were also Englishmen in whom the child showed interest, which saved them from the wrath of the beast. These captives taught the boy human speech and manners, but grew slowly insane through the constant proximity to wild animals. Most lost their way in the forest, trying to escape, and died falling into the treacherous ravines or in landslides; a few were devoured by wild beasts. Those who returned to Panayur were imprisoned in the dungeon across the river that Kombiyachan had built for the deranged. There were

Englishmen who had boasted that they would bring back the heads of both child and beast. They returned screaming in terror about a bestial devil longer than a forest fire and taller than an elephant, which carried a strange warrior on its back. Sometimes it was a native hunter, sly to the ways of the leopard and the fox. Bullets wouldn't touch it, swords melted in the heat of its roar. The dancing figure of death in the dark, the leaping ghoul with half-golden, half-black hair, descending upon them with *urumi* and sword . . .

'And Kombiyachan would gnash his teeth in rage and swing his sword at the narrator, who, if he escaped decapitation, was thrown back into the madhouse. There, Kombiyachan was to join them later, deposed by his nephew, the bastard of Charteris and Neeri. Neeri, who claimed royal lineage – having once been the concubine of the king – had plotted with the priest to seize power from Kombiyachan. The British collector of Palghat had sent a troop of redcoats with their bayoneted carbines, and Choorikathi Kombiyachan was dragged screaming and cursing to the dark stone cellar across the river. There he lived to the end of his days, trying to trap the grass snakes hunting rats and frogs in the grass outside his cell window. He tore their heads open with his teeth, holding the beating ends of their tails to his empty eye sockets, cajoling them to give him the serpent's power of sight. He howled in anger as the lashes ebbed into weak squirms, unable to banish the darkness that haunted him – the darkness that had come at the end of the savage's sword after Kombiyachan's hunting party had been destroyed by the great tiger. It had suddenly appeared, roaring, out of the night. A terrifying figure had leapt off its back in a classic *kalari* leap. A sword swung down in an arc to scoop out one of Kombiyachan's eyeballs, and the king watched helplessly as the blade returned. And then there was only red agony and darkness. Kombiyachan's howls carried across the river, and the Puzhanairs, who were the royal river guards, shouted warning cries to drown the demented noise of their deposed insane king.'

'Why didn't Parangi Cheykor kill him?' Swati asked.

'I don't know,' Mother answered, with an endearing shake of her head, a gesture that sometimes brought a sharp twist of pain into Swati's heart. It was one of those things by which he understood that love is undying, that we continue to mourn all dead loves in little ambushes of memory.

'I know,' Antara had told him that night, when he found her mourning her father. She wriggled away from Swati's arm and sat facing him, her small face acquiring the nocturnal gravity of the storyteller.

Swati laughed.

'Don't laugh, Your Highness. This was told to me by my mother, who was told it by her mother, who heard it from her mother.'

The boy smiled at the seriousness of his newfound playmate.

'He was the king of Panayur,' Antara said, 'and the king could not be killed by one of the princes. It was forbidden.'

'You mean the tiger forbade it?' he asked, mocking her with an eyebrow.

Antara ignored his scorn. 'There were codes in the old days,' she answered, 'codes for kings, codes for princes, codes for subjects.'

'Codes for tigers, too.' Swati laughed again.

'Do not mock, my prince,' she said. 'It was that code my father followed when he went to China with your father. It was the code of the vassal that sent him to protect his king.'

Suddenly the river was a smell in the wind. A smell that reminded Swati of a search, a voice that had told him to look for the navy that would come sailing down the river. Antara's hand rested on his cheek, at the same place his mother's had left its touchprint.

'Parangi Cheykor came to Panayur one night,' she said, 'riding the tiger. The palace was guarded by the collector's men who fled when they saw the giant beast and the Cheykor riding him.'

'What did he want, this White Knight of yours?'

'The kingdom. And he challenged the impostor to a duel.'

'Did he win it?'

Antara shook her head. 'It was a strange victory,' she said. 'He had the kingdom and then he didn't want it any more. It is a long story.'

'Tell me, my friend.' He squatted beside her. The night was full of comforting sounds, the faraway songs of nightbirds, and frogs croaking in the wet fields. Fireflies waltzed in the darkness.

'Parangi Cheykor stood in the courtyard, his long *urumi* trailing beside him . . .' Antara began . . .

Tall and straight, one half of his hair blond the other black, the knight looked like a savage god, standing bronzed and muscular in the light of the torches. The tiger had retreated into the dimness beyond the arc of the torchlight, slipping quietly into the gap between the trees and the shadows.

'Come out, impostor,' Parangi Cheykor shouted. 'I am here at last.'

A window opened in the upper storey of the palace, and the white face of a woman with haunted eyes and black serpentine hair looked down at him. The Cheykor lashed out with his *urumi* at the massive front door built of teak, reinforced with copper bands and studded with iron. At last, it opened, and a tall Englishman in a black cloak stepped out on to the portico. In his hand he carried a small bundle of red cloth.

Cheykor recognized Charteris and laughed. 'So they send me an old man, who is also a white priest,' he said sarcastically. 'Is the royal house of Panayur left with only old men to fight me?'

The priest cackled and raised the little bundle in his hand. 'Wait, my eager tiger-cub. Don't you want to know what is inside?'

'Your magic will not work on me,' the knight growled. 'It was you who killed my father with your intrigue, you who deprived me of my kingdom.'

'Well, then, it is time to meet your father.' Charteris laughed. 'Here he is, inside this little bundle. Come and fetch him, my pup.'

Parangi Cheykor's *urumi* snaked towards the priest's face in a silver flash, entwining itself around the wattled, leathery neck. He held out his hand. 'Give it to me,' he ordered.

Charteris chortled and threw the bundle towards Parangi Cheykor, who caught it deftly in his hand.

'Open it, and you will find a memento Kombiyachan kept for you,' the priest said.

Parangi Cheykor untied the bundle, and stared at the horror he held in his hand. It was a shrunken head, which had once belonged to a white man. The eyes were screwed shut; the skin around the mouth and ears was stretched in furrows of old wrinkles. The head looked disproportionately wide; there was one crude stitch, which ran from the base of the skull to the forehead. The hair was ragged and blond, and the face still had the remains of a moustache.

'Meet your father, Fernando Gomez,' Charteris said. 'I personally supervised his embalming. After the elephant cracked open his skull, Kombiyachan had it mounted on the western wall for all to see. He hoped that you would come looking for it.'

With a savage cry Parangi Cheykor drew the sword

away from around the priest's neck with a twist of his wrist, decapitating Charteris. The Englishman dropped headless to the floor; from the window above rose the demented wail of a woman. Charteris's head rolled to a stop at the Cheykor's feet, the leering expression in his eyes tinged with surprise.

Parangi Cheykor sank down to his knees in the courtyard of the palace, his sword falling from him. He held up his father's face to his own, learning the features of a man he had never seen. In its wrinkles was the intense grimace of pain, and a longing that the son tried to decipher. With his fingers he tried to smooth them; he held the odourless, dry mouth to his and tried to breathe into it. In his terrible orphaned sorrow Parangi Cheykor blew his life's breath into the skull and in the caress of his hands the severed head of Gomez slowly healed. The stitches fell away, the skin grew over the wounds, the wrinkles softened and vanished. The eyes opened, a cloud of surprise in them from the final memory of Ponni, her belly swollen with his child. And Parangi Cheykor felt the taste of his mother upon the dead lips of his father, the touch of her skin in his eyes. In the trance of this enchanted grief he did not notice the impostor king of Panayur open the door and spring upon him with drawn knife. He did not see the tiger leap out of the shadows and carry the pretender into the night.

Parangi Cheykor carried his father's head in his hands until he reached the Papanasini's shores. Gomez had alighted on these same shores; he had rowed with Ponni along the river to meet his death. And Parangi Cheykor held up his father's eyes to the horizon for one last time before he gave the head to the river. The sunset wind entered the dead man's mouth and moved his tongue to whisper his wife's name to his son.

Father of the distant lands, dying under an elephant's foot under the hot sun of Malabar, how often have I come down to the river with my tiger to look for signs you might have left behind. Parangi Cheykor, the new king of Panayur, mourned. Far away, from the dark glades of the Dhoni foothills, a tiger roared into the night . . .

Antara was crying.

'He found his father,' Swati said.

Antara looked up at her prince, a small smile showing through her tears, and he kissed her cheek gently. Her skin tasted salty. She gave a little sniffle. 'We will take Kombiyachan's boat and sail away to look for our fathers,' she declared bravely. 'We will find the tiger, who will lead us to them.'

Swati nodded. The moon was dipping beyond the fir of the mountaintop, the sky was growing lighter.

'Will you come too, Swatiraja?' she asked.

Swati clasped her face in his hands and kissed her lips. They tasted of flowers and sugar. Antara's eyes flew wide open.

'Sailor.' He laughed, and ran back to his room.

* * *

Swati looked at Antara and realized that he was smiling, too. The umbrella of a mutual memory covered them. He laughed and took her face in his hands, kissing her on the lips, tasting the flowers and sugar of another time. 'My harbour,' he whispered.

Suddenly Antara broke away, her hand flying to her throat. She hurried across to the window. Until a moment ago someone had been watching them.

Swati followed her. He saw a man walking away quickly across the front courtyard, through the criss-crossing shades of the trees. His gait reminded Swati of someone he knew well.

'Do I know him?' Swati asked. 'He looks familiar, though I haven't been here for years.'

'My son,' Antara said. 'He must have come looking for me.'

'Your son?' Swati was surprised. 'I didn't know you were married.'

Antara did not answer. Depths shifted in her eyes. Swati did not ask any further.

'He looks handsome, your son,' he said.

Antara lowered her eyes but not before Swati caught the gleam of pleasure that glimmered there. He put an arm around her shoulder, but she was suddenly stiff and unyielding. 'What is the matter? Are you upset that your son saw us together?'

'The day is getting on, Swatiraja,' she said formally. 'I must give you breakfast then pack Salim his lunch. He must have got work in the Dhoni today.'

'I don't eat breakfast,' Swati said, looking across the

room at the urn, which glinted in the sunlight, remembering. Marrying someone twelve years older had brought out in Nina a protectiveness he had found charming. She had wanted him to look broad-chested and flat in the stomach, and had forbidden heavy breakfasts. He smiled.

'Go, my dear, and look after your son,' Swati touched Antara's shoulder. 'What work does he do?'

'He has been looking after the land, and also does the *aazaan* in the mosque when the *mullakka* is away,' she said. 'There are men who come from Tamil Nadu and Kottayam to hunt in Dhoni. He acts as their tracker and guide.'

'I must hunt with him one of these days,' Swati said.

'Perhaps,' she said. 'There is time for that. Meanwhile, read the newspapers and I will fetch you your coffee.' She held out the morning's *Malayala Manorama* to Swati. He scanned the headlines and discovered that the Indian prime minister was negotiating with the Americans over the nuclear bomb.

'Do you think there will be war again?' Swati found that Antara was hovering at his shoulder, her eyes anxious.

Fathers of the war, sleeping in the Chinese ice, Swati prayed, answer her question.

'I am afraid,' Antara said. 'It was not our war but our fathers died in it.'

Swati understood. King and vassal, journeying into

129

strange mountains to die in a fellowship more ancient than a dispute over new borders.

'True. Panayur is not at war with Pakistan,' he said, with dry humour, 'but, then, we are not a kingdom any more.'

'Don't say that. You are the king,' she said fiercely. 'Saying that will make everything so futile. The journey of our fathers and your grandfather, the grief of Raniyamma . . .'

Swati held out his arms to her, but Antara seemed to have acquired an unyielding distance that separated her from him.

'What is the matter with you today, old friend?' he asked. 'Are you concerned that we might all die in another war?'

'I must go now,' she said. But she stood there looking at him. In her face a conversation was beginning, one that he realized had been a monologue for many years. Her eyes were filled with trepidation; the tautness around her lips reminded him of other arguments and anxieties. To Swati she now looked as she had years ago, when he was leaving for Cambridge, although her long, plaited hair had been gleaming and fragrant then, and her ivory face, with its elfin chin and the little black mole on her lower lip, decades younger. 'You will never return, Your Highness,' she had said.

He took her chin in his fingers: old playmate, friend, first teacher of my skin. 'This is not goodbye,' he promised. 'I will return soon.'

'It will be different,' she said. 'What you return to will be different. And you will be different. That is how all journeys continue, from difference to difference.'

'Our journey never ends, Antara. You will never be different for me.'

'Time makes it so,' she said, with a wisdom he had not suspected in someone of seventeen.

Only later did Swati find out that she had become the eyes and ears of his mother, the foster-daughter of the Gandhari of Panayur. Mother was a great spinner of parables, who saw allegories in every aspect of daily life. In her linen blindness there were only shadows and echoes. A learner of shades and an interpreter of reverberations detects the ellipse of the earth in the hum of a revolving wasp, finds the muted colloquy of mankind in the current of the river. And it was this language she taught Antara, the daughter of her faithful companion Fatima, who had died of malaria. After Fatima's death, Antara had become the queen-mother's constant escort.

The car had honked in the front yard, the driver telling Swati to hurry. He stepped up and touched Antara's cheek. Her skin was cool, but a cloudburst was waiting behind her dark, dry eyes.

'What is it? Is it that you think I will abandon you?'

Antara shook her head.

'It will not be you,' Antara said. 'You will become someone else.'

Then he heard Mother's voice from the doorway:

'He will never abandon you. He is the king.'

Antara's hand flew to her mouth. 'Raniyamma, I did not see you coming.'

Mother reached for Antara's hand, but Antara had fled into the palace.

'It is time for you to go,' Mother said. 'The world awaits you.'

Swati had bent to touch her feet. And even now, after all these years, the picture of her fair, small feet sometimes came to him: the perfect toes with their little gold rings and clean pink nails. Behind her veil, she was smiling, he knew.

It was not that Swati was in love with his mother, but she had formed his nascent impression of beauty. Throughout his years in the world, he had hunted for her smile in the women he had known, persuading even a tint of Mother's wistfulness to come into their mouths. Swati would exercise their mouths, kissing, joking, torturing, but Mother's smile eluded him. Perhaps it was a smile he had imagined rather than seen, how it had changed as it moved on his mother's mouth. It manifested itself in her posture, in the tilt of her head, the stance of her shoulder, and the way her right arm hung down while her long restless fingers played with her *melmundu.*

Memories make monsters of us at times, and some exist purely in the speculative realms of the imagination. And it was thus that Swati remembered Antara, in his years of absence when, unknown to him and watched over by the woman in the linen mask, his childhood playmate became the fiduciary of what he had left behind.

Today, he knew that.

Vel:

AMERICA

A RESTLESS PRINCE DISCOVERS SECRETS
THAT URGE HIM TO SET OUT AND SEEK
TREASURE. HE FINDS DARK
STORYTELLERS AND A FAIR MAIDEN

The Spell of Protection

BY WHICH THE CURSES OF OLD
PHANTOMS, UNEASY SPIRITS AND THE
MACHINATIONS OF ENEMIES ARE
NEUTRALIZED

May the goddess Neeli manifest herself through the symbols and materials of this spell:

Bathe at dawn the night after the full moon. Paint the body with a mixture of saffron, twenty-one leaves of the pipal tree, the spittle of a young frog and ashes from a funeral pyre blended together. Take the sacrificial knife from the altar of Neeli, and slit the throat of a red rooster, chanting the *Neelisamhara* mantra. Dip the index finger into the fowl's blood and write on the ground:

Hreeng Samhara Phud Hoong

Afterwards, draw the sigil of Mrityunjaya within a circle of charcoal. Set fire to the circle, stay within the sigil and meditate on the goddess in her destructive form, with a garland of skulls around her blue neck,

her black eyes blazing, the scimitar in her left hand
and the trident in her right.

The name of the goddess Neeli be blessed.

Source: Jayakandam, Neeleebhagavadimantramala

Chapter Seven

Vel Kramer, son of Jai Kramer and the grandson of Rama Varma of Panayur, woke up on his thirtieth birthday morning in Manhattan in sheets that smelt faintly of perfume. He stretched then propped himself up on his elbow. Thirty was supposed to change things. Did the sunlight look different on the creased bedsheets, the waves, swells and slopes? Guess not. In fact, it looked much as it had on the morning of his twenty-sixth birthday, when his agent called and said that Doubleday had bought his book for thirty thousand dollars.

'Vel, izzat you?' Nat's cheerful voice had said. 'We made some money.'

That morning he *had* felt different. To be a writer and twenty-six was a good birthday present. It wasn't a million dollars, but he wasn't Stephen King. If he kept writing about the Thing that lived in a refrigerator waiting to emerge when the nuclear winter came or about shadows that retained memories long after their owners were dead and tried to attach themselves to the heels of strangers, he might one day be on the *New York Times* list. He got there on his second book – called *An Old Map* – which he finished a week before he turned twenty-eight. It was a story about the first road on earth and how a couple had stumbled upon it unwittingly when they went for a walk in the woods on a clear summer afternoon. And what they saw and where they reached . . . The book fetched him half a million dollars and a lot of good reviews. And Vel had bought old Fred Kramer a new boat that Christmas.

'Grandpa Kramer,' Vel said softly to himself, smiling. A tall man with a Hemingway beard and big knuckles. Doc Kramer, they called him, at St Thelma where he lived in a large white three-storey house overlooking Lake Thelma. As he looked at his grand-father's big hands with the restless, knobbly fingers that were always twisting around something, Vel often wondered why people had once trusted their bodies to his scalpel. But when you saw how he took the thorn out of Crackers' paw, you knew God had made silk with Kramer's fingers – or if you watched him standing against the golden triangle of a lit-up window with the violin against his grizzled chin and listened to the music his hands made that hushed even the nightbirds' singing. And many a time, Vel thought, the wind, which came down the wooded slopes to race with itself upon the lake and climb the maple trees, dropped when Doc Kramer played. Standing on the porch, leaning against the wooden rails, looking out at the lake, which at night was a sheet of black slate, hearing the loons calling to each other across the surface of the still water, Vel remembered Grandpa Kramer holding him close, ruffling his hair. He was six years old, and he wore a red T-shirt and blue dungarees.

'Your dad ain't coming back,' Grandpa had said. His tone had held great depths of compassion.

Looking up, Vel saw the white fringe of beard around the strong jaw, the twilight cobwebbing around the kind eyes.

'Jai ain't coming back, son. Now it's just you and me. Grandpa Kramer and Vel. Is that all right?'

Vel had sat down on the wooden step, feeling its flatness and dryness. He ran his palm over it. Grandpa squatted beside him, and rubbed a large hand over his back, his motion small and soothing.

'Where's Dad gone, Grandpa?'

'He went to the forest.'

'Like Mom went?'

Fred Kramer looked at the boy and lifted him on to his lap. The child smelt of playsweat and candy. 'No, not the way Sally went,' he explained carefully. 'Your father went to war in a jungle, in a place called Vietnam. He is lost there.'

Vel could hardly remember his parents. Dad was a tall, laughing man who threw him up in the air and whooped, catching him with strong sinewy hands, and Mom was small, soft and golden. Later, when he was grown-up, he heard from the mother who had walked out on them when he was barely two, with a travelling salesman she had met in a bar one evening.

141

He had stared at the mouthpiece of the telephone half expecting to see her face coming through the small perforations. She was calling him about the success of *An Old Map*.

'Oh, I saw you on television and I'm so proud of you, son.' The voice was low and smoke-broken. 'You look so handsome, just like your dad. Where could—'

He put down the phone. Where could – what? he often wondered. Where could we meet? Where could I see you? Where could I get an autographed copy? Where could I see Dad once again? Where could?

Where could Dad have been lost? A soldier going to war – a fate all too familiar to his family, he learnt later. Walking down the war cemetery in Washington, finding his father's name on the wall, touching its script on the cold marble with his fingers, learning his father's name with his fingers: Jai Kramer. His father's chopper crashed in the jungle, sounds of flat gunfire coughing through the forest, the smell of swamp and cordite and burnt trees. Those were in his dreams, just like in a war movie with Martin Sheen waking up to the rotation of the electric fan, clack-clack-clack, morphing into the whirring of chopper blades.

'Just you and me, little man,' Fred Kramer said, ruffling his hair again and shifting him on his lap. 'Everything will be okay.' He had gone to sleep on his grandfather's lap, comprehending a great loss that never had a shape, just a little bare patch inside him where nothing grew. An owl cried in the trees across the lake, a solitary loon called across the water. A star fell across the sky.

Vel shook himself, suddenly feeling older than thirty. He sat up on the bed, smoothing the sheets absent-mindedly. Yellow light glimmered at the corner of his eye. The glass-domed lamp patterned with green and orange leaves was still on, the light weak against the daylight. May. There was a nip in the morning air in Manhattan.

On the glass table by the sofa with black striped cushions, there were two wine glasses. There was still some left in one glass, which was rimmed with lipstick. Vel got out of bed and sipped it. Warm.

There were things to be done and a sudden urgency gripped him, but he didn't know why. It was like an engine working within him. He could hear it at times when he wrote at night, and he could swear that the blinking green cursor on his Mac screen was powered by it. He felt its thrum when he made love or when he kissed a new mouth.

'Vel Kramer,' the mechanical beat of its pistons hummed in his heart, 'there are things to be done.'

Things like what? he asked it. Like go and look for my dad who was rotting in the swamp of a Vietnamese jungle, or find my mother, who was a beat-up brassy blonde on her third marriage, who chain-smoked and drank vodka on a Sunday back lawn in some nameless town?

'Vel Kramer,' the engine pitpatted, 'wait . . . hold on . . .'

143

Vel Kramer. It was a strange name for a kid growing up in America in the seventies. Not entirely American. Six-one in his socks. Sally's skin, Caucasian fair, with an undertone of dark, chromosomal ink. Pigment of the past.

'If you're not my real grandpa, who are you?' he remembered asking Fred Kramer, a tall man sitting on a porch of a wooden lodge, cleaning his gun. Summer was over and Vel was leaving for college.

'Your father was an Indian prince,' Fred Kramer answered.

'You mean like Sioux or Mexican?'

'No, in India, a faraway country, south of China.'

'You been there?'

'Calcutta, when we were fighting the Japs in Burma.'

'Did you adopt my father from there? Why didn't you tell me all this before?'

'Long story, son. Your grandfather was my buddy, many years ago.'

Vel's hands were in his pockets, and he had the hunched stiff look that the old man recognized as anger, bewilderment and hurt. He put an arm around Vel's shoulders, which Vel shook off. 'And you just spring it on me, like that, when you're cleaning your gun and I'm watching you and talking about college?' His voice was sharp, full of injured surprise.

'Just you and me, little man, I said to you a long time ago, remember?'

Vel's eyes shone with bewildered tears. Crackers the

144

dog came up and licked his hand. 'He wants to go get some rabbit,' Doc Kramer said. 'Is that okay?'

Vel's chest broke, and with a gulping cry he turned and put his arms around the old man he called Grandfather. 'But you are my grandfather,' he said, 'the only one I have.'

'Easy, little man, easy,' Kramer murmured, patting his back. 'And you're the only one I got, too.'

The little engine picked up speed, and his heart-beat sounded in his ears. Vel got up. He knew what to do. He would spend his thirtieth birthday night with Grandpa Kramer. Maybe the old man would play Bach on the porch. He picked up the phone to call him, then put it down and smiled. Let's surprise the old timer tonight, he thought.

It was dark when Vel turned into the road that ran along the lake, then into the lane above which the maple trees huddled together, hissing and shivering in the wind. He glimpsed the lake through the trees in flanks of shining water. The sound of Mozart came from within the house, and Vel smiled at the thought of Grandpa Kramer sitting in his winged chair upon the Navajo rug in the sitting room, listening to music. He cut the ignition, letting the noises of the night rush around him, hearing the rolling tyres crunching along the gravel. He didn't want old Kramer to hear him drive in. He got out of the car, and saw the familiar water of his childhood. The red boat he had given Kramer was tied to the small jetty east of the house. He climbed the white wooden steps, and reached out to punch the gleaming brass button of the doorbell. There was a shuffle of feet, furniture creaked, and he was ready to yell 'Surprise!' The door opened and a woman was standing before him. She looked familiar.

'Is that you, Denise?' he asked, after a pause.

She looked so different now from the young woman he had once hoisted upon his thighs with her naked legs wrapped around his waist, her arms holding his neck while she thrust her small, red nipples into his mouth . . . How long ago was it? Eleven, twelve years? The first girl he had made love to. Denise saw him remembering, and blushed. 'Where's Grandpa?' Vel asked. 'Has he gone out for—'

Denise raised a finger to her mouth, and Vel noticed that her lips were thinner, as if she had kept them pressed together for a long time. There were citric lines at the corners, silent retorts turning sour there. 'He isn't feeling too well,' she whispered. 'He's in the bedroom upstairs.'

'What happened to him?' Vel's voice had dropped to a hushed undertone.

Stepping into the familiar sitting room, with its deep sofas and the piano by the window, he fancied there was an invisible visitor in the room, sitting and waiting in the armchair by the window, which overlooked the western side of the lake beyond the pier and the small island in the middle to which Grandpa had rowed him on Sundays with a picnic basket and

146

a fishing rod. Crackers had sat on the prow, squinting at the sun, his pink tongue lolling out. Kramer's Rock, the people of St Thelma called the island. Fred Kramer's father, who had built the house beside the lake in 1918, had constructed a gazebo in the middle of the island, with slender white pillars and a mock-Greek triangle of a roof. In the 1920s, gentlemen in linen coats, hats set at a rakish angle upon their brows, had rowed ladies who sat in the boats with their little umbrellas held high, giggling and calling across to one another upon the lake. After church, Fred Kramer's father hosted Sunday luncheons on the island, the men smoking fat cigars, drinking beer and talking in small groups, while the women played whist, sitting on iron chairs set around the white marble table in the centre of the pavilion. Now there were cracks in the pillars, and vines twined around them. He had been leaning against one of the pillars when he had first kissed Denise, and on weekend nights, when the wind was hot and moved sluggishly among the treetops, he had lain upon the cool marble tabletop with her, licking the sex-sweat off her neck and belly, rubbing his nose on the pebbles that tipped her breasts.

'Old Fred had a stroke this morning,' Denise said. 'I called you, but your answering machine was on.'

'I must have left, already on my way here,' Vel said, 'but why you?' He bit his tongue, regretting the hurt that leapt into her tired eyes. Then she shrugged and smiled a small bird of a smile. 'I have been nursing him since March,' she answered. 'He asked me not to tell you. I *am* a trained nurse, you know.' There was a look of defiance in her eyes, willing him to contradict her.

They walked softly towards the bedroom and Vel put his arm around her waist, realizing how alien her body seemed to him now.

Fred Kramer was propped on the bed against a pile of white pillows, his eyes shining from his creased red face. He was ninety-six. Vel went over to him, his arms outstretched, and held Grandpa Kramer to his chest. He felt as light as cotton. There was an old-man smell in the room, of syrups and pills and something unnameable, stale. Vel got the feeling again that someone else was in the room, the invisible stranger who had been sitting on Kramer's chair beside the western window in the sitting room. He looked around: the curtains were drawn, and the television was turned on, with its sound off.

'He says he likes to watch Jay Leno with the volume off,' Denise said, and Vel noticed how her voice, too, had changed – it was tinny and thin. 'He says it makes him laugh.'

'At my age everything makes me laugh,' Fred Kramer said, his voice hoarse and hollow in his chest. 'Not much time left to do anything else.'

Vel took the old man's hand in his. He stroked the knobbly fingers, rubbing the fingertips between his thumb and forefinger. 'Just you and me, Grandpa Kramer,' he whispered. 'It's going to be okay.'

Kramer laughed. 'Oh, no, it isn't, my boy. I'm going, and going soon. Meanwhile, we have things to do.'

He asked Vel to go across to his writing desk and take out a small box from the bottom drawer. Vel opened it, and inside lay a fat envelope the colour of old ivory. He took some papers out of it, and an old black and white photograph, of three men in their late twenties. The man in the middle, who sat on a heavy stuffed leather chair, had Vel's look in his eyes. He was dark and handsome, and wore a dark suit with a thin tie. Vel recognized Fred Kramer as the tall, thin man in a fedora with a cigarette dangling from his lips. The third man was short and plump; he smoked a pipe and wore a tweed coat. 'That is your grandfather, Rama Varma.' Kramer pointed at the man in the middle. 'Rama, Fred Kramer and Richard Baulmer,' the old man wheezed, looking at the photograph. 'The Three Musketeers. Oh, God, what a long time ago it was. Nineteen thirty-four, Berlin . . .'

Vel looked at the photograph, trying to read the expression in the eyes of the dark man whom Fred Kramer said was his grandfather. The eyes held his gaze, commanding him to look into the stories that lay in their depths.

'Open the papers,' Kramer said, his voice rougher. He seemed to have trouble breathing. 'These are letters your grandfather wrote to your father.'

'Did Dad read them?' Vel asked.

'No, because I never told him the truth,' Kramer said. 'I was waiting for Richard Baulmer to call me

149

from London with a piece of news, or the puzzle would have been incomplete. He was looking for something your grandfather had asked him to find. Two days after your father left for Vietnam, Baulmer called.'

'Had he found whatever he was supposed to find?' Vel asked.

'Yes.'

'But then Dad didn't come back.'

'Your father didn't come back,' Kramer agreed. 'Then it had to be just you and me, little champ.'

Sitting on the bed beside Grandpa Kramer, Vel picked up the letters, and looked for the first time at the handwriting of his long-dead grandfather, the elegant script that tilted slightly to the left. Denise had left the room, but Vel hadn't noticed.

'I am so far away from home, and I wonder why the gods have chosen me to die in Berlin . . .' Vel read, in the letter his grandfather had written to his father.

I have tried to escape to America, but I should have tried a year ago, before they put a J in Else's passport. But Else's mother was ill and could not travel. I am the king of Panayur, through which the river Papanasini flows. She is the calmer of sin, her waters are always warm. The river flows by the palace, a silver bow strung taut across the emerald paddy-fields. I remember swimming in it with my brother. I was a better swimmer than he, always. You must learn to swim. You must go one day to Panayur, go to

our palace and swim in the Papanasini. It is the royal
river of our fathers. I know Fred will have taught you
to swim by now. I entrusted him to you, as I realized
that it would be difficult for Else and me to make the
passage to America. You see, we couldn't leave
Maman behind – your grandmother. She was very ill.

I never knew I was going to die until a few months
after you were born. That is neither here nor there. Go
to London, to my solicitors, Baulmer and Baulmer. Mr
Baulmer was with me in Berlin. They have been
handling the family business for many years . . .

'What family do I have besides you?' Vel asked
Fred Kramer in surprise.

'Your grandfather spoke about another son in India.
He was the prince,' Kramer answered. 'Perhaps he is
still alive.'

'But how did Dad reach here?' Vel asked. 'Did you
bring him?'

Fred Kramer looked at Vel and was reminded
of the boy his friend Rama Varma had given
him to smuggle into America. His own wife Vera
had died in the Berlin hospital, his son stillborn.

'Your grandfather was a doctor,' Fred told him. 'I
got to know him well . . .' Else and Vera, sitting on the
chairs by the fire while he and the tall Indian drank
Scotch from wide-brimmed crystal glasses.
Glenmorangie, he remembered. Strong golden
taste, chattering fire. Vera, dark-haired, pink-cheeked
and bright-eyed, in her seventh month of pregnancy;

151

Else, with her Madonna face and golden hair, swollen with Jai. Berlin, 1934. Good year to be friends.

Berlin 1936: 'Packing up, Fred?' Rama Varma was at the door, watching him put stuff away in cartons. Vera's dresses, her hats and perfumes, baby clothes they had bought together – all went into the big brown trunk. The dresses made crisp noises; actually, Vera's wedding dress was crackling at the weight of the other clothes being laid on it. A little wooden rocking horse, a gift from Else and Rama Varma, stood in the sun. Rama Varma tapped it lightly, making it rock.

'You take the horse,' Kramer muttered, 'for your son, Jai. I know Vera would have wanted you and Else to have it. She loved the little horse.'

Rama Varma lit his pipe. He carried its smell with him everywhere he went, a tall dark man dressed in dark tweed, with restless, supple hands. English tastes for an Indian, Kramer thought. He imagined they'd have hated the Limeys for running their country.

'You and Else should get out too,' Kramer said to his friend. 'This Führer guy is up to no good.'

'I have a favour to ask of you, Fred.' Raised eyebrow, small smile.

It was not a time for favours. Vera and the boy were dead. Favours needed warmth inside, some sun. Kramer felt like a dead wind.

'Will you take my son with you?'

Fred Kramer felt cold. There was no answer inside

152

him. Rama Varma gave the wooden horse another light tap. It bobbed back and forth.

'Jai? Take Jai with me?' Fred asked him.

'We'll join you later, maybe next year,' Rama Varma said. 'Else's mother can't travel.'

The eyes of the two men met, and locked. Fred Kramer knew suddenly that Rama Varma would not come to America. He knew that Rama Varma knew this, too.

'Okay,' Fred Kramer said.

'Buy you a drink,' Rama Varma said.

The old man had begun to cough, and Vel helped him up on the pillows, sat him straight and patted his back. Denise came in, and gave him some red pills from a little bottle.

'I'm dying, aren't I?' Kramer asked her.

She gave him a false, bright smile. 'Of course not,' she said, 'I need you to take me to the dance next week.'

'Oh, I'll be going dancing soon, never you mind, girl,' Kramer said, laughing. A fresh spasm of coughing shook him. 'But it won't be with you. I'm a doctor. You can't fool me, honey.'

He turned to Vel. 'You'd better go to London soon, young Vel, and look up Richard Baulmer. You got things to do.'

Vel looked at the beloved face of the aged man he called Grandfather Kramer. It was the map of the place in his heart that he loved most. He understood then that this is how we remember our loved ones – a smile or a gesture as a landmark, a voice or a footfall heard and gathered to keep. He leant over and kissed the old man. 'I didn't know you were married, Grandpa,' he said softly. 'I always wondered why you never had a woman in your life.'

Kramer waved his hand feebly, as if to brush away something that was bothering him. 'It doesn't matter how many women you have had, my boy,' he said, 'but once you have found the woman you love, there can never be another after that.'

Vel felt someone move behind him near the curtains, the impatient visitor who had followed him in. He saw Fred Kramer's eyes looking beyond his shoulder, lighting up with fierce disbelief and a wild joy. He looked round to see who stood behind him, but there was nobody. When he turned back to the old man, Kramer was dead.

After the funeral, Vel was the last to walk out of the cemetery. The papers Fred Kramer had given him were in the pocket of his overcoat. The house was locked up and left in the charge of a caretaker, and Vel got into his car and sat, for a short while, looking out at the white building with its gleaming façade set among the trees – the welcoming face of his growing years. It seemed hollow now, a familiar, beloved shell, but a shell nevertheless. He wondered at how it took so little time to change reality with such finality.

'Grandpa Kramer!' he called out, half expecting the old man to come out on to the porch and shout: 'Hiya there, Vel!'

But there was no answer. That was what death was: a lack of echo, the absence of a response that was always taken for granted.

'Mandalay, I go away,' he murmured.

A wind rippled the trees and stitched wavelets on the water, and he started the engine, turned left from the drive of the cemetery to take the road that would lead him to the highway and New York. Across the road, he saw a woman dressed in a neat black coat with a veiled hat. She was just standing there, looking at him. He thought he should stop, get out and give Denise Witmann a hug. Instead, he gave her a small wave as he passed her, but she did not wave back.

Chapter Eight

Vel sat in the London office of Baulmer and Baulmer, watching the rain wash across the grey window. The elder Mr Baulmer was in Durban on business, Vel had been informed on the phone by the clipped female voice, and the younger Mr Baulmer could see him at four, if he would come to the office.

Vel met the voice at four, on the second floor of a quiet building in Mayfair. The reception area was large and clean, with glass-on-chrome tables and deep leather sofas. The fragrance of cigar smoke hung in the air, as did an aftersmell of pipe tobacco and wood. Behind a severely polished desk he saw a small, neat, middle-aged woman who offered him that particular grimace of drawing in the mouth and puffing out the lower lip in what, for the British, was an upper-class smile. Vel smiled to himself. If the younger Mr Baulmer had to face a look like that every morning when he got in to work, what kind of a grimace did he himself favour?

But the younger Mr Baulmer had an open smile in

a long, equine face. His sandy hair was brushed back and his loose frame was clad in grey tweed and flannels. The tip of a Cohiba cigar peeped out of his jacket pocket. He invited Vel into his office for a brandy. Measured British voice, very Eton. 'I'm Robert. I didn't know you knew my father,' Baulmer said, settling Vel down on the leather sofa beside the window and handing him a balloon glass of Armagnac. He rubbed his hands, walked over to the fireplace and took a deep breath. A grey London pigeon was pressing itself to the window-pane, seeking shelter from the rain. Its head was wet and spiky.

'I do not know your father,' Vel answered, sipping the brandy. It felt warm and golden in his throat.

'Ah,' said Robert Baulmer, and fell silent for a moment.

'But my grandfather and yours were friends,' Vel continued.

'Ah, the Three Musketeers,' Baulmer said, with an inward smile, 'Richard Baulmer, Rama Varma and Fred Kramer.'

'Tell me about Rama Varma,' Vel said.

'They were the Three Musketeers of Hitler's Berlin,' Baulmer went on. 'How Grandfather used to go on.'

'About what?'

'About his times in Berlin with his friends. When the Wall came down, Grandfather was eighty-one. That night he drank so much champagne that he fell asleep on the sofa, even though his doctor had told him to go easy. He took a flight to Berlin the week after.'

'He must have loved the city to do that,' Vel said.

Robert Baulmer looked at Vel with a smile in his eyes. 'Enough to fulfil an old promise he made to a friend.'

'To my grandfather? Or was it to Fred?'

'In a way it was to himself. Fred Kramer wrote to me last year and said you would be coming to London,' the lawyer said, looking at Vel searchingly. 'Vel Kramer, prince of Panayur.'

'Fred is dead,' Vel said flatly. 'He sent me here.'

'I know,' Baulmer answered. 'By the way, I like your books. My wife hates them.' He looked at Vel, then pulled the cigar from his pocket. He removed the cellophane sheath and clipped the end neatly. He did not light it, but placed it between his teeth in the corner of his mouth. 'A trust fund set up by your grandfather, which we have been managing, has been taking care of your business in Berlin. I suppose you want the details?' he said.

Vel raised his eyebrows. He did not know there was a business in Berlin.

'A property in Berlin,' Baulmer continued, 'with a restaurant, the Ackermann.' He saw Vel's expression and smiled. 'I assure you, it is very well run. I would particularly recommend the Zanderfilet with braised cucumber. And the wine list is brilliant.'

'But why do I own a restaurant?' Vel asked, puzzled.

'It's a long story.'

Baulmer picked up an envelope that was lying on

his desk. 'Your grandfather left these for your father,' he said. 'My grandfather – Richard Baulmer – said he would be here for them one day. But I believe you are a generation later.'

'My father went down in Vietnam,' Vel said. 'That's why I'm here.'

'I know, and I'm sorry,' Baulmer said. 'Fred Kramer had written to me about that, too.'

Vel shook his head, thinking about Doc Kramer and his secrets. He opened the envelope and recognized the neat handwriting on aged paper. He sat down by the window – the pigeon was still there, wet and spiky – and began to read his grandfather's letter.

It was on a golden Sunday afternoon in the gardens of Sanssouci that I met your mother first. I had gone with Baulmer for a lazy meal at the Chinese tea-house in Sanssouci Park, with its dragon-scale pillars and the gilded figures that supported them. The gleaming Oriental sculptures were frozen in a conversation that only their builder, Buring, would have known: perhaps the secret monologue in the imagination of an artist's mind. It looks like a golden cake from a distance, set in a clearing in the trees, and the top is circular with an umbrella on it. I used to like walking with Baulmer in the gardens. Above the terraced vine-yard one could see the palace Frederick the Great built. On that afternoon, the trees in the park looked as if they were rimed in gold, their leaves syrupy in the sun-light. I was sitting on a bench, looking at the shadows on the grass. Baulmer was snoring gently next to me. I leant over and slapped his shoulder. 'A good day to be alive, my friend.' I laughed at his irritation in being woken. I saw two women strolling through the park. Even at that distance I knew I had to put my arm around the waist of one. It was a slim waist, and all her poise seemed to be attached to it. Her hair was part of the sunlight, and I could imagine her eyes even from that distance. Her companion said something and she laughed.

'Pretty, isn't she?' Richard Baulmer asked me, but his voice seemed insubstantial.

I saw her pause as she came out of the trees into the clearing. She was tall and slim, her skirts coming down to her boots, the little black beret she wore slightly tilted on her hair. I got up. 'I can't let her leave and never see her again,' I said to Richard.

She was crossing the lawn, walking towards the tea-house, and I saw her features become defined by the sunlight with each step she took. It was like a painting emerging from another distance. I willed her to look at me, my heart lurching, and she paused for a moment as if the wind was pushing her back. I saw her eyes widen. I smiled and raised my glass. Her face opened into my heart, her blush spread from her creamy neck to her cheeks. She smiled and bent her head, turning swiftly to walk away. I got up to follow her. Everything seemed so slow. She walked with her head low, but her carriage crisp and straight. I ran after her. As I neared her, she heard my steps

160

and turned. As I passed her, I caught her scent, the smell of her skin mingling with that of her hair and her perfume, and felt dizzy for a moment. She stopped. I faced her and knelt at her feet.

'Please don't go,' I said, looking up.

She had raised her gloved hand to her mouth, and her eyes were wide and dark. 'Who are you?' she asked. Her voice still trembles in my memory . . .

Vel looked up to meet the young lawyer's curious gaze. 'I have often wondered about your father, whether I would ever meet him,' Robert Baulmer said. 'This is the stuff of legends, you know. Rather unreal.'

'Life often is,' Vel offered. 'What was your grandfather doing in Berlin?'

'He was a legal attaché at the embassy there; he even got a medal for his work. I suppose he was a secret agent of sorts. Then he came back to England and joined his father in the business. We are an old firm, you know, going back to Queen Victoria's reign.'

'Why did he leave Berlin? Why couldn't he have helped his friend escape?'

'Grandfather spoke about it once,' Baulmer said. 'He would sit by the fire with a glass of port and talk to me and my father. His friend and counterpart at the American embassy, Fred Kramer, had a German wife who died in childbirth. Your grandfather was her doctor. That is how they became friends.'

Richard Baulmer looked across the room at his

friend, Rama Varma. 'Come back with me to England, Rama Varma, or go back home, to India. There will be a war soon. And here there is already a war against the Jews.'

'I am sorry,' Rama Varma replied, 'I can't. Else won't leave. Her mother can't travel.'

His gaze turned to the window. And Baulmer knew then that Rama Varma would not come to England, and he knew that Rama Varma knew it, too.

'It must be all there in the letter,' Robert Baulmer waved a lazy hand in Vel's direction. 'Grandfather talked about it many times . . .'

Else lived with her widowed mother on the edge of Berlin, in Friedrichshagen. At weekends, I would often travel out to Friedrichshagen to walk with her around the lake, the Müggelsee. Afterwards we'd always have a drink at Ackermann's. Karl Ackermann was a widower, a good man.

Else and I loved the tranquillity of Friedrichshagen, a lakeside haven, part of Berlin but with a quiet life of its own. After our marriage we lived there together in the family apartment, several high-ceilinged rooms on the first floor of a rather grand and ornate building on Friedrichshagen's main street, Bölschestrasse – a miniature Kurfürstendamm. But we also loved the bustle of Berlin. People rarely stood idly about: the city was infused with a sense of purpose. The streets were always busy, the Kurfürstendamm full of motor cars and buses, shop windows lit with brilliant display, cafés, cinemas and theatres. Twilight in Berlin is magical and, in those years, I felt it held the fateful undertints of a terrifying enchantment.

Ackermann's restaurant was only a short walk from our apartment, on Müggelseedamm, not far from the point where the Müggelspree river flows into the lake. The quiet lapping of the water somehow reminded me of the Papanasini. It was there I told Richard about astrology.

You see, astrology is the royal pastime of the kings of Panayur. Our ancestor, Choorikathi Kombiyachan, learnt it, and after that all the princes were required to learn it. When I was courting Else, she would laugh at the stars and call me her dark gypsy. But when I cast her horoscope and compared it with mine, it matched perfectly. It was a June evening, I remember. I was sitting in my study in my favourite wingback chair, the charts spread over the walnut table by the window. Birds sang in the trees, people strolled in the streets. An automobile spluttered past, a baby cried . . .

My beloved sat in a Biedermeier chair, her hands crossed in her lap, hair spun into gold by the sunlight. She looked into the mirror mounted by the window; it reflected the world outside. We rarely used the balcony, with its white stone balustrades jutting proudly over the busy pavement below. I think it was just a decorative detail of the architecture of the period, and I would have arguments with Else about all this ornamentation. Why have balconies at all, if you couldn't sit there and smell the air?

My wife had a soft, indulgent smile on her lips, and I wanted to kiss that curve. Suddenly I felt cold and my heart clenched within me. Else's mouth was red; to me, it looked stained with blood.

'Is something wrong?' she asked.

The dread had passed, and I took her in my arms. 'On an evening like this can anything be wrong?' I asked her.

Later, when I was reading your horoscope, my son, I understood that what I had felt that June evening in 1934 was death.

I told Richard Baulmer this story in Ackermann's restaurant, later that same night. Inside, it was smoky and warm. Ackermann was serving – he always insisted on doing so when we went to his restaurant – asking the barman to attend to other customers. He said, 'Perhaps it is time for all of you to get out of Germany. You could leave with Mr Baulmer.'

There is something called fate: it does not always accompany you. Sometimes it is a road you walk, sometimes it is an afternoon garden full of golden sunlight, sometimes it is a beast stalking you along the forest path. Or a gang of young Nazis you meet as you walk home in the evening, who swing at your head with batons, clamp your teeth on the kerb, jump on your head. I saw it happen to an old man one night. They had caught him under the railway bridge.

He was spreadeagled under a pillar, his teeth scattered around his crushed face like pieces of chalk. Fate, for him, was a pavement in the night. And for Richard Baulmer it was the ship on which he had a berth, sailing for London three days away.

Richard asked for another Pils. I was drinking whisky.

'That is English whisky,' a man next to me said.

He was a tall German, about thirty, his eyes dark and beady.

'I drink Scotch whisky,' I replied.

Karl Ackermann coughed. The old man had an ingratiating smile on his face. There was fear in his eyes, I noticed with surprise.

'Security police,' the man said. 'It is not German to drink English whisky.'

'Ackermann serves it,' I said, 'and I am not German. It's a big world.'

'Isn't it?' The man laughed. 'And soon it will be German.'

I watched him get up and doff his hat at me, with a faintly amused twist of his mouth. '*Auf wiedersehen.* Maybe we will meet again,' he said.

Karl Ackermann's face was white, his smile strained. The fear in his eyes had widened his pupils. Again it surprised me: Karl Ackermann had fought in the last war, and had won an Iron Cross for bravery.

'I must show you something,' I remembered him telling Else and me, when we were in the restaurant one evening. He went behind the bar with a glass of

Moselle and a plate of food, which he placed on the counter.

'Chopped liver with hard-boiled eggs!' Else squealed in delight. 'This is Jewish food I haven't eaten in ages!'

Ackermann smiled and offered her his plate. She took a nibble and sighed.

The place was empty. It was a cold, clean night outside, and the wind prowled the streets. The lamps spun shadows around, scattered with spirals of moths. From a cupboard behind the bar, Ackermann took out a battered old helmet. He held it out to us, and we could see the little bullet hole in its front. 'He came upon me when I was topping a ridge, as if he was waiting for me,' Ackermann said. 'It was thick fighting, almost hand to hand. Suddenly there was this little Englishman, his face all bloodied and his teeth white against all that blood. Blue eyes he had; I remember them looking at me. Die, they said, and I thought, How can all this which is happening so fast be so slow? The Tommy coming at me, his bayonet aimed low at my belly, ready to scour my intestines out. I pointed my gun at him and pulled the trigger, but it jammed. The man was getting closer now. Oh, shit, it was so slow, and I saw him grinning as he realized my gun wouldn't fire. Then, still smiling, his face went slack, and his eyes rolled up in their sockets. I saw blood jetting out through his helmet.

'Hans was right behind me; he had shot the Tommy through the head. Hans was from Baden-Baden. He picked up the helmet and gave it to me. "Keepsake," he said. Hans was killed the next day, when we were trying to take out a machine-gun nest. I didn't see him die.'

Else shivered and drew her wrap closer around her shoulders. 'Will there be another war, Karl?' she asked. 'I'm afraid.'

Karl Ackermann put back his gruesome memento. 'You are safe, my dear. You are in Germany.'

Ackermann came from Bielstein, which was wine country. For them, the Jews of Moselle were like anyone else – winegrowers and Germans – and had been granted their right to settle in Moselle by Kaiser Heinrich VIII in the fourteenth century.

'Hitler is against the Jews,' I said.

'Hitler is not Germany,' Karl said, puffing his chest. 'You are my friends. If ever you need a home, come to me.'

I gripped Karl's hand, and Else's eyes were moist.

Vel looked up from the letter at Robert Baulmer. 'Why couldn't your grandfather force mine to leave with him?' he asked.

'He spoke about it,' Baulmer answered, 'but by then it was too late.'

Richard Baulmer gripped Rama Varma's forearm. Ackermann was watching the policeman walk out into the night, his eyes suddenly old.

'Come with me, Rama Varma, you and Else,'

167

Baulmer pleaded. 'You can leave her mother with friends. Leave before it becomes impossible.'

Rama Varma sipped his whisky. 'It is pointless,' he said. 'If there is trouble, we will move into Karl's apartment above the restaurant. He wants to sell and go back to Bielstein, drink Moselle from his family's vineyard. But, Richard, I need a favour from you.'

'Tell me,' he said wearily.

Rama Varma understood the tiredness. He clasped his friend's shoulder. 'If I die here in Germany, nothing of me will be left for my son,' he said. 'I have to keep something of me here for him to find when he comes looking for me.'

'What do you want me to do?'

'You are a lawyer, Richard. After this nightmare is over, and if something happens to Else and me, I want you to buy this building of Ackermann's. My son will come looking for me, and I will be here waiting for him. Even if I am dead.'

Richard Baulmer, Englishman of reserve and breeding, discovered his eyes were full of tears.

'So Richard Baulmer went to Berlin after the war to buy the building?' Vel asked, incredulously.

'It wasn't as simple as that,' Robert Baulmer replied. 'Friedrichshagen was in the Soviet zone of Berlin. The building became the property of the East German state and stood empty for many years. After the Wall came down, it was eventually returned to its legitimate owner — some cousin of Karl

Ackermann's. Karl didn't live to see the end of the war and had no children. My grandfather finally bought the building, which was by then almost derelict, in 1992.'

'And your grandfather restored the restaurant?'

'He didn't live long enough to do that.' The young Mr Baulmer chewed on his cigar. 'But Father had heard so much about it from Grandfather that he took up the challenge to restore the restaurant and apartment to what they were in the 1930s.'

Suddenly Vel felt dizzy. 'My grandfather, Rama Varma,' he said, 'he is there, isn't he? In that apartment above the restaurant.'

'I think you might want to go to Berlin,' Baulmer suggested, noncommittally, 'and after that the road is open to wherever you may wish to go.'

Vel lifted an eyebrow at his cryptic words. 'Where do you think I might want to go afterwards?'

'To a small place called Panayur in the south of India,' Baulmer said, his eyes expressionless. 'You have family there. After all, you are a prince of Panayur.'

'What kind of family?'

'I received a letter a few days ago from the king of Panayur – that is, if kings are still left in India,' Baulmer said. 'His name is Swati Varma. My guess would be that he is your first cousin. Your father and his were half-brothers. He wrote to me asking for details about your father.'

'And what did you do?'

169

'Nothing as yet,' Baulmer said, offering Vel a cigar. 'Maybe you could fill him in after you two meet.'

Vel declined the cigar.

The lawyer opened his safe and took out a sheaf of papers tied with red string. 'These papers belonged to your grandfather,' he said, going across to Vel. 'I was instructed to hand them to you when I met you. You will find the deed of sale to the property in Friedrichshagen where I suspect your grandfather had been hiding before he disappeared. *Bon voyage.*'

Vel passed the papers back to Baulmer. 'You have been looking after them for so long, why don't you continue to do so?' he said. 'Perhaps one day my son might come here, as I did.'

Baulmer nodded. Vel lit a cigarette. Baulmer eyed it with faint distaste. 'A pity . . . you should be smoking cigars,' he said.

Robert Baulmer showed Vel out with a regretful smile, and Vel tried the well-bred British smile on the receptionist. She didn't smile back. Back in his room at the hotel, he poured himself a drink and called Lufthansa. A flight was leaving for Berlin that night.

Chapter Nine

Berlin was bright as Vel drove west across town
to Potsdam. The gardens of Sanssouci Palace were full
of tourists, their buses and cars parked beside the vine-
yard terraces. Vel walked up the steps flanked by
marble statues on to a promenade, and found a semi-
circular seat that looked over the trees, away from the
palace. A woman sat at one end, her arm thrown
around the curve of the marble backrest, her face
turned away from him. She was looking at the statue
of a naked young man astride a groaning monster.

Vel lit a Dunhill. American cigarettes were always
too rough, a coarse smoke. The woman turned round
to look at him. She had large grey eyes, with a fine
mesh at their corners. Clean jaw, nose a little too small.
The way her neck turned reminded him of a ballet he
had once seen in New York. There were wispy curls at
the nape. Vel offered her a cigarette.

'Kay,' she said, accepting it.

He told her his name, liking the way she smoked,
holding the cigarette as a man would. She did not wet

the tip, but held the yellow filter between the outer rims of her lips. Nice lips, a little thin, a soft vermilion. Her lower lip did not bulge in profile at the edge, he noticed. He often noticed women's lower lips: they told him more about the coarseness of their kisses than anything else. Bulging a little, like a small sac, as if greed and abuse lodged there. Kay had a nice lower lip.

'Tourist?' she asked, blowing smoke. Her nostrils flared a little like a mare's.

'Not particularly, just satisfying curiosity.'

'You don't look like one anyway,' she said.

'What do tourists look like?' he asked, laughing.

'They have that air of being familiar strangers, you know,' she said. 'The hurry they show singles them out.'

'And what do I look like?'

Her eyes were speculative, and hesitation lurked in them, suggesting that she saw more than she spoke of. 'You look like a hunter,' she said, self-consciously. 'Where are you from?'

Vel laughed. 'How true. A hunter. In a way, I suppose I am. I'm from New York, but would it tickle you if I told you my grandfather was an Indian prince?'

'Oh, a maharajah?' she joked.

'I believe there are no kingdoms left in India any more and Indian maharajahs run hotels these days, eagerly waiting to be invaded again from the West. Only this time, they charge for it.'

Kay smiled. 'I'm from New York, too. I work as a psychiatrist.'

172

'Really? I write books.'

'Not *the* Vel Kramer?' she asked. Then she made a face.

'I take it I'm not your favourite author,' Vel said.

'Horror stories are not my bedtime reading,' she confessed, 'though I did like *An Old Map*. At least, parts of it.'

'Ah, well, one has to live with critics. I learnt that early enough.' Vel shrugged.

'So tell me what hunt brings you to Berlin. Some new ghost story?'

'No, in a way it's an old ghost story. Some hunts have strange beginnings.'

'I grew up in the woods in Louisiana,' Kay said, 'spent a lot of time with my grandfather. Had a dog called Sporty, a golden retriever. We used to go hunting in the woods, all of us. Those were good days.'

'I grew up in Richmond, and my dog was called Crackers. I used to go shooting hare and woodcock with Grandpa, too,' Vel told her. 'Did you ever bag anything?'

'I was good at reading sign. Been doing it ever since.'

'Are we going hunting, Grandpa?' Kay asked the old man. They stood on the porch to watch Mama drive home after leaving her with Grandad. Mama had a black eye, and her face was swollen. 'I don't want to go back home to Dad,' she whispered to Grandad, as they watched Mama's car disappear. 'He hits her.'

The old man tousled her hair. 'Then what do you want to do?'

'Stay here with you and Grandma. We can take Sporty and go hunting every day. Can't we do that?'

'Yeah, Grandpa Kramer taught me to hunt,' Vel said, their thoughts running in parallel. 'He said, "Vel, before I teach you to hunt, I'll teach you to stalk".'

A man is a stalker first before he becomes a hunter, Fred Kramer's lesson began as they walked slowly into the woods, along the thin path that led deep into the trees. He becomes a warrior in the end. And to be a stalker, you must read sign: of how the fox has passed on his scent, where the badger has taken twigs to build his nest. You must notice the branch on which the owl sat last night, see the blood left on it after the mouse has been eaten. Owls are finicky eaters.

First you stalk little things, then big ones. The little ones teach you to stalk the big ones, because they know them better than anyone else.

'I don't know why I told you about Mama and the hunting,' Kay said, with a short, flustered laugh.

'It's OK. There's a tiger I haven't hunted yet,' Vel said. 'Maybe you could come with me and hunt it.'

'Come where? I didn't know there were tigers in New York.'

'The tiger I want to hunt,' Vel replied, his eyes serious, 'is in a small kingdom called Panayur, in India. But before I find him, I have to find his spoor.'

Kay's clear grey eyes held Vel's. 'Maybe,' she said, after a long pause. 'Where do I begin?'

'The spoor is right here,' Vel said softly. His pulse quickened. There was a smell to this woman's hair that made him want to touch it, a stealthy musk around her that strengthened in unexpected moments, catching him unawares.

'Are you flirting with me?' she asked.

'How well do you know Berlin?' he asked.

'Well enough. When I first came here and wanted to go across the Wall, I took a tour bus,' Kay said. 'Checkpoint Charlie was full of uniforms and dogs. An East German guard boarded the bus and walked down the aisle, carefully checking faces against passports. He was a boy, with pale skin and grey eyes. He had the same expression everyone in East Berlin wore: a bit of the Wall. Looking up from my passport picture, his eyes met mine once, twice. They were suspicious.'

'The East Germans were always suspicious of Americans.'

'What was funny was that the guards were thumping the sides of the bus. They made the driver get down and open the luggage hatches. With so many people trying to get out, I wondered why they should look for any trying to get in.'

'What were you doing in Berlin?' Vel asked.

'I was researching the Holocaust as part of my work on mass psychology,' Kay said. 'Way back in the eighties.' She looked at Vel's raised eyebrows and smiled. Her smile held a shadow. 'After Hitler, the

Communists,' she said. 'I always wondered why it should happen to Germany, most of all to Berlin, as I looked across the Brandenburg Gate, or watched the gunboats patrol the Havel, sometimes concealed in the rushes, and at the Wall, with the watchtowers, the searchlights and the dogs.'

Kay shivered, and Vel realized that she had moved closer to him, seeking warm refuge from a cold memory.

'When I travelled under East Berlin by U-Bahn, the train would pass through dimly lit ghost stations. Sometimes you could spot a guard lurking in the shadows. Through the chinks in the fence between Lehrter and Friedrichstrasse stations, I could see the border, bristling with barbed wire. There were always two bicycles propped up against a watchtower by the Spree.'

'That was another time,' Vel said.

A cluster of tourists passed them, talking in hushed tones. They were led by a pale, tall woman with a limp, who wore a baggy brown overcoat. She looked at Vel and Kay, then smiled apprehensively. She described the sights in singsong, stilted English.

'Wonder how she got the limp,' Kay mused. 'She can't run, poor thing.'

'Someone who mattered to me didn't run either,' Vel said. 'More than sixty years ago. I'm looking for him.'

Kay looked at Vel, eyebrow raised quizzically. 'A relative?'

He nodded.

'How nice,' Kay said. Her voice was like lemon — sharp. 'A homecoming.'

Vel looked at her and her eyes smiled.

She is reading sign, Vel thought, in a city where my ancestor left his spoor; a city that he and his wife had made their tomb. And I have discovered that I have a guide, with a level gaze and dark gold hair.

'Tell me about it,' she demanded.

A bus honked behind them, and she looked away. The tourists were climbing aboard, the guide with the limp was talking to the driver. She stood up.

'It's a long story,' he said. 'The bus will leave without you.'

Kay paused. Then she smiled and sat down again. 'There are taxis in Potsdam,' she said softly.

Vel watched Kay read his grandfather's letters, sitting on a bench that Rama Varma and Else might once have sat on, near the golden palace with its white dome, its fantastically framed roof-windows and baroque sculptures on the walls between tall white doors. He wondered why he had shown her the papers, this sympathetic stranger with the clean mouth and the quick, smiling eyes.

'. . . and you shall find me some time, my son, even after I am gone,' Kay read aloud. 'You shall listen to the echoes of the past; there will always be twilight and ghosts. Gather the echoes for the time being, like a lapful of leaves, and keep them within your pages.

Keep them within these letters, which will tell you your story, mine, and that of our family . . .

There is a river far away. I swam in it, Else swam in it. We walked by its shores, we held hands and looked at the forest growing upon the Western Ghats. We walked up the steps of the old ruined church that overlooked the Papanasini river, and I kissed Else, leaning her against the altar. She tasted of angels. I have woken up in the master bedroom with its huge windows that open out into the Malabar night, where Else and I honeymooned. The claw-foot tub in which I bathed her with gram paste scented with herbs and sandalwood holds memories of her skin. Call them out from its porcelain sides: it is me touching her. And waking up from that touch of her sleeping length beside me, looking at the night of the tiger outside. The tiger of antiquity, the tiger who comes to drink from the royal river.

After Jai was born, Else dreamed of moving from Friedrichshagen to the countryside, to the Spreewald, which she said reminded her so much of the forests of Panayur. There the firs grow close to each other, and the woodland is filigreed with streams and rivers. She wanted me to buy a house in Lübbenau, one built on the small islets between the channels where she could watch the punts glide past her white-framed window and wake up to birdcall. But by then there was no refuge . . .

'Your grandfather must have been very special,' Kay said with a soft sigh, 'he loved her very much.'

She looked up from the letter and found Vel watching her. She reached out to take a cigarette from his packet, which was lying on the bench between them. He lit it for her. His hands were strong, the fingers blunt, with well-cared-for nails. A capable hand, an assassin's hand. Her thighs were suddenly warm.

'Haven't blushed in a long time, have you?' Vel asked.

This strange man, reading her thoughts. Cartographer of her mind. 'No,' she answered. She got up and smoothed her hair. 'Now you can buy me a drink at the restaurant in Friedrichshagen,' she said gravely.

'If we can find it,' Vel said.

'I'll be your guide,' said Kay, 'but first I want to take you somewhere else.'

They crossed the street and, without realizing it, she slipped her arm through his. They walked to where Vel had parked his rented BMW. He noticed that she walked with an easy stride, yet there was caution in the way she held herself as she moved.

They drove across Glienicker Brücke, through the suburb of Wannsee and on to the four-lane Avus. The pines of the Grunewald flanked the road; an S-Bahn train kept pace with the traffic.

'Those are the rail lines,' said Kay. She pointed ahead to a station in the forest. 'That's where they herded the Jews from Berlin and bundled them on to the trains.'

'The death lines,' murmured Vel.

179

Ghosts. The tread of jackboots, the shuffling of feet. The earth was a vast, infinite fossil-mother of time, of flesh, bone and sound. Cattle trains along endless death routes, their rhythmic clack like a meaningless automated mantra drowning the insane tumult of those dying inside.

Clickety-clack . . . clickety-clack . . .

Grandfather of the cattle trains, shuffling on hope-abandoned feet as he waited to board for Auschwitz.

They drove on through the forest. Suddenly the old radio tower loomed against the science-fiction sheen of the International Congress Centre. Speer's east–west axis, still lined with lamp-posts of Nazi design, ushered them through Charlottenburg. In the lush green of the Tiergarten, they swept around the Siegessäule, studded with cannon and crowned with the city's golden guardian angel.

'The Brandenburg Gate.' Kay pointed ahead. 'Once only royal carriages were permitted down the avenue. Then Napoleon and later Hitler paraded their armies through it. Before it divided East Berlin from the West.'

Vel drove down Unter den Linden, slowing as they went past Humboldt University and the National Library; Kay reached to switch on the dashboard light to see her map. Vel glimpsed the sharpness of her profile from the corner of his eye; a strand of hair fell from her forehead in a line of fire, held back by the slender curve of her forearm. Kay was looking for Monbijou Park, north across the Spree from Museum Island. They turned off Karl-Liebknecht-Strasse and skirted the Hackescher Markt.

Vel parked the car at the edge of the green, and they walked arm in arm under the trees. Oranienburger Strasse was lined with bars and restaurants. Prostitutes in leather boots watched the traffic with dead faces.

'We're in the Scheunenviertel,' Kay told him as they walked slowly along the street. 'Before the war, it was Berlin's main Jewish quarter. It was from this neighbourhood that thousands of Jews were force-marched and trucked to Grunewald station.'

A train passed nearby, like an unexpected memory, an urgent clatter and length of sound. Looking up, Vel was dazzled by the reflection of the last rays of the evening sun on a vast golden and turquoise dome. 'The New Synagogue,' said Kay. 'For half a century, it was the main one in Berlin. The Nazis closed it, their army used it as a warehouse, and the Allies bombed it. What was left has been restored as a museum.'

'It's getting late,' Vel said. 'I have to drive on to Friedrichshagen. My family is waiting. Perhaps you'd rather not come? I can take you to your hotel.'

Family. The word contained a question, Kay understood, needing an answer. A small answer of a few words, which changed everything, placed the world on its head. A small bird fluttered inside her throat, its wingbeats vibrating in her heart . . .

181

* * *

Her father of a long time ago, the father who had never
wanted her to be born. Memories of childhood; her
mother cowering on the bed, while her father raged in
his drunken hatred. 'You Indian squaw,' the words are
reborn in her mind again and again, the nightmare
words of her father. 'Doesn't your kind produce
nothing but squaws?'

Kay's eyes studied her father, the tall bulk of him in
his yellow jacket, the fist red and huge, shaking in her
mother's face. It looked like a piece of meat, and she
swallowed her fear, thinking of what it might do to her.

Her mother was half Irish, half Sioux, and taught
school in the little town of Creek's End. Her father ran
the garage at the end of the town, the only garage in
ninety miles. Years later, she drove through to Creek's
End on her way to Chicago to meet a friend who
wanted to slit her wrists after a failed marriage, and it
seemed as if she was passing through a world familiar
only because she had read about such places in cheap
paperbacks: the small semi-detached houses with their
little green squares of land, Harry's store on the main
street, which still had the board hanging upon iron
hinges painted with the slogan 'You just bought it.' It
was on the wooden sidewalk outside the store that Joe
Kapovsky, the little boy with the cowlick pasted on
his freckled forehead, had pulled her pigtail one
afternoon after school. He screamed in delight and ran
off, and through her tears she watched the small
spindly legs in blue jeans grasshopping away, crossing

182

the red fire hydrant and the elm tree that grew at the corner of the kerb, and Mrs Mayhold's big blue Buick, which suddenly appeared from beside the Presbyterian church.

Kay screwed her eyes shut, screwed them shut, shut, shut . . . but not before she saw Joe Kapovsky bounce off the shining blue bonnet. She ran home with her eyes still shut, trying to make Joe Kapovsky go away, running into people and telephone poles, until she ran straight into a big warm smell – a large-man smell, of cigar and flannel, of cologne and skin.

'There, there, kid.' The voice came back to her after all these years, big gentle hands ruffling her hair. 'It's all right, everything will be OK.'

It was a man she had never seen before, but he drove her home, patiently stopping strangers and asking directions because she was keeping her eyes shut, trying to make Joe Kapovsky go away. She kept them shut when she was lifted out of the car and put on the steps, the man ruffling her hair and saying goodbye. Her eyes were tightly shut, though she longed to see him.

She didn't know what he looked like, and she would never meet him again. He was someone who must have been passing through the town. But in all the men she had known ever since, from Rick Yardlow whom she had kissed behind the apple tree that grew in the backyard of his mother's house one April afternoon, to the men she had offered her hair and skin, she had looked for that touch and voice. It was still with her when Dad opened the door, and took her inside.

'Joe is dead,' Kay told him. Dad laughed, and ruffled her hair. She opened her eyes in surprise, at the unfamiliar magic. Dad smelt of whisky; his chin had yesterday's blue stubble on it.

'I'm takin' you out for a picnic,' he said. 'C'mon, let's give Mommy a surprise.'

An afternoon of miracles, but behind them was suspicion. She had heard them fight the night before, Dad banging Mother's head against the bed. She could hear it from her room next door, and she had seen it happen a hundred times. Mother's black hair, which she wore to school in a neat braid, coiled around Father's fist, her eyes burning with hatred, her face grimacing like a shrunken skull while he battered her.

'Squaw, squaw, gettin' all so uppity with white airs and all . . .'

'John, please, please, the kid . . .'

'John, please, please,' Father mimicked. 'You want it from me all the time, don't you, Sioux bitch? One of these days I'll take that little squaw of yours and throw her to the bears in the zoo.'

Later, when Mother was getting divorced for the fourth time, she rang Kay asking her to visit.

'Why didn't you leave him, Mom?' she asked.

'I was afraid he'd kill you,' she answered, taking a gulp of bourbon. It was a quiet fall afternoon, with the birds chattering in the trees. Mother's kitchen was white and clean as always, but instead of the warm smell of cooking, it stank of cigarettes and stale doughnuts. She walked over to where her mother sat, on the yellow rattan chair by the Formica table. Mother poured herself another drink.

'He tried to, remember?' Kay said, and lit a cigarette.

Going for a terrible picnic with Dad, unable to say no to him. Legs feeling like lead, a stone that cut off all breath inside the chest. Sitting in Dad's yellow pickup, watching the streets leave her.

'Here, wanna Mars bar?' Dad offered her chocolate with one big red fist.

She reached out timidly, and Dad drew it back.

'Well, you ain't havin' it, li'l squaw.' The loud rough laugh quietened as the sheriff's blue car with its silver stripe passed them, and old Bill Halloran, in his aviator glasses and starched blue policeman's shirt with a silver star pinned on its chest, looked at her quizzically: father and daughter on their way on a quiet suburban afternoon, the milky green blur of the shadows of trees coming at her through the windscreen. She wanted to cry out to the blue car for help, but her father's big hand was on her thigh, gripping her flesh, forbidding her to move.

'Dad, I want Mom . . .' she whimpered.

'She's gone, bitch, left you.' The man she called Father was laughing. 'Now all you got is me . . . and I'm taking you for a picnic.'

'Dad, can we go see Grandad?'

'We'll see better things than your grandfather. Now shut up unless you want me to give you a mouthful with this.' He held his hand in front of her face.

'Dad, are you going to feed me to the bears?'

The stinging slap, hurting the lip, cutting it open, the salt-sugar taste of blood. Dad laughing, and singing 'Old Man River' . . .

The car leaving the Interstate, turning into the flat wooded roads that led to the hills, climbing upwards, an old memory of life's first terrible loneliness. Walking with her father, being dragged on, falling down and bruising her knees, cutting her elbow on hard flint, being lifted by the collar until she started coughing and choking, the rough bark of the tree against which he flung her.

'Don't come back,' he warned, 'or I'll kill you.'

Father threw the Mars bar into her lap; it fell on to the ground. A fat brown ant, clumsily tottering along, stopped to probe the wrapper. She watched it turn its conical head, and suddenly she could see it large and clear, the oversized, segmented body, the thin spindly legs like Joe Kapovsky's. She didn't look at her father, and heard him walk away. The sky was cold and blue, the wind a stranger's hum. The ant moved away, and she began to feel cold. Where was that warm-man smell, of cologne and flannel, where was that tender-rough voice? She smiled, rocking to and fro, her hands holding her shoulders, her legs drawn back under her . . . Oh, he will come, tousling my hair, taking me home. A bright house with a fire at the grate, and Mom looking clean and smelling fresh in a yellow spotted dress, her black hair loose around her shoulders. Lifting her up in her slender strong arms, holding her up and laughing, the man taking her from her mother's arms. Opening her eyes, looking at the man lifting her and holding her, an unknown smell. Sheriff Halloran, smelling of pipe tobacco and aftershave. Mother crying beside him. Voices of people, lights in the forest, cops, neighbours . . .

'He tried to kill me, but I lived,' she told her mother, sitting beside her on that autumn afternoon, pouring herself a glass of cool apple cider, 'and they never found him, did they?'

'No, Kay, they never did,' Mother slurred. 'I looked for him, too, the John I knew before he turned ugly . . .'

'Mom?'

'Four marriages later, no John,' Mother said, pouring herself another bourbon, with lights of sunshine dancing in it.

'Stop looking, Mom.' She caressed her mother's hair, which had been bleached a dirty blond. 'Stop looking and come stay with me awhile in New York.'

'I'll call you, Kay, once I get things organized here,' Mother said. 'Shut up the house, park the car at Helen's, maybe, find a home for Princess . . .' At the sound of her name, the old retriever looked up then flopped her head down again on her paws.

And a month later, she was shutting up the house, driving back with Princess in the front seat beside her, after Mom's funeral. The car had been a wreck when Mom ran off the road into a tree at an alcoholic ninety miles an hour.

Mom. Always looking for John.

*   *   *

'Kay.' Vel was calling her through a fog.

'You want an answer,' she said. He was going away, she realized, leaving her in a city that was at once alien yet home to her.

An answer is like a spell, she understood: by saying those words one changed lives irrevocably. She watched the man she had met only a few hours ago, whom she felt she had known for years. She touched his cheek tentatively. 'You have to go,' she agreed. 'There is something waiting for you out there.'

Vel did not move.

Kay frowned, a small ridge appearing on her forehead. 'I am afraid of what we might find there,' she said, 'and I am afraid that, for me, the hunt will continue.'

Vel was silent. She was trying to walk away from a subject that seemed to pull her into its own vertigo, and needed to reaffirm her world against the doomed, exotic picture he was drawing for her. He terrified her, with his retinue of strange memories and quicksilver sentences, this man was on a journey through another's past. Somehow Kay knew she was part of that journey. That was how, in human relationships, journeys acquired new directions. Sometimes love was a map, desire created destinations. She was not sure she wanted to go.

'Well, is it goodbye, then?' he asked, holding his hand out to her.

'I guess so,' Kay said, haltingly, answering the hand.

She felt his touch grow into her, a root searching for her even though she knew that at his core he was determined in his strange solitude. A solitude that would end only after he had found what lay at the end of his adventure.

Suddenly she reached up and kissed his eyes. 'I love your crow's feet,' she said.

They returned to the car and drove into the night, heading east along a wide and seemingly endless boulevard, flanked by high-rise apartment blocks. It was a long journey. At some point they stopped to check the map, and opened the window to let in the warm night air. 'I can smell the river,' said Vel. 'It's flowing to the same destination: the lake at Friedrichshagen.' Finally they were driving almost alongside the water, and Vel realized they had arrived. This was the street, Müggelseedamm.

He read the illuminated sign. Gaststätte Ackermann. He felt the night's nest open, and time alight on his shoulder like a great bird, its wings beating over his head. He stopped, afraid to move forward, afraid to discover what waited for him inside.

Vel and Kay walked slowly across the courtyard, where people sat drinking at tables beneath the trees. Vel looked up at the windows above. He tried to close his eyes into another time, but he could not see any-thing. Then he looked up again, feeling the force of eyes upon him from a height, and thought he saw the heavy curtains move, as if someone had been watching.

'Come, let me buy you that drink.' He took Kay's arm and reached for the brass handle of the main door.

The dining room had a high stucco ceiling: the floor was richly polished wood. Circular mirrors on the arched walls reflected the lights of chandeliers. Candles shone on the wooden tables, giving a glow to the leather panels on the high-backed chairs.

A waiter showed them to a table. Vel felt the flutter of moths in the pit of his stomach.

Kay placed her hand over his. 'You have begun to remember your grandfather,' she said. 'Strange that I should be here with you when it's beginning.'

Vel ordered Jack Daniel's for both of them; Kay noticed that his voice was low and hoarse. He looked like a man who had wandered into a play he had been watching; his movements were casual, but showed suppressed excitement. Kay sensed what was happening to him. Her hands never left him; they stroked his shoulder and back with a reassuring pressure that she knew was his only present reality as time cast its shimmering net over him. The walls were letting go of their ghosts, and the stones, so carefully reconstructed by Richard Baulmer, were turning old with collective memory. In that transference, shadows came to life to cluster around Vel, whispering passages of long-dead dialogue.

He felt a touch on his elbow and turned to see the smiling face of the restaurant manager. 'Mr Vel Kramer?'

Vel nodded, surprised.

'I had a message from London that you would be here. The description of you was ... uh ... very accurate.'

Vel smiled, thinking of the wry Robert Baulmer.

'Perhaps after dinner you would like to see the apartment upstairs?' He thrust a set of keys into Vel's hand.

Vel got up. 'No, I would like to see it now.'

The manager took a step back, startled by the intensity in Vel's voice. 'Certainly,' he said, 'if you would come this way ...'

Vel and Kay followed him out of the restaurant to the side of the building, and waited while he unlocked an entrance door.

'If you could leave us alone, perhaps ...'

The manager smiled. 'One floor up, the door on the left.'

'It is beginning,' Vel said. 'Behind this door, it is waiting to begin.'

Beginnings with ordinary façades are suspect, Kay thought. Behind what we have begun lie tigers of power. And something more, she suspected.

Vel turned the key and threw open the door, standing aside to let her pass. He closed the door behind him, aware of the room opening around them, soft, yellow-lit. Suddenly Kay leant into him, pressing him back against the door. Her mouth found his, and Vel felt the whole length of her against his body. He lifted her and carried her across the Venetian carpet, past the grand piano into the bedroom. The apartment had odours that lay in stealth for them, and Vel felt the heavy curtains brush his shoulder. They fell on to the bed on which Vel's grandfather had lain with Else, upon the heavy velvet bedspread against which Kay's hair looked like fiery gold. She moaned and called Vel's name, and he thought it was perhaps another voice from another time.

He began to learn her mouth, his tongue touching its softness. Hers answered, and as he kissed her, the soft, strong pink skin stretched, moist. She had the breathlessness of a woman who knew her breasts were blooming, becoming heavier and rounder, her nipples aching. Suddenly she realized that this man would haunt her for ever . . .

A search ending in heat, the bed of ancestral matings celebrating the return of a child of its own. He lay watching the street-light come into the room through the white curtains, the soft gloom gathering in the drawing room. His head was against Kay's white shoulder, he could feel the soft rise of her breast against his neck, smell the scent of her armpit as she raised her arm and pointed sleepily at the mantel-piece. 'Look, over there,' she murmured.

He got up, unaware of his nakedness, but aware of Kay's eyes. He felt a strange sense of duality: that it was not really Kay who was watching him. He walked across to the mantelpiece upon which stood a framed photograph of a man in a dark suit with a woman who had long fair hair.

Rama Varma and Else.

Next to it was a silver box.

Under the photograph was a familiar yellow envelope. He picked it up. Vel read Baulmer's address in the lower corner. It was addressed to his father and inside was a letter from Richard Baulmer:

I made my friend, Prince Rama Varma, a promise, but it was a difficult one to keep. Though not impossible. The search for your father took many years. It took me through the records of Berlin, the mass graves of Auschwitz and even to Israel. The details are not relevant, but I found him. I knew his dentist in London when he was at Cambridge, and we were able to identify him by dental records. I always knew Rama Varma was a determined man, and he would have left enough signs behind. I arranged for him to be cremated and you will find what is left of him in the silver casket next to the photograph. The photograph had been given to me by Rama when I left for England. His remains lay for a long time in a vault in my London office, since I did not know when I would be able to return them to Berlin, which was in Russian hands. So here he is now, a few fragments of bone and a little ash. Rama Varma is waiting for you to take him home to his river.

I have done what I promised to do.

Vel touched the silver box in which Grandfather had waited patiently through the years for someone to take him home. Someone who would prepare the final pyre of clay and straw, someone who would stand waist deep in the beloved waters of the Papanasini and release him into the tides of its flow.

Part of that covenant, Vel felt the metal of the box sting him with ancient electricity, a wild gladness that invaded each nerve and muscle. He felt Rama Varma move within the silver container with the impatience of someone who had not found rest for a long time. Vel sank to his knees with his grandfather cradled to his chest. Kay was beside him, calling his name, holding him, and Vel sat on the soft thick carpet of his grandfather's bedroom, leaning against her.

'We are going home now,' he told the box.

Panayur:

INDIA

IN WHICH TWO PRINCES DISCOVER
THE OATH OF BLOOD, OLD GHOSTS
AND NEW DEMONS, AND TAKE
UP AN OLD SPORT

The Spell of Blood

BY WHICH, NEARING THE END OF A JOURNEY,
ONE INVOKES THE GODS OF PAIN
TO END ALL SORROW

May the goddess Neeli manifest herself through the symbols and materials of this spell:

At the crack of dawn, bathe in flowing water, standing facing east. Sit upon the pentacle prepared with powdered rice and lotus leaves. Upon the green leaf of a *kuvalam* tree, plucked from the topmost branch facing west, place by turn a silver coin, a gold coin and a copper coin, chanting each time: '*Sokanasaye neelisamhaaraye namaha.*'

Light the sacrificial fire and place the leaf upon the southern base of the *yagnakund*. With an unused iron knife, make a small cut on your left thumb and let four drops of blood fall on to the leaf. Offer it to the fire, summoning the Great Goddess in your mind to appear to you in her terrible beauty with her hordes from hell. And chant one thousand and one times: '*aeeng brhm hing*'.

The cut on your finger will have healed at the end of the chant.

The name of the goddess Neeli be blessed.

Source: Amavasyakandam,

Neeleebhagavadimantramala

Chapter Ten

'Allahu Akbar . . .'

The cry woke Swati to a terrible dawn, from the canopy of a dream in which the underbelly of the sky was a skin stained with blood.

'Help me, someone help me,' Nina's voice faded in the dream, as she lay dying in the rainy morning.

Swati got up and took the urn in his hands. He opened the window, showing her the vast Panayur morning, which had the splendour of a bride, showing her the mosque Great-great-grandfather had built for Tipu Sultan's soldiers to come to prayer when he visited Panayur. Its small dome was dark green in the twilight, its four white towers gleaming cleanly through the soft mist, which was withdrawing slowly into the darkness of the forest afar. 'Look, I have brought you home, my darling,' Swati whispered, holding her to his face, fiercely pressing the rim of the urn, with the red scarf, to his lips, cutting into them so that they bled. 'Blood to blood, silence to silence. Now you will never leave me . . .'

The river flashed silver in greeting.

'Soon you will be free,' he promised Nina.

A small wind opened the leaves of the trees outside, a sigh of a wind, an answer far away.

It was time. In the final loneliness of an empty dawn, it was time to bathe in the river, which held shoals of memories. To pass holding her in his hands while the phantoms followed the last king in a ghostly funeral procession through the incomplete museum of the Panayur palace, where the desiccated elements of his forefathers haunted the shadows and his father had planted his seed and his promises.

From these dark halls full of ornate furniture, and unused shields, swords and guns, I carry my dead wife into the morning, Swati thought. The river had always been the eternal companion of his imagination. Now he must call it forth as the sibling of water that has flowed for ever beside the royal house of his ancestors. Into its kindred flow he must release the dust of Nina, that sacred grey powder, and small, vulnerable fragments of unburnt bone. His wife, his love, now Nina of the river. That is what she will become: Nina of the river.

Om bhur bhuvarswaha
Tat saviturvarenyam
Bhargo devasya dheemahi
Dheeyo yona prachodayat

Salutations to the three worlds –
The corporeal, the intermediate and the heavenly.
May that glorious and brilliant Savitha, the Sun,
Inspire our Being.

The *gayatri* of life. Swati stood and chanted, waist deep in the Papanasini. The river seemed to rise up from the rushes and the rocks, emerging as it had always done in greeting and solace for its royal child. He raised the urn above his head to the sun and the blue sky of Panayur. Clouds floated by, and the western wind cooled his wet hair.

Swati opened the red cloth that tied the vessel's mouth and let it fall into the water. He looked inside, at Nina, and the last of his cries for her flew from his throat. It was a relinquishing of his grief. Swati immersed himself in the river, dipping the urn in the water, letting the Papanasini enter it, swirl within it and carry away the particles of Nina. The opaque green of the water was around his eyes; it was the medium within which Swati lived for that moment. It was the medium of Nina now. The singing in his ears became green and translucent – the riverspeak of sound, the blindness of water, the eternity of where all life began. Into that I let thee go, companion of a few years, and ghost of the rest.

Swati rose, letting the urn free from his fingers, watching it bob away into the distance, flashing farewell in the sun.

He felt free.

Little does one know that freedom is a small hiatus between one discovery and another. Discovery changes the world, lets one know that something unexpected existed all along. And one changes tactics, devises strategies to deal with altered reality. But, on the other hand, one passes without noticing the point where one had first begun to change it, just as a small stone thrown into a pond can make a leaf on the other side of the water bob upon the ripples, long after it has sunk.

But that was to come much later, when Swati opened his black box of divination once more and called out the old sorcerous knowledge Puliyeri Panikker had taught him at the command of the last queen of Panayur, his mother of the white veil. Now he stood at the bank of the river, watching its flow curve beyond his gaze into the circle of the jade hills far away.

The forest grew as a patina of blue; blue and green and yellow, the quilted shade of a mirage on the hills. The white cranes flew slowly and gracefully above the paddyfields, their wings moving rhythmically like rowers in the current. It seemed as if the river itself was an endless allegory of time. Along this had sailed the Portuguese boat of Gomez, and from here Kombiyachan had sent out his navy. It returned voyagers and bore away the dead, and Nina was now part of its mythology. The silver fish would taste her ashes, the sand of the riverbed would receive the little pieces of her bone and absorb them slowly and stealthily. Once again Nina would belong to everything, and the spiders that wove their webs would try to catch her ghost, which fluttered above her ashes.

Swati was sure she had sailed far away, beyond the reach of those gossamer traps, to the river mouth at which the sea churned in surf and noise, and he felt her diving into it, seeking out the ancient algae from which all life began.

Such is the reasoning of sorrow. And the hope of all sorrow for the safety of our loves after they have departed from our flawed protection. And how grief changes into sorrow, as a river changes into the sea. The tributaries of sadness garden our pastures; in their loamy regeneration our memories mature into vast, shady, benedictory trees.

A garden of sorrow, he thought, tended by the gardeners of grief. The parable of remembrance.

Swati walked away, crossing the graves of his ancestors. Time to pause a bit, beside these beloved strangers. The flames of the little oil lamps cast weak shadows; the morning was becoming brighter. He lingered near his mother's grave, noticing the fresh flowers placed in the little alcove of the headstone. He smiled: it must be the work of Antara, the beloved foster-child of the queen. He sat down, leaning his wet body against Mother's grave. The stone felt cool against his drying skin. Swati caressed the sides of the brick canopy, smelling the holy basil that grew over her. He broke off a leaf, a green, lucid young leaf, and held it to his nose. Mother always wore some *thulasi* leaves in her hair – she seemed to give the plant the fragrance of herself. He discovered old odours returning, of Mother's skin and hair, the perfume of her clothes.

Swati closed his eyes and nibbled at the leaf, tasting it slowly and deliciously; it was the link between a hunger and a recollection. Sitting there beside his mother, having said goodbye to his wife, Swati knew he belonged to this small space. A shadow fell across his closed eyes and he opened them to see Antara standing beside him. She had come up in her quiet way as usual. 'Is it over?' she asked.

It occurred to Swati that it was the first time she had mentioned Nina.

'Yes, it is,' he said. 'Won't you sit down?'

'I want to ask you something,' she said. 'Forgive me if I am intruding, but why didn't you have any children with your wife?'

Swati did not answer.

'For a journey like that, we need valediction from our children, don't we?' she asked. 'At least, that is what the books say.'

'I just put my child to rest along with his mother,' he said, pointing at the river. 'Perhaps the house of Panayur is fated to be heirless.'

Swati saw that Antara had withdrawn into an intense melancholy; she was grieving for his grief. It was as if a curtain he had never known existed was being withdrawn. But then, suddenly, a crow cried in a tree far away, a cloud sailed across the sun casting the countryside into gloom. Antara's face cleared. Swati patted the ground beside him. 'Come, sit down next to Raniyamma,' he said. 'You were perhaps the daughter she never had.'

She frowned – a small, endearing frown, taking him back to the years of their adolescence. Antara sat a little away from Swati and the sun gilded her face and skin – just as, many years ago, they had sat by the river, watching the wind whip the paddy and the small boats punting along to Ponnani with their catch of river fish. The forest taunted them with its secrets; occasionally, on the sand near the graves, there would be the pugmarks of a big cat. It was then that they would both remember their fathers, and the elder who had gone to look for his children. The last ship of Kombiyachan lingered there, retaining a sad majesty in its abandonment. They remembered the boat, fastened securely to the sides with tough coir rope, the boat that was to take both prince and playmate in search of their lost elders.

'The boat is still there,' Swati said.

Antara smiled, remembering.

They recalled how they had once found the queen-mother's linen mask on the ship. He often wondered how it had come to be there. He had not asked his mother, afraid of her wrath, because the ship was forbidden. Thinking back, he could not recollect a single incident when Mother had punished him, but he felt that her presence itself was the warning of deprivations and penalties if he ever crossed the line. Such is the way with queens.

Antara stood up. 'Let us go inside,' she said. 'You will catch a chill in the wind.'

But Swati felt incomplete and restless. Antara's eyes were outlined with the soot of a premonition, which darkened her glance. Behind her, the sky was heavy with rainclouds.

Another monsoon.

Chapter Eleven

After his bath, Swati sat on the shaded veranda on a planter's chair with elongated footrests. From there he had a view of the eastern side, with the sun climbing into the sky, lightening the dark green of the Western Ghats and glinting among the tufted grass that grew uncontrolled upon the riverbed.

He thought idly of getting up and walking the half kilometre down to the river again to the *samadhis* of his dead. He was filled with a strange restlessness. It was there in the shadows the mango tree threw on the ground; it teased him in the shapes of the clouds the western wind herded through the sky. The house of Panayur slept with the river's gentle song – and now Nina was also part of them. Antara would have lit the lamps on the headstones of the graves. Little tongues of fire protected against the wind, they warmed the sleep of the kings and queens. But he did not have the heart to go there again and sit in desolate kinship among the bones of his forefathers.

Swati wondered whether he should walk across to the temple on the crest above the river as he had done the day before, taking the old gravel path along which the sorcerer kings of Panayur had walked, wet with ablution, holy crimson smeared on their foreheads, ready for worship and the trance of knowledge.

Secrets . . .

Antara came into the room and stood behind Swati. She cleared her throat. 'Will the Maharajah be eating early?' she asked.

Swati laughed. 'How many times have I asked you not to call me that?' he admonished her gently. 'Didn't you vote for the Marxist Party in last year's elections?'

'You are the king,' she said. 'That doesn't change.'

Antara, with the quick-cornered eyes and the smile of a lamp. Swati looked at her, the grey in her hair, among which there were a few strands of *thulasi*, the matronly spread of her waist and the wrinkles around her neck. But her face was still smooth and soft, her wrists were slim.

'Sit down,' Swati said.

'It is getting late,' she said softly. 'I have to feed you first, then go home to cook for my son.'

'Stay a while,' he persisted. 'When we were children, do you remember how I used to keep you after sunset so that your mother would spank you?'

'Then we were children,' she said.

'And now?' he asked playfully. 'Have things changed so much?'

Antara's eyes warmed with her smile, and Swati could feel their gaze wrap him like a shawl. He drew her to his lap, putting his arm around her waist, which had broadened with childbirth and time. But her skin was cool. She hesitated, as if adjusting to a tide in the water, and Swati held her close. 'Sit down, my dear,' he said. 'At this age, scandal is delightful.'

His palm was on her stomach, and he felt her navel with his finger, a soft wrinkled dimple in the mound of her belly. Her *melmundu* slipped, and her breasts swelled against the blue fabric of her blouse. Antara sighed as Swati kissed the small mole on her chest. 'Your Highness,' she whispered, 'it is late.' Her voice rasped, as if she had been thirsty for a long time.

Swati caressed her gently. Her womb fluttered to his touch: he could feel its heat lick the lines of his palm. Antara stood up, and Swati laid his head against her. The soft weight of her breasts rested on his greying head. Maybe this is how I would like to go. The thought came to him like a bird. Cheek against the warm belly of a beloved friend, the smell of familiar yet long forgotten skin soothing me to sleep.

He hadn't thought about death until that moment when he held Antara against him. It startled him.

'It doesn't matter,' Antara whispered.

'What doesn't, my dear?'

She leant down and brushed her lips against his forehead. 'Whatever it is,' she said, 'it does not matter.'

Through the eastern window, the sun travelled into a cloud and the day became the undertide of a dream. The sun was blurred; it reminded Swati of his mother's face. Mother, who now slept beside the tame waters of what had become the ghost of a great river.

Swati felt that the river continued its flow now below the grass-covered sands, having dug its grave along an ancient course. It flowed deep through the earth, an immense vein, waters of penance for those who had bathed in it once and for those who slept beside it.

'You are thinking of Raniyamma.' Antara had read his mind, startling him.

'But I cannot recall her face,' Swati said.

'I can,' Antara said. 'I was beside her when she died. I took the cloth away from her face because she was thirsty.'

'Tell me how she looked,' he whispered.

Antara clasped his wrist, and Swati felt her shiver against his skin, cold as a grass snake.

'She had no face,' she whispered. 'When I took her mask away to give her water, Raniyamma had no face at all.'

Swati tried to remember Mother's face, from those rare times when she removed her linen mask while she performed her husband's funeral rites. He remembered the last time he had escorted his mother to the Papanasini for this purpose. The river had already started to thin, folding into itself as the foothills had begun to brown. Mother had paused beside the riverbank, placing the plantain leaf bearing the milk pudding upon the sand.

'The river is going away from Panayur, Swati,' she said. 'I can feel it disappearing into where it came.'

Swati remembered Mother's river tales – of the sudden

flash floods that came without warning and the tale of three women who were swept away.

'They were Meenakshi, Ulpalakshi and Kamalakshi,' Mother said, as he lay on her lap on the *aattukattil*, the swing-cot suspended by chains from the oak rafters. The wooden ceiling of the palace was smooth and black; the chairs creaked as they swung. A spider was weaving a web above, suspended from the ceiling by an invisible string, a tiny, furry acrobat, designing accurate pentagrams with all the patience of its karma. Up in the air it hung, swaying in the breeze, a filamental trap for fruitflies and mosquitoes.

'That is a ghost catcher,' Raniyamma said, following his eyes.

'What is?'

'That little brown spider can catch ghosts in its web,' she said. 'When they fly in the air, they get caught in it. The spider waits for it to get dark.'

'Then?'

'The ghosts thrash about in the web, trying to break free, but it is a magic web. When the moon is high in the sky, the little spider ventures out from the centre of its home and drinks the ghosts.'

'How do you drink a ghost?'

'Male spiders do,' Raniyamma continued, ruffling his hair. Her palm smelt of sandalpaste and lilies; her wrist was slender and blue-veined. 'And the female spider takes the ghost from her mate when she eats the male.'

The child Swati shuddered. That terrible cycle of

consumption had a sense of endlessness about it: death, and then the aftermath in a web. Ghosts in the air, nomadic and free, colliding with silver traps, being fed on by little brown spiders, which are fed on by their mates.

'I wonder how ghosts taste,' the queen-mother said.

'What happens to the ghosts then?' Swati asked.

'They are reborn as spiders when the female spider's eggs hatch, and they spin webs in the air to catch other ghosts.'

'How do you know all this? You are just spinning a story.'

Raniyamma's eyes twinkled. Her smile was red with betel leaf, her teeth were white against her lips. 'Maybe, my little prince,' she said. 'But when the river flooded and the three sisters were crossing it to come to the palace, a spider was spinning its web on the veranda.'

'Why were they coming to the palace?'

'It was one of the customs of Panayur. They were bringing me turmeric and honey from Madurai,' Raniyamma sighed, 'which Fatima would grind to a paste with her pestle for me to apply to my arms and face. Before them their mothers used to, and earlier their grandmothers. They had strapped their daughters to their backs, tied up in the pouches of their saris.'

'You mean the children got swept away, too?' he asked in horror.

The queen stroked his cheek. 'They sang to their babies as they waded in, while the monsoon clouds

212

were spreading their hoods, darkening our sky. *Mazha varunu pozha pole, kazhai kettada Pazhanimala . . .'* The rain is coming like a river, Quickly build a dyke, O Pazhanimala.

Swati imagined the river and the rain becoming one, a great curve of water that coupled somewhere between the earth and the sky, a curtain of translucent darkness, a great throat opening above the three women crossing the Papanasini, their babies sleeping against the warmth of their backs. And the women were like small brown dolls in bright flowery saris.

'That night I woke up on my bed to the sound of their song,' Raniyamma said, 'and there was a spider's web on the ceiling. Kamalakshi, Ulpalakshi and Meenakshi were fluttering in the web, and their song was its dirge.'

'Didn't you free them, Mother?' Swati asked, in horror.

'No, my prince, because I did not know whether I was dreaming or awake. What you do in a dream has no consequence, and sometimes what you do when you are awake seems like a dream.'

Father going to war had created swings in Mother's moods, and Swati saw that she was often given to melancholy. It was as if, with her morbid fantasies, she was trying to foresee what would happen to Father, and ward it off. He looked up at her face, which was framed by her curly black hair, her eyes dark and lustrous with kohl. Her cheeks were soft and dimpled, and there was a mole on her chin.

That is how Swati remembered his mother's face, even after she took to her veil. Over the years, he had noticed that her features had blurred. Her small sharp nose with its diamond nose-pin had somehow lost its contours, and her eyes swam in her face like the black eels of the Papanasini. Her mouth was becoming a pale gash in her face; it had begun to lapse into her cheeks. There was a certain shimmering upon her features, as if an invisible waterfall fell over her, blurring them. Her skin had become very pale, almost transparent – he could see the blood flowing through the veins underneath. The Raniyamma was fading.

Sometimes when he saw her moving between the planes of reality and invisibility with eerie ease, Swati felt that he was in a lucid dream. Then he would command her face to swim forth from the archives in his mind, beautiful and sharp-featured, so that he could console himself that the last queen of Panayur, who had once sat with her son in her lap and told him stories in her low, melodious voice, was indeed real.

After Father died, Swati spent a long time on the banks of the Papanasini. After the night he first met Antara, he spent days under the mango tree, which threw its complex shade into the water. Some of its roots stole out through the riverbank to clutch and spread on a huddle of rocks beneath. It was one of the royal trees of the palace, and somehow custom had forbidden its cutting. When he was very small, his father had lifted him on to its lowest branch. 'Swatiraja, all the men of this house have climbed this tree,' Father's voice was slow and pleasant, 'and when you are old enough, so will you. When you become a grown boy – as I once was – you will climb up to the topmost branch and look at the river. Sometimes, when the summer shivers in the afternoon air and the evening mirages fall like curtains of mirrors, you can see the tiger of Panayur come down from the forest to drink.'

The tree had been an ancient companion, and afterwards in its solitude it seemed even more nearly laden with uneasy remembrance. When the afternoon was darkened occasionally by a passing cloud on its way to rain over the slopes of the Western Ghats, the shadow of the mango tree became a ghostly arabesque in the water. In the wind it shivered and eddied like a woman's garment, and among its branches would be revealed the silver threads of spiderwebs. The fruit was pulpy and sweet, and there was a spicy odour in the air. Swati fancied he saw faces in the current – simulations of dim visages, which were themselves reflections. They rarely had any sharpness of feature; they resembled his mother's face years after she took to the veil.

On one such afternoon, Antara came and lay down next to him, a small fair girl with pigtails and a red cotton ribbon in her hair. Her mother, the widowed Fatima, had drawn thick lines of kohl around her eyes, and woven a string of jasmine buds into her hair. 'Are you missing your father, Swatiraja?' she asked. She put out her small palm as if to touch his cheek. A yellow butterfly pirouetted down in the breeze and flickered briefly on her hair. He reached out to hold her hand, but she pulled back.

'Let us go and look for the tiger ourselves,' she said.

'Look for him? How? He lives in the forest.'

'Let us take a boat,' she said, 'and at night we will row upstream and enter the forest. I know where the tiger lives.'

Swati's curiosity overcame his fear. 'Where does the tiger live?'

'In a cave at the source of the Papanasini,' Antara said. 'There is a great waterfall in the forest, which thunders down all the way from the sky. It falls from the top of a mountain that rises all the way to the clouds. Only the god Ayyappan lives there, and the forest is deep and dark, full of wild elephants and alligators. Under the waterfall is the home of the tiger of Panayur.'

He scoffed at her. 'How would you know?'

'Mother told me,' she said. 'Once, I asked her where my father had gone. My mother told me that the tiger of Panayur was looking after him. She told me he was safe, and your great-uncle had gone to hunt the tiger.'

Swati was quiet for a while, thinking of his father and great-uncle: Father, for whom he watched the Madras Mail from the bridge over the river, and Great-uncle, who had gone into the forest in search of the tiger. Now only Swati was left, the last prince of Panayur. 'Where do we get a boat from?' he asked Antara.

She pointed north behind the house, where the river curved to form a small bay. Upon its sand and mud was docked the ancient ship of Choorikathi Kombiyachan. Its topmast grinned brokenly at the sky, a black femur of wood to which clung shreds of mouldy canvas. Grass had begun to grow on the deck, which flowered sometimes, after the rains, with pink *chettipoo* and *nandiarvattams*. The ruined portholes squinted down into the muddy swirl of the river as the ship lay on its side. A rusted cannon had sunk into the mud on the deck; kingfishers meditated upon it.

'But it is forbidden to climb upon the ship,' Swati said.

'No one will know,' Antara whispered. 'Inside the ship is a boat.'

'Inside the ship?' he said disbelievingly. 'How do you know?'

Antara's mouth was set in a line of determination, and Swati knew that she wasn't going to tell him any more. He knew that she was not going to reveal her mischief, thereby absolving him of any need to denounce her to the grown-ups.

'Tonight, after Kannachar has gone to sleep,' she whispered.

Kannachar was the watchman, whose father and grandfather before him had been royal sentries. They held the title of Puzhanayar, a caste created by Kombiyachan for those who patrolled the riverbank of the Papanasini. Once upon a time their duty had been to watch the movements of the fishing boats that went up and down the length of the kingdom, and to see that the sandalwood smugglers who sailed by night on log-rafts did not escape into Moolathara and Ponnani.

But Puzhanayar Kannachar was an old man with rheumy eyes and legs shrivelled with polio. Still, he went every night to take up his post by the river, a shelter of thatched bamboo built over a small rock on the riverbank, swinging along the ground upon strong muscular arms, his useless limbs flapping cross-legged beneath his torso as if they belonged to a wounded grasshopper. From there, he commanded a full view of the approach road to the gate, the spread of the river and the paddyland beyond. To the right corner of his eye was the ruined ship of Choorikathi Kombiyachan and to his left the church Charteris had built. Fatima would go to him before the house locked its doors for the night with an earthen bowl of *kanji* and dried fish. After slowly munching the fish between huge gulps of gruel, the last Puzhanayar of Panayur would lean back against his rock and sigh. There were no more Puzhanayars, and Kannachar had no children. Many times, out of curiosity, Antara and Swati accompanied Fatima as she took him his dinner. He would curtsy to them and look at Antara longingly. 'I wish I had children too, Fatimabi,' he had a gravelly voice that rumbled in his throat, 'to take the maggots out of my legs.'

Their Puzhanayar could not even walk, let alone run

to catch anyone who trespassed into the grounds, but he had a voice like a trumpet. In the still of the Malabar night, it could carry miles across the river and the paddyfields to reach the huts of *cherumis* who worked on the fields and the grounds. Once two *pandis* from Tamilnad looking for treasure had sneaked up to the grounds at night, wading along the riverside in the shallows. Kannachar saw them jumping over the low palace wall as they ran across the bay to board the marooned ship. '*Kalla, kalla,*' boomed the Puzhanayar's voice, and, '*nikkavide kalla.*' Stop, thief! Stop! The *pandis* were framed in the moonlight against the sky, and one held something glinting in his hand. Suddenly, from the shadows of the palace balcony, a shot rang out: the intruder dropped the thing in his hand and let out a howl.

In the morning, an old brass spittoon, which had belonged to Kombiyachan, was found with a bullet hole neatly through the side lying on the mossy deck. The sound of the shot woke the servants and the lights came on. For days, they whispered about what they had seen in awed voices: how Raniyamma had appeared on the balcony like a wraith in white cotton, her husband's rifle in hand, its barrel smoking.

'I wondered how Raniyamma could have seen with the cloth over her head,' Antara said. 'Yet she shot the man at a distance of nearly forty feet. His finger had been chopped off by the bullet – it lay pulsing on the deck like a lizard's discarded tail, according to one of the servants. He threw it into the water for the fish to eat.'

Swati tried to picture his mother aiming the gun, her forefinger curling round the trigger that his father had squeezed so many times when he had gone to the hills to shoot partridge and hare. He spoke about this to Antara and she felt that in the communion of sightless shot Raniyamma had entwined her fingers with those of his dead father. In her self-imposed blindness it must have been a moment of intense enjoining, around the cold steel of a trigger, feeling the phantom pressure that steadied her aim and sent a bullet into the night. It was one of the legends of Raniyamma, Swati's mother of the unseen face. Later, in the middle of the night, Swati was awakened by Antara's touch and her whisper urgently coaxing him out of sleep: 'Swatiraja, let's go and find that boat.'

Stealing away to the harbour, the children heard the Puzhanayar's snores. They climbed the broadside of the ship, like monkeys scrambling along the mossy anchor chain. It was slimy, rusty and cold. The deck was overgrown with grass, a false meadow with flowers growing along the cracks on the deck. A frog, surprised by their presence, croaked and leapt into the water.

Antara laughed. She held Swati's hand and led him to the back of the ship. Under a canvas, he saw the covered shape of a boat. Two heavy oars with brass rings were placed upon it to keep the canvas from slipping off. 'We shall take it,' Antara said, 'and go looking for the tiger. He will lead us to our fathers.'

Swati turned her round to face him, holding her by

her slim shoulders. 'Antara, do you know where to go?'

She bit her lip and lowered her head. 'No,' she said, in a small voice, 'but the Papanasini will take us there.'

Swati gathered her to the circle of his arms, feeling her crying softly against him. Then Antara broke away with a gasp. 'Look,' she said.

Something white fluttered in one dark corner of the ship, a ghost face that moved in the wind.

Swati went over to look. It was one of his mother's veils.

'Raniyamma was here,' Antara said in awe.

They did not sail anywhere that night.

'Is the boat still there?' Swati asked. 'Or do you think we are too old to climb the ship to find out? Middle age and creaking bones and all that . . .'

Antara answered him with a slow smile, which warmed her eyes. She got up and held out her hand to Swati. 'Want to find out?' she asked, with the playfulness of another time. 'To be children again?'

Oh, to be children again. The ritual of an incomplete chronology was being devised here. Swati got up from his chair and walked with her to the old ship rotting in the creek, its broken hull kneeling into the water. The topmast was long gone, leaving a stump in its place, pointing broken-toothed at the sky.

'When your mother was dying, I was beside her. I

had lit the old five-tongued lamp she was so fond of, do you remember?'

Swati nodded. A prologue was beginning here, being told by the foster-daughter of his mother, the greatest troubadour tongue he had ever known, the sculptor of his childhood imagination. In what Antara was about to say, he knew there was a special riddle that his mother had left behind for him, and even if she did not know of it, he would. Suddenly he was full of haste.

'And she asked me, "Antara, do you remember Kombiyachan's ship, which is docked out there? Swati and you used to go there a lot, didn't you?"'

'How did she know?'

'She seemed to know everything,' Antara blushed. '"On it there is a boat," she said. "You know the boat, don't you?" I nodded. In the next room my son was crying and I knew he was hungry. But Raniyamma's voice restrained me.'

Mother on the bed, the sunset coming down from the hill, the big window opened out into the Malabar wind.

'That boat is for me,' Raniyamma continued, 'and you know what to do, don't you?'

Suddenly Swati knew too. It was a puzzle coming together. Suddenly his mind and Antara's were mating.

'That was the only place where she took off her veil, and she would stand there looking out at the

222

river flowing down from the forest,' Antara said.

'And she would look for the tiger to come down from the forest when the moon was full to drink from the Papanasini,' Swati said, with sudden clarity.

'And she would call out to the tiger and it would come swimming across the river and leap aboard the ship . . .'

'And the tiger would put its great head on her lap, the lap of the last queen of Panayur . . .'

'And she would slowly rock it in her arms, the tiger of our fathers, the tiger of her husband and her king . . .'

'And from her fading face, the features would be called out by the tiger's warmth, and in its rough fur her fingers would plant caresses . . .'

They did not realize that they had already climbed upon the ship and were standing on its deck.

'Mother told you this, didn't she?' he asked Antara.

'No, I already knew,' Antara said, 'and that made her happy. That someone knew without having to be told. The only other person would have been you.'

The ship assailed them with old smells, odours that came back in a rush as if a cloth had been lifted. The deck was overgrown with grass, and where it sloped down to the river, it was thicker and greener. Flowers grew wild, riotous with colour, turning the deck into a garden. Antara had come to stand close beside him, and Swati put his arm around her waist. Nina's death seemed far away, and his life between departure and arrival seemed to belong to someone else. For Swati, there was only this old childhood companion who stood soft and familiar beside him, her contours welcoming his weary fingers. Together they walked around the cabins to where the boat was. It was gone.

'After she died, I placed her ashes on the boat in an open golden chalice,' Antara said, 'and my son took the boat out and lowered it into the water. The river took the queen and the boat, and we stood there for a long time watching your mother sailing away down to the ocean.'

'And?'

'And then we heard a roar from the other bank, we saw something long and golden leap into the water – it was the tiger. My son said we should run, but I knew there was nothing to be afraid of. I saw the great beast swim after the boat. It put its paw on the side, tilting it over, and caught the queen in its mouth.'

'It swam back to the forest,' Swati said. 'Mother of the forest?'

Swati turned Antara towards him, holding her by her shoulders. Her eyes were soft, dark and heavy-lidded, and her mouth trembled in a smile that was also a sob. He kissed it gently and tasted the familiar, forgotten flavour he had thought he would never taste again. He drew her close, inhaling the scent of her cheeks, caressing the wrinkles at the hollow of her throat. They had not been there when he had kissed her first. Kissed her first on the grass that grew upon this ship many years ago, discovering the delight of her skin, the singing of blood at her throat. Discovering the palm sugar of her nipples, the dip of her navel.

Antara was breathing heavily. Her arms were around his neck, her breast was free in his palm. It was still firm as he remembered it, but it bore the marks of maternity on its side. The nipple was taut in the wind, the large areola prickly and swollen. Then Antara disengaged herself, and pulled down her blouse.

'I do not know, Your Highness,' she said formally. 'We are old now.'

Swati did not say anything. He was surprised at himself, how an ancient desire had filled him, relegating to distant borders his bereavement and the knowledge of his mother's final journey. Antara was his soil, Swati knew, which he had always known.

'It will rain soon,' she said, 'and my son has already gone for a hunt. There is a party from Munnar that wants to hunt boar. He is their guide.'

'When did you marry, Antara?' Swati asked her. 'Mother never wrote about it.'

'I do not want to talk about it now,' she said. 'My son wants to do the Hajj pilgrimage this year. He helps our Hajjiyar at the mosque in the mornings, calling the faithful to prayer. He has a fine voice.' Antara shrugged like a dove adjusting its wings after a long passage. 'Swatiraja, I am worried,' she said. 'I need you to do something for me.'

'Anything,' he replied.

'You are a sorcerer,' she said, 'and an astrologer. My son's horoscope has never been cast. Will you do it for me?'

'With pleasure. Why? Are you thinking of finding a bride for him so soon?' Swati asked. 'Shall I do it for you now?'

They walked back to the palace, her small palm in his, and Swati read its restless pulse. It tattooed her anxiety on to his skin. She drew the grass mat to the middle of the floor, and lit Mother's oil lamp. He took the rice powder she brought him, drawing the pentacle upon the old black floor as he had been taught, beginning from the bottom left and going clockwise. The old disciplines came without effort, the placing of the hibiscus flowers at the four points of the pentacle leaving the southern corner free. And then, after decades, he opened the black box.

Fingers touching the powerful wood, the tips feeling the cool metal of the latch as it was lifted . . .

The box welcomed Swati, and the unused skills returned to his fingers. He uttered the invocation of divination, closed his eyes and dipped his hands instinctively into the second compartment where the cowrie shells were. They filled his palms, small, smooth and white, throbbing with portents.

Swati picked them up and raised his forearm, feeling their answers, getting ready to open his palm so that they might fall upon the ground in the pattern that was waiting within them. Discovery and continuity, he read. Grief and renewal. He did not understand. For once, his old knowledge was veiling itself. He looked at Antara. 'What do you want me to see?'

'See for my son,' she said. 'I am worried for him.'

'Why?'

'He is getting mixed up in politics,' Antara said, 'politics of the kind that will get him into trouble. He has been arrested twice for getting into fights with the Hindu Sabha people.'

'What for?'

'The divisions are getting strong and violent.' Antara sighed. 'There is so much hate now. The other day two policemen from the CID came asking for him. They were acting on a complaint that my son was smuggling arms and bombs for Islamic militants who were hiding in the Dhoni forest.'

The cowrie shells fell again, in the same pattern. Swati put them away. 'I do not understand the signs. Perhaps I will draw his horoscope now. It should clear the confusion,' he said, taking his ephemeris and an unwritten palmyra scroll from the box. He also picked up the old *ezhuthani* to write with, a long thin needle of silver with runes carved on it.

'Name?'

'Salim.'

'Age?'

'Twenty-two, born in Makara, the sign of Kartika.'

'And the father's name?'

Antara did not answer. She looked at Swati, her face taut and tense.

'Go on, it doesn't matter,' Swati said. 'Tell me the father's name.'

'It does matter,' she said.

Swati met her eyes, reading the terrible knowledge

in them before she said, 'Swatiraja, you are his father.'

The afternoon tilted, darkened and rolled, the day detaching itself from him like skin pulling away, mooring him within a cool, neutral space in which all he could see was Antara's face looking at him anxiously. Her eyes had an intense plea in them, of a deer flinching from a pain it knew was inevitable and final. Swati reached out, his hand weak and boneless, to touch her face. And learn it all over again as he would learn a stranger's face, reading the routes of old tears and the passages of long-past smiles, the movement of muscles that called out with the voice, learning Antara all over again. And again.

In the branches of the trees, crows cried out omens. Swati looked at his old playmate, the companion of his mother, and the mother of his unknown son.

Antara looked away.

'Wait,' he said. 'Why didn't you tell me before?'

'I was afraid to. I didn't want to change your life from the way you wanted it to be. You are the king.'

'What king, Antara? Of what? A ghost of a kingdom that no longer exists? A small, obscure piece of land that exists as mine only in dead people's memories?'

'For me, you are the king. That is what Raniyamma taught me, and my mother before that.'

'Did my mother know that you had my child?'

Antara nodded. 'And she gave him a small charm to wear, a pendant of a tiger. It belonged to you when you were small. When he was a child he came home from school with his clothes torn and tearstains on his face.

He said he was never going to school again. He had got into a fight. The children were taunting him, saying that he did not have a father. When he used to ask about his father, I would tell him that he had gone away to war, like his grandfather. Today he is a young man, and sometimes I think he wonders, too, about his father who went away to war and never came back.'

Swati was suddenly aware of the great hall with its arched ceiling bound with oak, the crystal chandelier, which hung down from the ceiling and had been lit only on Valiyamama's birthday. The portraits of his dead ancestors looked down upon them. Useless, ancient swords were mounted beside them, upon studded shields. Swati sensed the pulse of old echoes, revisitations of bloodstains upon the blades, a tableau of shadows passing.

Wordlessly he took Antara by the hand and led her to the king's bedroom, with its great mahogany bed and the purple velvet canopy. Its headboard was a carving of two tiger masks at both ends, snarling silently in a protective, frozen roar. Antara had spread a white linen sheet on the bed on which Great-uncle had last slept before he went off to the forest in search of the tiger. On the mantelpiece was a silver frame from which Swati's parents smiled out at them. The guns were in their wooden racks, lined neatly along one wall. Swati sat down upon the bed – the bed of his forefathers, and of his own begetting.

'I have to go now,' Antara said softly, trying to free her hand from his.

Her eyes were scared, as if she stood facing an unexpected stranger. A stranger readying for departure, and becoming a stranger because of that departure.

It all came back to him: the night two decades ago, when she came to him in his sleep, waking him with a kiss as light as a shadow passing in a dream, the night before he left Panayur for England.

Her eyes were bright with tears.

'You're crying,' he said in wonder, feeling for the first time the heat of a woman's tears in his palms. The heat passed into his skin, the heat and her wetness, and Swati held her face in his hands with the fragility of a thirsty man holding a chalice. He was finding her as he had never found her, in this great room full of the sighs and whispered sentences of dead kings and queens, upon this bed, which was the garden of his lineage. He breathed in the scent of her skin, her hair, the sandal odour of her forehead. He smelt her cheeks with the soft fur near the ears, and rubbed the tip of his nose on the small diamond she wore in her ear.

Antara sighed, a small tired sigh of valediction. The moon came in through a skylight on the roof, turning her skin to golden butter and he searched for her mouth with his. He laid her back on the bed, and peeled away her garments with the delicacy of one dusting the colours from a butterfly's wings. She opened to him, his palms over her breasts, searching for lotus flowers in the temple pool. Swati travelled her skin, pausing over the velvet mound of her belly. From the bed arose the energies of bygone matings, ghostseeds sprouting as a grove above them, and the heat of Antara's cry reached out to them and she was the river of Panayur, the Papanasini of her king, strong, powerful, viscous, opening out to Swati. And into the asylum of her body, Swati summoned from within all that he was. And in receiving him, Antara finished the ritual they had begun many years ago upon a ghost ship docked behind the palace, of a journey that had in it a boat, a river and a search.

And the search was about to end for Antara. For Swati, another was beginning. He was in turmoil, sitting on the great bed on which he had planted his seed in Antara long ago. The knowledge spread from his loins to his brain like a giant banyan tree. In the upheaval of that learning, he became aware that someone was knocking at the door. Antara had already heard it, and with a startled exclamation broke away from him and ran out. Someone was waiting in the drawing room, a tall young man who reminded Swati of his father: Father, young and tall, in a black shirt and white sarong, with his hair combed back. Antara hugged him.

The man smiled down at her tenderly. 'What is it, Mother?' he asked gently. 'I have just returned from the hunt. We have bagged some fine boar and a few deer.'

Swati got up, and looked at his son. He took a step

231

forward, wanting to embrace this young stranger, but stopped, catching the warning in Antara's eyes.

'Have you greeted the king?' she asked.

Swati detected a faint flicker of amusement in the corner of the young man's mouth, before he bowed. There was a slight mockery in his posture.

Swati nodded curtly, his face a mask. 'I have to go and bathe now, Antara,' he said, 'and after that write some letters. There are some matters I have left unfinished.'

That evening Swati fell ill. The physician was called, and diagnosed that he had caught a chill by bathing in the river. But Swati knew better. The dark vapours of the past had settled upon his brow in a cloud of fever, and he felt he was being haunted by the pain of those who had lived and died here. He slept, and dreamt deliriously of Raniyamma and Nina, and the young man who was his son. Fever burned beneath his eyelids and racked his body.

The physician came with poultices and unguents, which Antara applied to his forehead, throat and chest. Sometimes it was Raniyamma's hand stroking his brow, wiping the sweat from his eyelids, Antara's palms on his skin, Nina's fingers on his cheek, Antara holding him close. Through it all the sounds and omens of Panayur ebbed and fell away. The fever was a continuous nightmare: there were wings in the night that cut his sleep with thick, sharp edges; scorpions laid clusters of eggs in the hollow of his neck; spiders wove their flimsy threads on his eyes, trapping his dreams and giving them up to the greedy ghosts of Panayur to feed upon.

But in his brief moments of lucidity Swati felt Antara beside him, her eyes sooty and deep, her touch like the underside of the waterlilies that grew in the temple pond. Then he would slip back again into the dreams. Beyond them, a great violence of sounds filled his delirium: the roar of old wood burning, cries of women and children, the movement of mobs in the night. The wind brought screams and gunfire, the heat of flames and the smell of burning parchment.

Antara's fingers were on his skin, increasingly insubstantial. Sometimes the pressure was strong, travelling over his burning forehead with the fragrance of herbs, sometimes her touch was the delicate flutter of shadowy moths. Then, one day, he woke up to find that his fever was gone.

He called for Antara, but she did not answer. The house was silent, but for the wind, which scraped fallen leaves along the veranda. A snatch of film music playing on some distant radio came to him, and far away a train wailed long and loud.

Swati got up to look for Antara.

Chapter Twelve

On the journey to bring Grandfather home, Vel felt that it was not he who was travelling: it was Rama Varma's final homecoming. As he and Kay sat in the car bearing them towards Panayur, Kay linked her arm through his. 'What is it?' she murmured.

Her voice stirred him, reminding him of her lips. He raised her face to his and kissed her.

'Have you ever seen me as a king?' he asked.

'No,' she answered, 'only as a hunter.'

They passed through the rough beauty of the Palghat pass, where the giant hills were like granite burial mounds in the dawn. Kay gasped at the world emerging around her, the sun's aura in the mist outlining the mountains behind them.

'The tiger lives there,' Vel said, half in jest, 'in a cave in the forest.'

'We hunt the tiger, Vel,' Kay said softly. 'I will read sign.'

He laughed and stroked the curls at the nape of her slender neck. 'If there is a tiger,' he said, 'the great myth of Panayur.'

They kissed again. 'Then we hunt the myth,' she said.

Morning opened up the landscape to them, and they turned from the even asphalt of the highway into the vermilion country road. Yesterday's rain lay in gleaming puddles, and the car passed temple ponds, which were fringed with clusters of pink lilies. Brass flagpoles glittered in the dawn and the sky was a new blue, washed by rain. A bullock cart was returning home with hay, its lantern still alight and swaying. The red road ran through paddyfields and hamlets of small houses and shops under tamarind trees and bamboo groves. The car turned a corner, under an immense banyan tree, and slowed. Vel looked in surprise at the police roadblock. A sleepy inspector, his balding head tousled at the fringes, waved them down. He was accompanied by a constable who had an antiquated rifle slung over his shoulder. The inspector bent down and peered through the car window.

'We are going to Panayur,' Vel said. 'What is the matter?'

The inspector's eyes were curious as he looked at Kay. 'Where are you coming from?'

'America. Is there a problem?' Vel asked.

'You'll have to get out,' the inspector said, 'and show me your passports. There is a lot of trouble here.'

'What kind of trouble?'

'Islamic lunatics blowing up temples, posters of Osama bin Laden pasted on the walls of churches. A local boy trained to be a *jehadi* in Pakistan broke out

235

of prison, bombed a temple and escaped into the forest. There were riots in Panayur for two days and there is still a curfew out here.'

A motorcycle came roaring around the bend in plumes of red dust; it was driven by a young man whose head was shaven. Riding pillion sat a burly dark man in a white dhoti wielding a stick. They stopped at the checkpoint. 'Who are these people?' the man with the shaven head asked the policemen.

'They are from America,' the inspector replied, 'going to Panayur.'

'They must be missionaries,' the pillion rider growled, 'trying to convert our children. We don't want their kind here.'

The inspector raised his hand feebly, assuming charge of the situation.

'Are you missionaries?' The burly man raised his stick in the air.

'Why should we be missionaries?' Vel asked. 'Do I look like a priest to you?'

'Oh, they come in all forms, let me assure you,' Shaven Head said. 'Missionaries are banned here. They are trying to convert Hindus.'

'Why don't they convert Muslims instead?' Vel asked.

'Good idea!' The inspector sniggered. 'The best way to counter Bin Laden.'

'Look, I don't know anything about missionaries,' Vel said. 'I am a relative of the king of Panayur, Swatiraja.'

236

The constable spoke out – he had a thin reedy voice: 'Swatiraja, the king of Panayur, is here now. He has been staying at the palace since his wife died.'

Vel got out of the car and Kay followed him. The western wind blew against them, chilling them. The men couldn't take their eyes off Kay, her long legs and breasts. The breeze threw her hair away from her eyes, and she raised her face to its coolness and the countryside smells.

'Is your wife also from America?' Shaven Head asked, starting his motorcycle. The burly man behind him looked disappointed that there was going to be no confrontation with missionaries.

Vel recognized the leer hidden in his eyes, the barely suppressed hyena of desire that most Indian men felt when they saw white skin. Must be colonial karma, he thought, all those years of being ruled by the whites. 'Why do you ask?'

'There is a lot of violence here now,' the inspector explained. 'It is not safe for women. Especially a white woman. What if some *jehadi* attacks her, shouting "Death to America!"?'

Vel felt a knot form in his stomach.

'The Muslims attacked temples in Panayur,' the inspector went on gravely, 'and there was police firing. Curfew was on for days.'

'Where are we – in Belfast?'

'Oh, things are not today how it used to be in the old days of the kings,' Shaven Head said. 'They say that when Pakistan exploded the atom bomb, Muslims in

237

Panayur celebrated by distributing sweets and letting off fire-crackers.'

'But why would they want to do something like that?'

'Because for Muslims Pakistan is their true country,' Shaven Head answered simply. 'The Christians support them because America likes Pakistan.'

'Even after what's happened in Afghanistan?'

'You do not understand international politics,' Shaven Head shouted as he drove away, his voice slapped back at them by the wind. 'If America did not love Pakistan, why do they not let us bomb them?'

Vel was puzzled.

'Be careful,' the inspector warned, as they got back into the car.

They drove past the Panayur town, passing its crossroads at which the Marxists had erected a monument to the Martyrs of the Four Corners, men of Panayur who had been shot by the British police in 1941. Martyrs keep changing, Vel thought wryly, but monuments don't.

They passed the Panayur temple, and he saw policemen with guns posted outside. Vel winced as he saw the burnt roof, the blackened rafters that stuck out like charred bones through the broken, baked tiles. They drove into the palace, through the tall, crumbling gateway upon which a stone tiger roared its silent welcome – and a warning. The walls were green with moss, and so was the low brickwork that lined the driveway, which was carpeted with dead leaves that squelched under the wheels of the car. The heavy canopies of trees hung down, weighted with green damp, and a crow cried out its harsh greeting. A crowd of birds rose from the trees near the river, forming an arrowhead as they raced towards the ruins of the church upon the river.

Vel got out, carrying Rama Varma, and Kay followed him. He sensed the energy inside the box, a suppressed impatience that was cousin to some strange ecstasy. Vel felt it pass through his hands and enter his blood, commanding him to look at his ancestral home. The lizards cried omens of welcome, and the sky darkened. Vel felt Kay's fingers digging into his forearm, heard her swift intake of breath and looked up. Crows filled the sky. They were flying towards the house, from beyond the mountains and across the deepening gold of the paddy, lifting in dark squadrons from their nests at the top of the palmyra trees, then alighting on the ground. As Vel walked towards the house, with Kay at his side, the courtyard had turned into a moving carpet of crows, whose throats screamed the language of the dead.

'I've never seen anything like this except in a Hitchcock movie,' Kay said, with a shiver.

'Stop right there, I have a loaded gun,' someone said, from the dark space of the veranda in front of the house. 'Who are you?'

'I am looking for Swati,' Vel said, stepping ahead to greet the voice. 'I have brought Grandfather home. Grandfather, Rama Varma.'

Chapter Thirteen

Swati discovered that the illness had left him weak, but somehow replenished. It seemed that he had been sleeping out his fever in some primeval swamp. He smelt of dried herbs and unguents, of sweat and leaf. In his memory Antara had been with him like some dryad of healing.

He called out for her, missing her, but she did not answer him. He called her name again, louder this time. There was still no reply. He stepped out from the bedroom into the corridor, hoping to find her in the kitchen. He did not know how long he had lain in bed, and wanted a bath. He was hungry. A bath, then a shot of Lagavulin. Antara would make him dinner, and they would sit down to eat. And talk.

He thought of the ring Nina had worn, which now lay inside its little velvet box in his cupboard, the sapphire ring of the royal house of Panayur, the ring his mother had worn and her mother-in-law before her. He wondered if it would fit Antara's finger, and smiled at the thought. The end of one journey is always the beginning of another, he told himself.

Swati walked to his study, noticing the dust that lay everywhere and wondering why it had not been cleaned away. There was a cobweb in a corner and he swatted it away, watching its creator scuttle off on ungainly legs. He opened the cupboard, took out the ring from its box and slipped it into his shirt pocket. Let me surprise her, Swati thought.

He walked to the kitchen, hoping to find her there, but it was empty. Signs of neglect were everywhere: pots stood empty and uncovered on the kitchen counter, there was a pile of unwashed plates in the sink, which had mildew on it, blackish green. Dust lay everywhere and the oven was cold. Antara hadn't used the kitchen for some time. A knot of herbs lay near the grinding stone, drying stiff with fungus, and a cockroach gnawed at them, raising its swaying antennae questioningly at Swati's approach.

Swati was puzzled by Antara's absence. Why had she not been at his bedside when he woke? Why was the kitchen in a mess? Was she ill? He walked through the house, calling for her. Dust carpeted the great hall from whose wooden rafters crystal chandeliers hung; it masked the canvases of long-dead kings and queens, who looked down with disdain from the gloomy walls.

Perhaps she has gone to the graves of the ancestors, he thought, to light the lamps.

Swati stepped out of the palace, climbed down the steps of the back veranda, and walked through the dead leaves that lay on the uncut grass in the courtyard. He went towards the back of the house. As he came upon the headstones of the ancestors, he was surprised to see that the lamps were no longer lit.

Antara . . .

A terrible darkness clutched his heart. She had not been here for days. Had she left him?

Swati crossed to the eastern side of the house, climbing over the turnstile in the *chettipoo* hedge, towards the path that led to Antara's house. A brown cow grazed in the field; it looked up at him with velvety eyes. A red string of white conches was tied around its small, curved horns. Swati could see her house with its low red-tiled roof and yellow mud walls and, beyond it, the mosque Parangi Cheykor had built. The small towers were no longer white; the walls were sooty and the green dome had collapsed into itself when it was burnt down. He hurried, crossing the mud-paved front yard, avoiding the few brown hens that scattered at his approach. The door was locked and he banged his fist on it, calling her name. He went round the house, knocking on the windows and shouting for her.

'She is not inside,' someone said behind him.

Swati turned at the unfamiliar voice and saw an old man watching him at the gate. Flies buzzed around his swollen leg, and he swatted at them purposelessly with a small cotton towel. 'Chandu? The umbrella carrier?' Swati recognized him.

Chandu bowed. 'She is not there,' he said, limping away. 'I will show her to you.'

Swati followed him to the back of the house, a strange shrivelled figure with a small cloud of flies that seemed always to accompany him. He stopped at the boundary stone in the corner of the yard, behind Antara's house. 'There she is.' He pointed.

In a corner of the bare rice paddy next to the house, behind the burnt-down western wall of the mosque, was a freshly dug grave.

Swati heard the story of Antara's death, sitting beside her grave. He caressed the mound as he listened to Chandu, picking up handfuls of earth and rubbing it between his fingers.

'Someone came running into the office of the Hindu Mahasabha saying the Muslims had bombed the Devi's temple in Panayur,' Chandu said. 'He said, "Salim, Antara's son, did it."'

Swati steadied himself, placing a hand on Antara. 'Salim? But . . .'

Chandu sighed. 'Salim had been under police surveillance for some time. He had been seen in the company of fundamentalist mullahs and SIMI activists.'

'SIMI?' Swati's mind was reeling.

'Ferocious Islamic zealots. They want to turn Kerala into Afghanistan. One day Salim disappeared. Months later he returned and started preaching the holy war. He let his beard grow and started praying five times a day . . .'

'Antara knew?'

'She was very worried about him. The rumour was that he had crossed over the border to Pakistan to train with the Taliban and learn their deadly methods. They picked him up last week. He had explosives and plans to blow up the Malampuzha dam. Would have flooded the countryside for miles if he had done it.'

'And he escaped from prison? Did Antara see him?' Swati closed his eyes.

The mob surrounded the temple, shouting for Salim to come out from hiding.

'We saw him go inside,' someone shouted. 'He has gone to desecrate the idols.'

Antara came out of the record room, and stood facing them. 'My son is not here,' she said calmly. 'He is in the mosque.'

'You lie. He is inside.'

'I have served the king of Panayur all my life, so have my mother and grandmother. Believe me, my son is not here.'

'Stand aside, you faithless Muslim, we will see for ourselves.'

'You cannot enter the record room, it is only for those who serve the house of Panayur.'

'Where is the king?' yelled another voice.

'He is ill, and resting in the palace,' she said. 'Now, please leave.'

'She lies. She has poisoned the king! The *Ummachi* lies to protect her son!'

Antara stood with her hands barring the doorway, and the crowd moved at her in a roar. Knives and axes glinted in the mercury light of the street lamps, which were buzzing with flies and moths. 'I will not let you enter,' she said calmly. 'Please go away and leave my son alone.'

Someone threw a stone at the street lamp; another stone hit Antara's forehead. She fell, upsetting the oil lamp that had been lit in front of the sorcerer's platform. She raised her hands as a fragile shield against the blows that rained on her. Blood filled her eyes, and she called out to Swatiraja, the king she loved. The dry palmyra records caught light from the lamp that fell on them, and the flames climbed up the wooden rafters, devouring the old dry wood and spreading through the temple of Panayur.

Antara's last memory was of a great golden light.

Swati sat looking towards the ruined mosque, caressing Antara's grave-earth. He was afraid to know more.

'And Salim . . .' Chandu said softly.

'Yes?' Swati asked, chest constricting in fear.

'He was hated by the Hindu Mahasabha people,' Chandu said. 'After they killed Antara, they went to the mosque to look for him.'

'Did they find him?'

'No.' Chandu shook his head.

'Who knows where he is now?' Swati asked.

Chandu looked at him. 'Why do you want to know?'

Swati laid his hand on Chandu's shoulder. 'Chandu, he is my son,' Swati said.

Chandu did not seem surprised. 'I guessed that,' he said. 'The young man has your eyes.'

'Tell me, where is he?' Swati asked.

'Perhaps you can find him,' the old man said, pointing in the direction of the forest beyond, 'and I will come with you, as my fathers have accompanied your fathers.'

'You mean he has fled to the forest?' Swati asked in disbelief. The old chill gripped him, the myth of the tiger that carried away a royal son into its lair. Valiyamama had disappeared in his search for it.

'You forget that Salim is a hunter,' Chandu said. 'He has worked in these forests as a scout for hunting parties. He will be safe.'

Swati walked back to the palace without looking back to where Antara slept. The landscape had acquired for him the surface of another person's nightmare, one from which he could only be released by some magical spell. His heart was like a glacier, numbed by grief. At the steps, Swati expected Antara to be waiting for him in the shadows, with her dark eyes and soft smile. For a moment he glimpsed her looking out through the window, a flash of her eye and smile as she turned to him to say: 'We have visitors.'

Swati went across to the king's room, took a rifle from the stack and checked its loading mechanism. If anyone came to the palace looking for Salim, they would not go away alive. He stepped out into the shadows of the unlit veranda with the rifle raised to shoot. He saw the white Ambassador marooned in a black moving carpet. The crows were everywhere, screaming hoarse warnings, clustering on the ridge of the three-cornered roof and lining the wall and the branches of the trees. He watched a man step out of the car holding something; a woman followed him.

'Stop right there. I have a loaded gun,' Swati called. 'Who are you?'

'I am looking for Swati,' Vel said, stepping ahead to greet the voice. 'I have brought Grandfather home. Grandfather, Rama Varma.'

Swati stepped out into the light, lowering his gun. 'You seem to have brought a lot of these with you, too,' he said gesturing towards the crows.

'Is this the Panayur palace?' Vel asked.

'It is,' Swati answered.

The man with the gun looked familiar to Vel, the domed forehead, the thick black hair that fell to his shoulders with its scythe of white across the skull, the broad chest.

'Swati?' Vel asked.

'You seem to know my name.'

'I am Rama Varma's grandson, Vel Kramer, and I have brought our grandfather home from Berlin.'

Swati held out his arms, and Vel felt as if something in him was opening into a valley with a trail through it – a quiet little path that wound around itself among the rock and bramble of the hills. It was a trail he had come to take, all the way from Manhattan to London, to the offices of Baulmer and Baulmer, to the streets of Berlin, searching for mementos that told sign.

Kay had joined him. She was involved now in the riddle that haunted him, and as she watched Vel go into the tall man's embrace like a child going into a familiar touch, her heart lightened.

'Welcome home, my brother,' Swati said.

As their bodies touched, the crows took wing silently, a massive carpet of black blotting out the sun. Vel did not notice them. He felt disembodied and elated at the same time, witnessing his twin coming out from Swati's self to meld with his own.

Swati held Vel at arm's length and looked at him searchingly. 'You resemble my father, only he wasn't so fair,' he said.

'I don't really remember my father,' Vel replied. 'He was lost at war when I was six years old.'

'What games fate plays,' Swati said, his eyes bright with tears. 'I lost mine, too, the same way.'

Swati took Vel by the hand and led him to the study. He opened the drawer of the old table by the window, and took out the yellowing photograph of Rama Varma, Else and Jai. Vel touched his father's infant face on the print, looked at his grandfather's dark eyes and sophisticated smile. He held his grandmother's face to his lips – the grandmother he had never met, the grandmother of Berlin's afternoons and the angel of his grandfather's disembodied words.

Clackety-clack, clackety-clack . . .

Beyond the afternoon's folds, beyond the sibilant green paddy and the wind-rumbled palmyra trees, the Madras Mail hooted as it came through the Palghat tunnel. Its whistle carried across the palace, harsh and melancholy, an allegorical warning of arrival and departure.

Vel shuddered. Swati put his arm around his shoulder. 'So you found me,' he said.

'This is only the beginning,' Vel said, and handed him the box in which Rama Varma had come home. He knew that in releasing the ancient bones into the river and interring the restless ash in the old earth of his sleeping ancestors, both he and Swati would be performing the last rites of their lost fathers. From this bone and ash their seeds had sprung and, in its rest, many ghosts would be pacified.

Vel looked out through the window at the river, visible through the grass. Swati gestured at the sleeping elders. 'Come. They call you.'

He led Vel and Kay to the graves of the ancestors, and the spoor of their passings came to them. The wind carried voices. Vel reached out to touch the headstones, which resonated with greeting. Kay stood close to him, watching without intruding.

Swati placed Grandfather upon the grass beside his father's headstone. A yellow snake slipped down from Parangi Cheykor and slithered lazily through the grass in the direction of the river.

The ancestors had lain in wait for him to bring to them one of their own, Swati thought. Now he must bathe in the river, wearing a new loincloth of cotton tucked in at his right hip. He must cook the rice and milk upon a fire he would light, and place the milky rice upon a plantain leaf. In the middle of the leaf he must stand the six-tongued brass lamp of the Panayur house, light the wicks of cotton that he must split and roll with his own hands. And, on one knee, he must offer the rice to the ancestors, feed it to the crows.

> *Tryambakam yajamahe*
> *Sugandhim pushtivardhanam*
> *Uruvaruk miva bandhunath*
> *Mrtyor mokshya ma amritataat*

> May this sacrifice to the triad be accepted,
> The sweet-scented, energizing
> For the eternal liberation from death
> That binds us to the world.

The Mrityunjaya mantra, the words of immortality, the farewell to the soul.

Swati dug the burial mound for Rama Varma and lined it with straw and cow dung. He placed Grandfather's remaining bones in it, heaping straw and sandalwood upon them. He covered them, paving the mound with clay and dung, leaving four holes for the air and smoke to pass through. They watched Grandfather's bones smoulder on the coals, and saw the smoke fly into the freedom of the blue Malabar sky, to disperse over the curves and gleams of the

250

Papanasini. Next to Grandfather's grave were Swati's father's and his mother's. He saw Kay sitting on the grass, her back against the queen-mother's headstone. Her face looked drained and lonely.

Swati sat beside her. 'The spirits of our elders are with us,' he murmured. 'They rest now. Tomorrow, we scatter Grandfather's ashes in the river, and you will bathe with us.'

He poured oil into the lamps at the headstones, and gave the lighted wick to Kay. He held her forearm outstretched as she lit them one by one, and saw that she was shivering. Her eyes were swollen with tears; she trembled uncontrollably. There were faces in that flame. The wind of the dead played upon the fire and she saw the faces of those who had loved her and passed on: her grandfather calling to the dog through the sounds of the forest birds, her mother's laughter.

Someone touched her cheek, and Kay saw a man she thought she recognized. She couldn't immediately recall his name: he was tall, dark, with black hair. Many years later, when she saw her son turn back and wave, smiling as he left for school, she was to remember the dark man's smile.

But now she was standing in the middle of a strange landscape, on an alien golden afternoon. It was not part of the geography of her memories. Then someone called her name and, slowly, with his hand, coaxed her to lay her head against his shoulder.

'Kay, it's all right,' she heard him whisper. 'These are the spirits of our fathers. The presence of the ancestors brings out fundamental memories.'

It all came back to her: meeting Vel in Berlin, the journey to this strange green land with its breathtaking scenery of rough jade mountains and fields. She turned to look at him standing beside Swati and smiled.

'Welcome home,' Swati said gently.

'You found your people,' Kay said to Vel, her eyes shining with tears.

'They are here,' Swati spread his arms wide, 'they are everywhere.'

She looked around her and her gaze was that of a hunter reading sign. Swati recognized it and, with the clairvoyance of a sorcerer, he held out his hand, palm spread towards the river and what lay beyond it. 'You have to seek them out here until they finally rest,' he said, 'both him and Else. Tracking their footsteps, the smells and shadows they left behind sixty years ago.'

He knew Kay would walk hand in hand with Vel along the old path that led to the river, tracing the footsteps of Rama Varma and Else. It was the hunt of communion, with messages Grandfather would have left without knowing it, little delicacies left by Else that they must seek out and taste. Somewhere the fossil of a flower Grandfather had put in her hair; somewhere a little shell they had discovered and hidden under a rock in the Papanasini; somewhere a scrawl in Rama Varma's handwriting of his lover's name on the bark of a tree that grew in the courtyard . . .

In that search, which was Vel and Kay's, Swati was an outsider. Suddenly he felt Antara beside him: a gust of wind that caused the flame on the fresh grave to flicker. He smelt her fragrance, her touch flowed around him and through him. Somewhere a crow cried, its voice like pain.

'It is all right,' he heard Kay say. He saw her turn towards him.

'Come here,' Swati called out. His voice was low, like the rustle of dried leaves heard through sleep. He took the sapphire ring from his pocket and placed it in Vel's hand. 'This is the royal ring of the queen of Panayur,' he said. 'You know what to do with it. My mother wore it once, and then my wife.'

Vel gazed at the ring in his palm. Kay stood close beside him. Wordlessly he slipped the ring on her finger. Kay gasped; her hand flew to her mouth.

'No, the custom is that the man kisses the ring on the lady's hand,' Vel said.

Kay held out her hand, her eyes gleaming like wet mirrors. He kissed her finger and she shivered at his touch. He kissed her mouth, which was soft and deep, caressing her cheek, her hair and her neck.

Kay's breath came in short gasps and she broke away.

Swati had slumped on to the ground, his shoulders hunched, his head bowed. It seemed that a last lamp had been extinguished within him. Kay and Vel knelt down beside him, putting their arms around him. Swati leant against them.

'Whatever it is, it is all right,' Kay said softly.

Swati held her tightly, and she crooned to him gently. He began to talk, the words coming slowly at first, then tumbling over each other – of the child who had died in Nina's womb, of his mother and the veil, of his father, Antara and his son. When he finished the shadows of dusk were climbing the steps to the patio.

'Sleep,' Vel said. 'Sleep well, my brother. Tomorrow we hunt the tiger.'

Swati looked at Vel in surprise, but in the younger man's eyes he saw the understanding that came with an acceptance of strange destinies. 'We?' he whispered.

The Papanasini answered him in the wind, in a cold shiver of its passing.

Kay and Vel led Swati to his bed; he walked like a man in a dream. They watched him lie down, his head tilted on the pillow into sudden sleep, the lines on his face deepening as his dreams began again to mourn along old routes.

Swati had slipped into a slumber he had never known before, welcoming a weariness that flowed upon his bones like the currents of the Papanasini of his childhood. The weariness and the river were one, ancient yet familiar. He heard his mother call him to dinner, but he was too sleepy to answer. He lay under the mango tree, its shade cool and reassuring, the sunspots like warm coins on his skin. Antara sat beside him; he could feel her like a velvet shadow covering him, and her scent was the tree in bloom, her fingertips sunlit.

Mother was humming a song – or was it Antara? It sounded to Swati like the descending octave of the river's lullaby. It lifted him and carried him to the middle of the current, and the forest became a green cooling shadow in the river's flow.

'Let him sleep,' Kay said. She got up and held out her hand to Vel. Together they walked down the steps and turned to the path that ran along the side of the house to the river. Above its thin curve, they saw the spires of the burned church.

'I haven't been to church in a long time,' Kay said.

Vel followed her eyes. 'But there doesn't seem to be anything there,' he said. 'I can only see ruins.'

'Who knows?' Kay smiled. 'It has an altar, I guess.'

Chapter Fourteen

Vel would always remember Kay's head thrown back, her throat exposed, her hair flowing over the broken altar of the ruined church. The memories of old consecrations, of an innocent sacrilege: This is my body, this is my blood.

Ghosts – the hunter's instinct alerted him.

Ghosts of footfalls, a tall man smoking a pipe, a slender woman in a dark beret.

This was the church Charteris built. Inside the ruined building Vel heard his grandfather's voice telling Else about the church that the White Knight, Parangi Cheykor, burned down after the priest died.

Else's eyes widened as she looked up at the shattered Venetian glass in the crippled casement windows, the great domed ceiling depicting the resurrection of Christ, layered with cobwebs. A muffled bell clanged from the ruined tower and a flock of pigeons rose screaming into the sky.

'Why did the White Knight burn it down?' she asked.

She sat on the altar steps, her beret in her lap, her golden hair loose in the western wind that came in through the destroyed windows. Rama Varma saw the angel beside him, and slowly sat down to take her hand in his. He began to tell her the final story of Parangi Cheykor.

After Charteris had been killed and Neeri hanged herself from the rafters above the altar where the priest had said mass, the church was abandoned. The local Christians sent word to the British collector at Palghat to send them another priest. Parangi Cheykor had taken the throne of Panayur, and honoured his treaty with the British. He refuted the taxes of Tipu Sultan, who claimed the annexation of Malabar from Panayur southward. Tipu and Cheykor met in battle upon the great summer plains of the Papanasini's banks, where the Chittoor king had fought the *pandis* a few decades before. The battle lasted three days, the armies resting at sunset. The British had promised the Cheykor troops with rifles and cannon, and Colonel Falcott's regiment was stationed at Salem, but a hundred kilometres away. Help did not come.

After the day's battle was over, Parangi Cheykor would go to Tipu Sultan's tent and sit down with him looking at the carnage around: dead elephants, screaming horses, men being carried away. And Tipu would take his father's old chessboard, place it on the small folding ivory table and invite Parangi Cheykor to a game.

'Sometimes I feel we are playing someone else's game,' the sultan said, as he moved the black bishop to counter the Cheykor's white pawn.

The Cheykor smiled and tossed back his blond-black mane. 'Checkmate,' he challenged the sultan, taking the rook covering the black king with his white horse.

'You win.' The sultan shrugged.

'I don't think anyone wins,' Parangi Cheykor said, getting up. 'Tomorrow we fight the last battle.'

'Your grandfather and I used to sit here playing chess and talking of the times that are coming,' Tipu said. 'Then I was young, and he was wise.'

'We can still call it off, if you will yield the taxes,' Parangi Cheykor said, with a smile that had a mischievous sadness in it.

The older man answered by placing his beringed hand on the shoulder of his beloved adversary. 'I cannot do that, my son.' His voice was weary. 'The British will take it as a sign of weakness.'

'And if I pay, I am forced to take sides,' the Cheykor countered. He embraced the sultan, as his grandfather had many years ago. 'Until death, then, my friend,' he whispered.

'Until death, noble friend,' the sultan answered.

The *panans*, the local travelling bards of Kerala, still sing of the great doomed battle, where the last line of Panayur's defence met the Mangalorean soldiers of Tipu Sultan's army. The sultan himself did not fight, preferring to stand on the small hillock behind the fort, caressing the flanks of his white charger, watching his opponent in battle. Parangi Cheykor, surrounded at last by Tipu's crack Mangalorean guard, looked like a demon on fire, his hair flying behind him as he cut and swung, mowing down soldiers in his path. The sultan watched in amazement as the great tiger sprang out from nowhere into the battlefield: a giant beast roaring and clawing through his soldiers, carrying Parangi Cheykor away on his back. The animal sped towards the palace of Panayur and Tipu gave the signal to stop the chase. The last of the *chakorpada* fought to the end, and the earth and the sunset looked like mirrors of blood.

Lying on the floor of the church, leaning against the altar, Parangi Cheykor waited for Tipu Sultan to come. He was weary of battle, and his wounds hurt. The tiger had left, as swiftly as it had come. His sword loose in his hand, he waited for the clatter of hoofs outside the church, signalling the last fight of his life. But those he heard were not those of the sultan's army. Fists hammered on the church door and a British voice called out, 'This is Colonel Falcott. Is the king inside?'

Parangi Cheykor got up and pushed open the door. A group of red-coated white soldiers stood in readiness, bayonets shining in the moonlight. Their leader, a small man with white sideburns, alighted from his mount. 'I am Colonel Falcott,' he said, his hand on the grip of a pistol in his belt.

'Why have you come now, after the battle is over?' the Cheykor asked harshly.

'I have a message for you,' Falcott said. 'In the name of the king, please give yourself up.'

Parangi Cheykor's twisted smile was terrible to see. 'With allies like you, Panayur would go far.'

'The Crown is taking over the government of Panayur,' Colonel Falcott said, with a smug smile. 'Of course, you will continue to be king, but you will rule in His Majesty's name.'

Parangi Cheykor stared at him, holding the white man's eyes in a searching glare. Suddenly his arm shot out, he grasped the soldier and dragged him inside, heaving the thick oak door shut. A fusillade of shots peppered it.

'Surrender to your fate and we shall treat you well,' Falcott said. His voice contained an edge of fear that he was trying hard to conceal; this half-blond giant with the bloody wounds and burning eyes frightened him.

Parangi Cheykor threw back his head and laughed. 'What is a man's fate but death?' he asked the colonel. 'But lucky is the man who can choose the means of his own death.'

The king of Panayur drove his sword into the colonel's chest, slapping away the body as it fell towards him in a gush of blood. 'No one shall take me alive,' he screamed. He leapt upon the chaplain's podium, snatched the burning torches from the wall and set fire to the great velvet curtains that hung above the altar, the wooden pews and the huge teak-wood cross upon which the figure of Christ hung.

Outside, the soldiers tried to control their panicking horses as they watched the roof of the church collapse in a blazing inferno, the galleries snapping and crumbling, as a demented flaming figure, his sword raised high above his head, danced like a Fury, jeering at them. Fleeing in terror, the English heard the great roar of a tiger above the noise of the church in its destruction. They saw the fire become the skin of the beast, which leapt out of the flames with Parangi Cheykor astride it, his hair streaming in the wind as the tiger raced towards the trees into the night.

In the old church, Vel looked at Kay, leaning against the altar. The golden sun of the evening had turned her into something not of this world. He heard the birds nesting in the ruined loft and saw spiders swaying down from the scorched rafters. He kissed her, as she leant against the smoky stone, in the shadow of the ghost of a charred cross, her neck white in the light, her golden hair spread like a sacrifice, mingling with the gold of another's, her white throat emerging from another's . . .

Rama Varma kissed Else's neck, the skin of her shoulders, her breasts.

Vel followed in ancient memory, dreaming ancestral dreams over the vein-run, lily-cool skin of Kay. Love is an exorcism, he thought. The vapours of mating wash away old pains.

The church bells in the wind, the alabaster altar wall smooth against the naked skin of Kay's back, the words of the mass, the sacred words that Else's body learnt as Rama Varma moved into her, the choir opened up around Kay, the sound of harps and the chords of the organ, the sun flooding through the shattered Venetian windows, the ceiling spreading its wings under Else's eyes, the candles around Kay lighting up, their flames illuminating the faces of the saints in their nooks. Kay gave herself to Vel, in passionate repetition of another afternoon years ago, and her cry rose up like a flight of soaring birds, answering an echo that reverberated through the ruins of the walls . . .

She looked into Vel's eyes and saw the beginning and the end.

The night of the church had grown around them, blanket-like. Vel woke with a start to the flapping of nightwings, and something passed over them swiftly. Something unseen and urgent. It woke Kay too, and she looked into the empty air then up at her lover's face, turned away from her into the moonlight. From the forest, a great roaring came to them, a sound unlike anything they had ever heard before.

'The tiger . . .' Kay said.

They went out into the night, and saw that it was empty. The forest seemed to have come closer, and the window of Swati's bedroom shone in the distance as a rectangle of yellow. Kay and Vel walked back to the palace and paused to look into Swati's room where he slept his weary sleep.

But when they knocked on Swati's door in the morning they found the room empty and Swati gone.

Chapter Fifteen

The night was at its orphaned hour when Swati stepped out into it and on to the veranda of the palace. He didn't want to wake Vel and Kay, sleeping in the west wing of the palace. All around him he sensed darkness delaying its last tide; the sky was a shimmering mandala. A pale moon lay bevelled among the constellations, while the stars bled around it in milky lines of light. The palace of Panayur was a dark ship moored in the harbour of that night.

'Sailor.' The snatch of a girlish voice came to him in a warp of memory, along with spray from the river, spindle-brushing his face in a breeze.

Swati turned to look for her, and the riverwind tossed the boughs of the trees in a shadow play upon the moonlit ochre of the palace wall.

The mountains appeared nearer and denser in the night, and the lost silver of the Papanasini glittered in the moonlight among the clearings in the grass. The sorcery of the hour parted the curtains of distance, and he could see the river comb itself into the forest's

perimeter, foil flashes of moonlit water. His son –
Antara's son – had fled into that forest. The forest of
the tiger of Panayur, a shadowful context of Panayur's
royal house, into which his ancestors had entered
when their hour came, in a search both absolute and
arcane to each.

Tonight, it was the forest of answers.

A clock chimed somewhere within the palace as he
stood on the veranda, looking out at this hour into
which he was to sail. It was the hour when instinct
insinuated itself into the sleep of roosters, when they
slumbered with their beaks buried in the fluffy
feathers on their necks. He heard a hen cluck and
burrow into the straw. The wind was gentle in the
trees, sensing the nature of the cusp, murmuring over
the rough nests of the crows.

He had left his bedchamber, rising weakly from
sheets still sticky with the sweat of past fever. Antara's
flavours lingered in the room – creases on the bed-
clothes where she had sat and soothed his burning
forehead with the paste of *neem* leaves, a little smear
of turmeric where her finger had brushed against the
bedpost. The room held a sense of darkness corrupted
with insincere moonlight. The shadows that painted
the old walls had a narrative poise about them. The
headboard of the wooden bed, with its intricate carv-
ings, threw an arabesque upon the wall; the furniture
fell as a tapestry of phantoms that mixed their shapes
among the dusty dyes of the canvases and the dim glint
of weapons. He had paused by the northern wall of the

bedchamber beside the portrait of his great-uncle, painted in oils by a Ravi Varma acolyte, and briefly touched the absent, beloved face. Trembling fingers, weary with the unaccountable contacts of a lifetime.

The moth-wings of touch had grown and thickened, flitting along Swati's fingers, spreading upon his palms, racing along the sinews of his emaciated hand. Briefly he longed for the end of all touch.

Swati had lifted the Winchester rifle from its wooden brackets below the regent's portrait. He would be needing it, on his path to hunt for the tiger. He had sat down on the familiar chair by the window, and wiped the barrel and stock with the soft cloth that was kept in the drawer of Great-uncle's desk. He had checked the bolt and the spring action of the breech, working the trigger lever, which ejected the spent shells, and loaded the next one. As he put a handful of cartridges into his pocket, he remembered the pugmark Antara had shown him on the first rainy night he had come back to Panayur. It had been nearly as big as a baby elephant's, and suddenly the gun seemed hopelessly inadequate.

'What am I hunting?' Swati asked himself.

Sitting down once more upon the old chair with the rifle in his lap, Swati had reached out to stroke the tabletop where the urn containing Nina had stood. It seemed that until then what had flowed in his life had been part of someone else's journey and that he was just a witness without a voice. The moonlight had gleamed on a small circular patch in the dust where she had once sat, and he had opened his palms to rest his face in them, waiting for a distant source to disgorge its stream. At that moment he had known that the tears would come no more. Sorrow itself was like the phantom moon that burned outside over Panayur, belonging neither to the night nor to the morning.

He had walked down the stone steps, descending into the dying moonlight of his hunt: his voyage. His limbs were unsteady after the fever and lack of nourishment; the gun he carried on his shoulder felt heavy. He stepped slowly upon the cool earth damp with dew-sodden leaves, on the shadows of the trees above. He paused under the mango tree, looking out towards the Papanasini. A cloud passed over the moon, and the river's silver darkened. In the distance the topmasts of ships gleamed and their sails swelled as they bore down upon the palace . . . Swati shook his head, and the cloud cleared; the vision passed.

'Look for Kombiyachan's navy come sailing.' Father's words.

Swati shrugged. A dog howled somewhere far away in the village and the sound carried in the night over the open spaces of the paddyfields. Swati walked slowly around the house, passing the gravestones of his ancestors, which Antara had once cared for as a garden of eternal memory. Grass was creeping up the rectangular borders of the graves, invading their ancient sleep, and the headstones were shiny with the first signs of moss. He paused and felt their dreams among the grass, dotted with little yellow daisies. The earth was seeded with the memories of the dead; they were veined among the roots of the grass and the plants and he felt their amorphous kinship. The earth was full of loss.

Swati touched each stone in a ritual of farewell, which also was a seeking of benediction. He followed the route he knew Vel and Kay would have taken to the ruined church, a path that crossed the crumbling palace wall and skirted the burned-down mosque beside which Antara lay. He would pass her abandoned house too, he knew. He wanted to be clear of the palace grounds and well into the forest by the time Vel woke. He squatted beside the small mound that was Antara and laid down the gun.

'I don't want to lose them, too,' Swati told her, smoothing the surface of the grave, which had just been cemented and whitewashed. 'You would have liked him – a brother you never had.'

Beyond his closed eyes Swati felt her touch on his shoulder, but he did not turn to look. The night shifted and slid between planes and he surrendered himself to it. From then on, he knew that the quality of his search for his son and for the tiger of Panayur would be that of time and space, which constantly meshed into each other, often throwing him off his trail, but soothing him with the presence of those who peopled it.

'Do not worry.' His fingers sought hers on his shoulder. 'I will find him.'

'I am afraid for him.' Her voice came in snatches from far away, like dragonflies skittering in the night wind. 'He never believed in anything. Not in Raniyamma, not in the king, not in the tiger.'

'He is the prince of Panayur,' Swati told the wind, and Antara in that wind. 'I will find him.'

He felt something crawling up his hand, so light he barely registered its weight. It was a small brown spider speeding to hop on to the grave. The wind bent the small *keezharnelli* plant that grew beside Antara: it shivered on the little cobweb that bridged the leaves as a star of silvery thread. Swati remembered the ghost-catchers of Mother's stories. A chill sped over his skin with the lightness of spiderfeet.

Antara . . .

Swati got up and lifted the gun to his shoulder. It was a weapon, he knew, that Father and Grandfather would have been familiar with. His palm sought out their long-dead fingerprints upon the shiny blue barrel and the cool, smooth walnut stock. Spectral fingertips seemed to greet the whorls of his own.

He thought of Vel and Kay, of the ghosts who watched over their sleep. They would see her asleep, smiling, in the crook of his arm, and the ring that encircled her long white finger as if it had always belonged there.

The moon's edges were like wax, and a cloud, ink-dark and wispy, passed over it in a long caress. The dawn had the sharp smell of paddyfields and the spicy aroma of the country flowers, which he left behind as the path narrowed. The overpowering odour was of vegetation: a great collage of chlorophyll and spice mingling with the sharp scent of wild blooms, the cloying redolence of frangipani.

As Swati stumbled through rocks and clumps of grass that grew along the way, he could hear the descent of the Papanasini; sometimes through a clearing in the trees he saw the gleam of her travel. Coconut groves and banyan trees grew wild along the old royal hunting route. For decades, nobody had used it, and it had shrunk into a narrow grass path. A yellow rat snake crossed his path, its mouth packed with an inert dead thing. It paused in its slithering and changed course into the *chettipoo* bushes. A nightbird flapped its wings close to his head, flying low towards its nest.

The wind was a witnessing voice in the leaves and the wild bushes: it spoke of the serpent sliding out of the cool anthill, the panther crouched on a branch painted with the lichen and moss of centuries. A school of bats arose from the rafter-bones of a ruined hunting lodge in a black, leathery somersault. The Papanasini was the ancient medium of the forest, flowing along the ridges and shoulders of the Dhoni, singing its secret chants.

The forest edited the light with its hues of green, and Swati couldn't tell whether it was moonlight that glowed among the ghostly spaces or the coming dawn. It was getting darker among the trees. Awareness came to him, slowly, that the darkness was alive: the forest had inveigled him into its core. The gloom was sentient with shapes that flickered in the spaces between the trees: glimmering, water-like reflections, faces stained with shadows.

'Try to sense the tiger,' Valiyamama's voice whispered in Swati's ear.

With each step he took on the forest path, Swati felt he was readying himself for something of which he had no foreknowledge. There were no reference points in this shimmering volume of green that belonged to neither day nor night, where the light played tricks with the senses and the strange cries of beast and bird might be of warning or surprise. In this search for his son he would perhaps find pain – or deliverance. The walking tired him; each step forward brought with it an agony sharpened by loss, and Swati wondered about the shape of that deliverance.

Perhaps pain itself would be deliverance.

But the only thing that mattered was the tiger. The only thing that mattered was that glorious moment when he stood face to face with the great beast his ancestors had hunted, which held the key to his son's flight.

'What do you seek?' the ancient voices asked him, from the shadows of the green gloom.

'The tiger,' he whispered in reply.

'Seek more than the tiger, or you will fail,' they told him sadly.

'I seek my son,' Swati said, 'and I seek vengeance.'

'Vengeance is useless against the tiger.' The voices began to fade, losing themselves among the velvet sounds of the forest.

'Remember the fable of Nachiketas, the boy who was sacrificed by his father and found immortality.' Swati heard his mother's storytelling voice in the distance. He thought he saw the glimmer of a white veil among the trees; a slender arm parted a low-slung vine and faded into the darkness.

Nachiketas, the boy who bested Death, the son of Wajashrawas who, desiring heaven, gave away all that he possessed. Curious, Nachiketas went to his father and asked, 'Father, have you given me away also to someone?' Wajashrawas did not answer, but his son repeated the question a second and a third time. Then, irritated, his father said, 'I give you to Death.'

What were the questions his own son had asked him? Swati wondered. As a child, had he looked for his father to come sailing down the Papanasini?

As Nachiketas had thought, Whether I die now or later matters little; but what I would like to know is what happens after Death.

'Did Death get Nachiketas?' Salim's voice haunted Swati on the trail that led through the forest. 'Did Death get me the way it got my mother?'

'Stop,' Swati cried. 'Stop!'

'Tell me, Father.' The young voice was mocking.

Nachiketas went into the forest and sat in meditation inside the house of Death. When Death appeared he said to the boy, 'A guest should be respected. You have lived three days in my house without eating and drinking. I offer thee three gifts.'

Nachiketas said, 'The first gift I ask is that I may be

reconciled with my father, that he may keep no grudge against me for having come to seek you out.'

Death agreed.

Swati heard someone laugh among the trees, harshly, contemptuously.

'Nachiketas asked for his second gift.' Swati remembered his mother's words, 'He sought the fire of sacrifice, which would take him to heaven.'

'Teach me the nature of the fire god Agni, and how to build the sacrificial altar,' Nachiketas requested. 'Only he can bestow the immortal world on his worshippers.'

Death told him that out of Fire had come this world, and how best to build the altar. 'Your second gift, Nachiketas! The fire shall be named after you. Now choose again, your third gift.'

Nachiketas said, 'Some say that when man dies he continues to be, others that he does not. Explain this riddle, and that shall be my third gift.'

But this gift Death was reluctant to give. He offered Nachiketas sons and grandsons, cattle and horses, elephants and gold, a great kingdom full of beautiful women. 'But do not ask what lies beyond death.'

But Nachiketas was adamant. He would have that knowledge.

At last Death agreed. 'I will tell you the secret of the undying Spirit and what happens after death. When the knot of the heart is cut, what is mortal becomes immortal. This is the law.'

'It is the knot of the heart one tries to unravel,' Swati said, bitterly and wearily, into the darkness, 'and discovers new knots one never knew existed. In the loosening of that string, more entanglements happen.' Swati felt very tired. He had to sit. He saw that he had reached a small clearing, where the forest shadows were interrupted by gleaming belts of water. He walked down towards the river, dropping the rifle behind him. The sight and sound of the Papanasini reassured him. 'Give me something to help me,' he begged the river.

He leant against an old tree on the bank. An owl hooted in the foliage, and a strong gust of wind shook the boughs. A bunch of dried debris fell to the ground: twigs and straw, the remains of a crow's disused nest. Something metallic glittered at his feet where it had fallen. It was a pocket watch with a long golden chain and Roman numerals inscribed on a white dial.

With a cry Swati picked it up, raising it to his lips. 'Valiyamama's watch,' he stammered. 'He must have come this way in search of the tiger.' The phantoms of the forest were answering his final riddle – the riddle of time. Time, which punctuates happiness and sorrow, like noon and midnight.

'Nachiketas!' Death said to the boy. 'I will tell you the secret of the undying Spirit and what happens after death. Some spirits enter the womb, some pass into stone and sand, according to karma. It takes the shape of what it inhabits, yet the self exists outside it.

Go backwards from effect to cause and you are compelled to reach the beginning of time.'

Swati sat upon the soft moss, the watch to his lips. His mind was suddenly a monsoon of memory: Great-uncle looping the watch-chain through the buttonhole of his waistcoat as he got ready to sail for England; the watch suspended from his middle, tucked into the waistband of his sarong when he held court at home; Swati sitting in his lap in the huge carved armchair on the veranda, holding the watch in his small hands ... 'When the hands point to twelve, it is twelve o'clock ...' Great-uncle's heavy voice teaching him to tell the time. 'All time begins at twelve o'clock.'

'And when does it end, Valiyamama?'

'Time never ends,' the old man answered. 'But remember, each time it begins at twelve o'clock.'

The mapping of the day, learnt at a patriarchal knee, inlaid with the parables of separate realities of time. The continuity of beginnings, the endlessness of the end.

Swati held up the watch to his moist eyes in an act of contrition to this teacher of movement, which extolled to him, in its relentless ticking, the small riddles of life.

'Seek yourself in the tiger.' Grandfather spoke to him from the rustling of the leaves. 'Seek the star along the path of the tiger.'

'And once I find him?'

'You know what to do.' The voice of his forefather

came to him, disguised in the conversation of the leaves and the branches.

'Do I?' Swati asked himself. 'Do I know what to do?'

It was the voice of his fear, the angel of his doubts that forbade him to accept the pains and sorrows of his years. He realized that all along what he had feared most was the loss of his loves. Today, as he walked along the forest's treacherous road, they came back to him as echoes of colour and voice: Mother's palm on his cheek, Nina's breath on his skin, Antara's touch on his face. He had pushed them to a distance all along; they were too painful to carry with him. It was the fear that everything had to end while he alone had to go on – in a sudden farewell of a childhood night, on a rainy curve of road, or in the terrible flashing of machetes and knives upon defenceless limbs.

Fear.

The path of the tiger was calling to him, the trail along which the beast came on great, padded feet from its lair to drink the moon-coloured water of the Papanasini, along which it took its prize to vanish into the myth of the centuries, along which it raced into the waters to reach the queen of the veil to place its great head on her lap.

The trail of the tiger.

There were so many spoors he had to scent out from the knowledge of the centuries. This was no ordinary hunt: it had its beginning in generations of memory.

Swati looked out beyond the water, to the height of the mountain. He could see the eastern ridge curve upwards and stretch away in front of him in a giant blade of granite, woolly with trees that grew all the way to the top. The peak of the mountain was a bare nipple of rock, and there was a conical gash on the hillside that faded among the last line of the trees on its summit. There the atmosphere was lighter, the trees grew less thickly. A pale light shimmered, turning the air incandescent with spray from a gigantic waterfall.

Dwarfed by the vision, he sat and gazed at the eternal birth of the Papanasini, which cascaded from the great height of the Sivamala. It was a sheer descent of live water, a vast roar that plunged into emptiness from the mouth of a god.

'Behind the waterfall is a cave.' Swati remembered Antara's childhood story. 'The cave of the tiger of the Papanasini.'

Swati squinted at the mountainside, trying to see through the watery mist. The fall shifted like an unruly curtain across the open rock when the wind blew through, revealing rents in its plunge. The mountain itself was a shape-changer; the streaks of past forest fires through the conifers looked like stripes on tiger fur. The night was playing tricks on him and the wind stoked his fever; mist haunted his eyes – the fog of exhaustion. In the distance, the spray cleared and spread again. Through the fall of primitive water, he imagined he saw the shoulders of the tiger; the wind kept pulling at the waterfall, revealing the mouth of the cave, open like a great animal's roar.

'Looking for a tiger?' asked a mocking voice

behind him. Swati turned. A man stepped out from behind a tree. The forest light illuminated his outline, and silvered the strands of his hair as it blew back in the wind. He wore no shirt, his body was lean and well muscled. In his hands was the gun that Swati had dropped.

'Parangi Cheykor . . . ?' Swati whispered, disbelievingly.

The man threw back his head and laughed. The sound chilled Swati. 'You are still hunting myths, old man,' he said. 'In fact, you call yourself the king of Panayur, don't you?'

'Who are you? My eyes are hot and feverish. I cannot see you.'

'You killed my mother,' the man said, and stepped into the light, the gun pointed at Swati. 'She loved you. She cared for your mother until her death, kept the house from crumbling to the termites. And what did she get in the end? Death!'

'Antara!' Swati called her name into the night, and behind the young man the forest gloom rippled and darkened.

'Why her? Tell me,' Salim asked savagely. 'Why my mother?'

'In heaven there is no fear,' Nachiketas said. 'In heaven, O Death, you do not exist. Nor your companion – old age and its terrors. Leaving sorrow behind as it crosses the two rivers of hunger and thirst, the soul rejoices reaching heaven.'

'This is Aditi, the mother of the gods, who was born through the mingling of the elements,' Death answered. 'Deep in the heart of things she has entered, there she is seated. This is what you seek. As a woman carries with care the unborn child in her womb, so is the Master of Knowledge lodged in the cinders. And day by day should men worship Him, those who live the waking life and woo him with sacrifices, for He is that Agni. This is what you seek.'

Swati's chest clenched. He wanted to embrace Salim, promise him that it was all over. He struggled to get up, holding the tree trunk.

'Stay where you are,' Salim said, aiming the gun at Swati. 'Don't think you can capture me.'

Swati collapsed back against the tree, and raised his arm feebly in protest. He beckoned the young man to come closer.

Salim laughed. 'Oh, don't try to trick me, King of Panayur,' he said. 'My mother may have trusted you and she is dead because of that. Your people killed her. And as for me, I am not afraid of death. I am dead already.'

'Don't say that. You are my son,' Swati said, and only then realized he was crying.

Salim's eyes flashed in the dark. 'My father?' he spat. 'I have no father. I am a bastard.'

'You are my son,' Swati whispered hoarsely. 'And thank God you are alive. I have found you at last.'

'I have no father,' the young man screamed. 'No father, do you hear? Mother told me he died when I was small, but I knew I was a bastard. The children at school taunted me with that.'

'I am your father,' Swati said calmly.

The young man's eyes narrowed. 'I have no father except Death,' Salim said, 'and that is the gift of the royal house of Panayur. My grandfather followed your father to his death, and my mother died defending your temple.'

'He to whom the sages are as meat and heroes as food for His eating and Death is an ingredient in His banquet, how shall one know of Him where He abides?' Nachiketas asked Death.

'Know the body for a chariot and the soul for the master of the chariot: know Reason for the charioteer and the mind for the reins only.'

'Come closer and let me tell you everything,' Swati said. 'You are my son, the prince of Panayur. I had loved Antara since I was young, but she never told me she had borne me a son, not until a few days ago.'

Salim's eyes were locked on Swati's, and the father held the son's gaze. He offered his hands to him, in greeting and in seeking forgiveness: forgiveness for the orphaned childhood and the shame and the ridicule, for Antara's loneliness and her loyalty, her terrible death; and the young man saw all of this replayed in his father's eyes.

280

That truth, and the helplessness of it, filled Salim with rage and a desire for revenge.

Swati saw his son lift the gun and a tongue of fire leap at him from the mouth of the rifle. Time had slowed to measured, deliberate pauses. The fire reached him, growing gigantically as it came closer. A burning fist hit him in the chest and as he fell backwards, spun away from the tree with the force of the shot. He tried to raise his hands in *namaste* to the fire – Agni, the Sublime, Supreme God – and felt the Papanasini receive him like an eager mother.

Above the vast, distant roar of the Papanasini's descent and the sound of the wind in the trees, a great roar came to Swati's ears – savage and powerful, silencing the waterfall. Before the shadows claimed him, Swati's last vision was that of a blazing length of orange emerging from the darkness, launching itself at Salim, who had been raising the gun for a final shot.

Swati shouted at the tiger of Panayur not to hurt his son. But his voice was an echo from a great distance. When he came to, the lapping of water was in his ears.

The night was vast and filled with serene light, the dawn a green awareness in the shadows. Through its stealthy opening, the Papanasini flowed in its eternal nature. Antara passed him with the lamps lit for prayer, Great-uncle smiled at someone behind him. He saw them as insubstantial, translucent images, real only in the tug of anguish that the sight of them caused him.

Mother was beside him, her face unveiled and beautiful. Her smile became a gentle mirage in the dawn, a persuading softness that seduced him into a sleep that opened and closed like wings that settled on his face, breathing from his breath.

Swati woke again, feeling a weight settle on his lap – something alive and majestic, great in volume, yet weightless like light. It exuded the presence of things awesome and unnameable. The great tiger stretched beside him on the water-ribbed shore where he lay, its head resting on his lap in contentment. It raised its head and looked at him, amber eyes burning in a huge face, its striped forehead sleek and broad, the hint of an ivory fang showing through a gap in its black lips. Its gaze was mesmeric but gentle, and Swati felt the power of its immortal wisdom. Suddenly the tiger winked, and Swati laughed. The dawn warmed the water lapping around his ears, the sky buzzed and shone and tilted . . .

Swati was flowing. The tiger swam with silent strength against the current; he could smell its strong odour, his nostrils buried in the rough fur of its neck. The smell wrapped around him, and the river soothed him . . .

It was Kay who found him, lying where he had fallen on the bank of the Papanasini. Water lapped against his head, a fringe of froth that caught the sun in its myriad bubbles. Vel found the rifle a short distance away, its butt shattered, broken from the barrel, which had been driven into the earth.

Kay dropped to her knees beside Swati's body, and cradled his head to her. 'Look at him sleep,' she whispered to Vel behind the tears. 'It is as if he has come home at last.'

'Let him be,' Vel said, and gently drew her away from Swati's still form. 'We will go back to the palace and tell people to bring him back. He was the king, and he must return to his palace as a king.'

As they retraced their steps down the forest path, the birds chirping the spreading morning in the trees, they did not know that when they returned with the royal bier – Chandu hobbling behind with his tattered umbrella to shield the king on his last journey home – Swati's body would have vanished.

And upon the riverbank, in the wet sand where the tiger had lain with its head on the king's lap, a giant pugmark could be seen leading into the Papanasini, its breadth wider than a man's arm.

THE END

Glossary

aattukattil: swing-like cot inside the house
aazaan: call to prayer in a mosque
achans: chieftains
arrack: locally brewed liquor

Bharatam: ancient name for India

chakorpada: suicide-warriors of medieval Kerala
cherumi: woman belonging to agricultural caste

gayatri: Vedic hymn

Hajjiyar: he who has returned from the Hajj to Mecca

illams: Namboodiri houses

kanji: rice gruel
kasavu: gold brocade
Kauravas and *Pandavas:* main protagonists of the
Mahabharata
kayampoo: herbal scent

kolambi: poisonous plant
kovilakam: palace
kudiyaan: serf

melmundu: upper garment
mullakka: Muslim priest
mundu: sarong

Namboodiri: the highest Brahmin caste in Kerala
nazhi: south Indian measurement, roughly one kilo

pandi: Tamil national
parangi: Caucasian

Raniyamma: queen-mother
rowka: blouse

samadhi: grave
sambandham: amorous tryst
shraddham: death anniversary
sivalinga: holy stone of Siva

thampuran: lord
thoni: boat
thorthumundu: linen towel
thozhi: lady-in-waiting
thulasi: holy basil

Ummachi: Muslim woman
unniyappam: sweetmeat

urumi: whip-like sword of flexible steel

veena: south Indian musical instrument

Acknowledgements

First of all, my gratitude to my father Etteth Gangadharan, for pointing towards an inner road the book could take, my agents Martina Dervis and Malcolm Imrie for believing in me and taking this forward, and my editor Simon Taylor for the marvellous treatment of the book. My thanks to Ashok Malik and Ramya Sarma for the careful reads, corrections and suggestions, Malavika Tiwari for burning the midnight oil, Sapna Kapoor for design suggestions and logistical support, Shyama Sharma for looking after me on the small house on the hill in Banethi and Mr Malhotra for all the packaging and handling. And last but not least, I acknowledge the phantom voice of my ancestor Krishnan, who perished in the Holocaust in the late 1930s because he could not leave the woman he loved.

THE VILLAGE OF WIDOWS
by Ravi Shankar Etteth

When a diplomat at the Madagascan Embassy in Delhi is stabbed to death, the ambassador asks his old friend and fellow chessplayer, Jay Samorin, to help find the murderer. Samorin is a man with a profound interest in the nature of evil and an unorthodox approach to criminal psychology. The Delhi police are also involved, and the Deputy Commissioner put in charge of the investigation is Anna Kahn – recently transferred from Kashmir where her ruthless pursuit of terrorists had threatened to cause a scandal. Wary of each other, Samorin and Kahn each have highly personal reasons for their obsession with such crime: his father, a war hero, was hanged for the murder of his mother, while her husband was killed by Kashmiri Mujahedeen, and they become uneasy allies in the hunt for the killer.

Untangling a web of corruption, of prostitution rings, medical malpractice and embezzlement of foreign aid, their quest takes them into the darkest recesses of their own lives, and beyond as they explore older, deeper mysteries that are outside the more usual boundaries of a criminal investigation. It is a trail that is fraught with danger, a trail that will eventually bring them to the village of widows. . .

Imbued with the magic, myth and wonder of India, the haunting new novel from the author of *The Tiger by the River*.

0 385 60404 1

NOW AVAILABLE FROM DOUBLEDAY